THE UNLEASHED MIRACLE

TIERNEY JAMES

Publishing Coordinator – Sharon Kizziah-Holmes
Cover Design by Sweet 'N Spicy Designs

L & D
PRESS
Owasso, OK

ISBN – 978-1-965460-44-3 (Paperback)
ISBN - 978-1-965460-45-0 (eBook)

DEDICATION

To all the angels in my life who have watched
over me through the years and
kept me safe from harm.

Hebrew 13:2
Do not neglect to show hospitality to strangers,
for thereby some have entertained angels unawares.

ACKNOWLEDGMENTS

Without my team of professional people, comprised of so much talent it boggles the mind. I would not be able to do this writing life that consumes me. Words cannot express how much they step up for me each time I get lost in a story. They stand ready each time to smooth out the wrinkles, put Band-Aids on my ego and give me the advice I need to solve problems that will pop up at the most unexpected times. These are a few of the people who continue to circle around me like the angels in this book.

Paperback Press with Sharon Kizziah-Holmes – Thanks for a terrific job of formatting and making suggestions to put the final polish on each book I write.

Decadent Publishing editors – Kate Richards and Nan Bauserman. You fix what's broken and teach me along the way. I hope I make you proud.

Sweet & Spicy Designs – Jaycee DeLorenzo has designed all my book covers during this journey of being a writer. She puts the fun and energy into creativity. I know I can always count on you.

Beta Readers – Becky Young and Gayle Bodenhamer. You ladies went above and beyond.

Proofreader – Author Shirley McCann can always find the little things I missed and has saved me many times from embarrassment. You make me proud and are such a joy to work with.

Chief ARC Reader – Author Willy Robbins never shies away from grabbing one of my books to read and promote. She has been on this journey with me from the beginning. She inspires me with all she has accomplished

Prologue

"Run," came a whisper at her ear. It felt like a tickle or the brush of a morning breeze. "Run."

Petra whirled around to make sure no one had slipped into the underground labyrinth of stalactites. She had promised not to enter, but when Chadwick left to check his instruments and geological map, she broke the first rule of exploration. *Don't go in alone.*

"Someone there? Chadwick?" Her flashlight dimmed. Palming it, she gave it a hard shake, but the effort did nothing to brighten the connection. An uneasy sensation rose inside her when she remembered Chadwick had replaced the batteries with new ones last night. Another shake, and a few curse words brightened the glow.

Turning around, she swung her light toward the back wall of the cave. In that second, she finally discovered what her parents had searched for before they died. The Vessel of St. Mary. She stepped closer and stopped to shine the light on her feet. Water was seeping from under the stone walls behind the altar where the vessel rested in a small enclave carved out of the stone. She lifted one wet foot then flashed the light toward the vessel. Hair-thin trickles flowed down the sides of the wall at first then widened to splash on the floor. She stepped forward then stopped again; her ankles were now completely covered.

Should she rush to grab the vessel without considering its fragile condition? The only path to it was between two statues of Caspian Tigers, animals thought to be extinct since1970. Their teeth revealed a viciousness, and the amber eyes were strange in the way they stalked her with each step she took. A trick, she thought, similar to those pictures of Jesus who often did the same thing. Without warning, thin flames of fire shot out of the tigers' mouths, creating a hiss when droplets fell from the ceiling. Although the fire turned to steam, she became engulfed in a fog that threatened to block the problem-solving side of her brain.

A rumble alerted her to flee. Chadwick wasn't here to tell her what to do. Besides, the walls gushed like the orchestrated Fountains of Bellagio in Las Vegas. Unexpected water terrified her. Chadwick explained it was due to her parents drowning as they tried to save her after being washed away in a flash flood, right here in Turkey. A lump formed in her throat as the wet spray turned into a fountain on both sides of the vessel.

"Run," whispered in her ear as she took two steps backward.

One of the stones broke free just as she turned awkwardly to run. Trying to backtrack down the tunnel and through the cavern-like room cloaked in stalactites, she dropped her flashlight. She instinctively stared down into the murky abyss swirling around her thighs. Tapping the light on her helmet gave her the glow she needed to forge ahead. By the time she reached the rope ladder to climb out, the torrent had reached her waist.

The ladder lifted as if it might float away before she added her weight to anchor it down. She had no trouble climbing until the second step from the top broke, and she fell back in what felt like the jaws of death. A scream escaped from deep inside her as the churning current dragged at her. The ladder, free of her weight, floated away. Slapping at the walls to catch hold of a rock, she hoped anything might stop the wet death grab. A rope dropped on her upturned face. She held onto the noose; her body being pulled upward until the last few seconds when a hand clamped onto the back of her shirt and yanked her upward. The sensation of being dragged onto dry ground gave her satisfaction she'd beat death once again.

She moved across the floor of the upper cave on her belly like a baby seal headed for the protection of the sea before she collapsed, gasping for air. Two boots appeared six inches from her nose, forcing her to sneak a timid look at the disgruntled face of Chadwick.

"Okay, I know you're mad," she choked. "In my defense, I found—"

"You'll never learn," he quipped then walked away.

ONE

Mikhail removed his bike helmet and secured it on the back of his restored Harley. The passing of a semi brought a sudden breeze, sending his hair into his eyes. He needed a haircut, but he'd been a little too busy to bother with such trivial chores. Like always, he took a few seconds to survey his surroundings in case he was being watched. Habit maybe.

The cool morning air led him to zip his leather jacket up to his throat, followed by tugging at his gloves before flexing his fingers. They'd stiffened on the ride over, and he wondered if people who hated cold weather would go to an icy hell if their sinful ways caught up with them. An odd thing to cross his mind.

Stepping up on the curb, he examined the area one last time, especially the shadows between buildings, strangers with hats pulled down low over their foreheads, and any parked car with a driver inside. Turning, he collided with a woman who staggered backward. He grabbed her and pulled her into his arms to prevent her fall against the plate-glass window of a coffee shop.

"I'm sorry." He smiled, staring down into the hazel-green eyes of a young woman of undetermined age.

She pushed away and tilted her head in a head-to-toe appraisal of him. The instant she smirked mischievously, Mikhail liked her. For all he knew, she could be one of his mentor's traps. With that thought in his head, he continued with caution. "Are you hurt?"

"Do I look hurt?" She continued, clearly teasing him. Was she flirting? Sometimes, he just didn't know about these kinds of things.

"Do you always answer a question with a question?"

A soft laugh escaped her generous lips as she turned and disappeared into the coffee shop.

He wondered if he should continue with his plan to go inside and get his daily cup of brew. Would she think he followed her?

He'd parked out front and clearly was headed toward the coffee shop. Why would she think otherwise?

When he entered, the intoxicating smell of all things coffee and pastries lifted his foul mood. He'd awakened at five to continue his routine and study. His mentor often showed up and other times called. Mikhail had accused him of not trusting him many times, but deep down, he knew it was just part of the job.

The woman he'd collided with already stood in

line. Several women glanced her way and sniffed, arched an eyebrow, or rolled their eyes. The young men, however, eyed her head to toe like she was shark bait.

Since he stood several people behind her in line, he took the liberty to observe the whole sideways package. The snakeskin boots and black stockings led up to a short leather skirt. A white blouse hung out from beneath a worn denim jacket rimmed in lace. Her painted fingertips stuck out from black gloves. He wasn't sure if they were old or just a fashion statement.

What he admired most was her long red hair pulled back in a messy braid. It reminded him of Scotland and how much he loved it there when he had needed to recover. There were a few purple streaks, as if she'd chose to add a punch of color to an already eye-catching head of hair. The interesting white forelock around her face gave her a mystical vibe. Those kinds of close observations made him feel things he knew were forbidden in his line of work. From this angle, he noticed several ear piercings and two necklaces clasped on the back of her neck. A slender neck with freckles.

A wave of guilt washed over him just as the woman glanced back and gave a half grin, one eyebrow lifted in mischief. He straightened and tried to appear nonchalant but needed to tighten his mouth to hide his pleasure at the attention. When he raised his chin in acknowledgement, she turned away to place her order at the counter. What did it hurt to enjoy the view and remember?

Once more, Mikhail took stock of his surroundings. One man in particular had a bulge under his jacket. He tried not to be judgmental, but with the gang tattoos around his neck and colors he wore on the hat, Mikhail guessed he could be a problem. Like himself, he'd been watching the red-haired woman but lost interest each time the cash register clinked or slammed shut. The man slipped his hand into his ripped jean jacket and jerked out his gun just as the clerk handed the young woman her coffee.

Between the screams of terror and the sound of chairs being flipped over, as customers attempted to escape, Mikhail stood calm, except for his fingers, twitching down at his side. The two people who stood in between him and the red-haired woman dove under a table, leaving her holding her coffee in midair, and the gangbanger pointing a gun at the barista.

Mikhail took a step forward, causing the gunman to back up and stand sideways.

"Just calm down. What's your name?" he asked with his hands lifted out from his sides to suggest he wasn't a threat.

"Shut up," the gangbanger yelled. He focused back on the barista. "Everything in the register," he said, wiggling the gun. "All of it. Now."

"Do as he says," Mikhail spoke calmly as the barista opened the drawer before returning his attention to the gunman. "Can you just lower your weapon so no one gets hurt?"

"Maybe I want to hurt someone. Maybe you who is buttin' into my business."

The gangbanger shifted his attention to Mikhail for a split second then reached for the money being handed over the counter. The red-haired woman let out a yell as she threw her steaming coffee in the gangbanger's face, followed by a kick to the knees, driving him backward into an awkward stagger.

Mikhail rushed in when he cried out and dropped the money. He shook his head in rage and leveled his gun at the woman. A confused look of surprise crossed his face, but when Mikhail shoved the gun upward, a shot rang out, causing more hysterical screams and flipped-over chairs. Mikhail quickly slid his foot under the gunman's, throwing him off-balance. The downward momentum landed him against a table full of teenagers before he hit the floor. At the same time, the gun flew up into the air as he waved the teenagers off to a safer place.

When Mikhail straightened, he heard a click. The red-haired woman pointed the gun with both hands at the would-be robber with a devilish expression that stretched across her mouth. The downed man tried to move, only to find her snakeskin boot in the middle of his chest.

"Careful with that." Mikhail reached for the weapon, only to have her step back and shake her head at surrendering the gun.

She bent over the thief, puckered her lips, and squinted. "That'll teach you to mess with my early morning mood stabilizer. Dumb jerk." Sirens blared for a few seconds, followed by screeching brakes of the police pulling up outside. When her attention shifted to the police swarming toward the double doors, she suddenly handed Mikhail the gun and batted her eyes innocently like an angel.

"Put the gun down," ordered an officer.

The almost-comical situation was not how he wanted to find himself first thing in the morning. He slowly passed the weapon to a young officer and immediately found himself handcuffed. The true criminal was yanked to his feet and also cuffed. The coffee-shop crowd appeared to be in shock, since no one spoke up for him.

"Hey, you," Mikhail called to the red-haired woman who strolled behind the counter and poured herself another cup of coffee. "A little help here," he insisted, annoyed she was oblivious to his situation.

She took a slow sip of coffee while shifting her focus to him over the rim of her cup as if this was a normal day. Curls of steam lifted in front of her face. Later, he would remember this was the moment he decided she was a menace, not some Scottish angel.

A young officer stepped to her side. "Petra, what went on here? Should have figured you were involved. Know this guy?" He made a hard visual assessment of him from head to toe.

"Nope." Letting her voice coo softly, she tilted her head sweetly. The officer blushed as he returned the flirtatious amusement. She took a deep breath then spoke. "Hey, can we meet for lunch, and I'll give you the whole story? I'm late for a meeting." She reached out and touched his arm.

"S-sure," he stuttered. "Back here at two?"

Definitely a menace, Mikhail decided as she strolled past him then circled back.

"I could have handled it myself, cowboy." Okay. Maybe he didn't like her after all. "Hold this." She handed him her coffee cup even though he was handcuffed. Without asking, she took the officer's pen, and pooched out her lips as if trying to avoid smiling at him. She paused and stared a little longer than polite. "You have pretty blue eyes." She took her coffee cup and set it on a table then pulled his hand open. She wrote across the palm, followed by retrieving her coffee. "Have a nice day." With a wink, she walked out with a shout to the remaining crowd, "Be safe, everyone!" Applause and cheers of thanks filled the room.

He lifted his cuffed hands to read what she'd written. It was a phone number. He was back to liking her.

The officer's phone beeped. He held it up to his ear and glanced out the plate-glass window. Mikhail followed his line of sight and saw the redhead talking and watching him. She also stood at the side of his Harley, running one hand over various sections. It was sensual, and the cop seemed transfixed by the motion.

"Okay, Petra. Noted. Thanks." He clicked off and came to remove his cuffs. "Petra says you got in the way but helped her take down the culprit."

"Helped her?" he asked incredulously.

The teenagers chimed in, "That's right, officer. This guy was a regular badass."

The officer took down his name and a quick way to reach him.

"I'm supposed to be someplace. Can I go, since you have my info?"

"Let me ask my boss."

"Ask your boss? You just let the redheaded ninja wannabe go with no problem."

"Watch your mouth, mister." He went to speak into his phone then returned. "You can go. I'll contact you later."

"Why don't we do lunch?" Mikhail snapped sarcastically.

"What? Are you a weirdo or something?"

Mikhail exhaled and calmed the inner beast inside him. "No. I apologize. Certainly, the experience has been traumatic for all of us." He fanned his hand out toward the customers then handed the officer a business card. "Would you like me to stick around and help in some way?"

The officer read the card and lifted his eyes toward Mikhail in disbelief. "Yeah. Maybe. Thanks. I would appreciate it. That little girl is crying, and her mother is having trouble soothing her."

Mikhail nodded and patted the officer's arm. "No problem. I'd be happy to speak to them."

"Oh. And sorry about cuffing you. Petra can be a real handful and thinks she's a badass."

"Yes. I gathered as much." He leaned in closer and spoke in a quiet, controlled voice. "Just to be clear, I'm a badass, too."

Two

Petra stood behind the a table, focused on a map using a magnifying glass. The map had recently been uncovered in the archives of the North American Museum of Natural History. A graduate student using their state-of-the-art computer system stumbled across it when he was cataloging a vault no one had touched in twenty years. She had studied it every day since. The musty smell and touch of brittle paper, long forgotten, never ceased to thrill her. It had begun to deteriorate to the point, the staff quickly worked their magic by photographing and applying a seal to keep it from further damage.

"Petra?" came a familiar voice from the open doorway. "How many times are you going to examine that smelly map before realizing it means nothing?"

Without turning to acknowledge the man who

probably leaned against the doorframe with his arms folded in a stubborn stance, she responded, "Chadwick, I know this is the map we've been searching for, and it was right under our noses."

Dr. Chadwick sighed, came closer, and peered down at the map. "You are right. As always. But Mr. Janson has requested to see you." He grabbed the magnifying glass from her hands and mimicked her examination.

"Then he better come down here to see me. I'm a little busy."

Petra had already had a harrowing day, starting at the coffee shop. She didn't bother to tell Chadwick, who might snort his distaste at her jumping into action. Although she believed he feared for her safety, he always acted perturbed at her antics, as he called them, and lectured her on how such behavior jeopardized the important work of the museum.

The image of the biker swam up to her memory as she stared into the distance. She bet those dangerous blue eyes had pierced many a heart. The shaggy dark hair with a little curl also had a few strands of gray. The tight-fitting leather was old, maybe from the Salvation Army store, and didn't leave much to the imagination. The scuffed boots went halfway up his calves, and, in her mind, branded him a rebel.

He liked her, too. She could tell by the way he watched her that he was interested. Why did she treat him with such a snarky attitude? After all, he did help her with the gunman. She probably would never hear from him. Picturing the whole scene as it unfolded gave her pleasure.

"Why are you smiling? And why aren't you on

your way to Mr. Janson's office?"

"Just waiting on you." She stood on tiptoe and kissed his cheek.

"Liar." Chadwick continued to examine the map.

"Actually, I met someone this morning at the coffee shop."

Chadwick lifted a skeptical glance at her then back to the map. "And?"

Petra shrugged. "And nothing. He drove an old Harley, wore leather, plowed into me by accident, and helped me stop a robbery."

I Suddenly she had Chadwick's undivided attention. "A robbery?"

She waved him off and eased back toward the door. "No big deal." She swooned to deflect the attention away from the robbery. "He was really a hunk."

"The robber or the biker?" He laid the magnifying glass down and joined her.

"Silly. Anyway, what is this meeting about?"

"It appears you're getting a partner." He flashed a diabolical expression of glee, followed by a chuckle. "Mr. Janson is tired of your going off half-cocked and jeopardizing acquisitions. He thinks your MacGyver slash Indiana Jones lack of decorum is repugnant and doesn't shine a favorable light on the museum."

Petra twisted her mouth and stomped forward. "La-de-dah. He doesn't complain when I strike archeological gold, though, does he?" She unbuttoned her white lab coat and tossed it on a nearby chair since the man kept his office to mimic a tropical rainforest along the equator.

The oak doors to his office lobby reminded her of

what the doors to the castle of the giant in "Jack and the Beanstalk" must have looked like. Once inside, his twenty-something secretary waved them to go right in. Why the man insisted on a supermodel type to be the first thing a person saw when they walked in was beyond her.

"Really? You have no idea?" Chadwick told her several weeks earlier. "She puts a little shine on all this old dusty world we explore. With one smile, she can get investors to fork over thousands of dollars to keep us in the game."

"I could do that," she insisted.

Chadwick expelled a belly laugh at that point, making her fume for at least ten minutes before responding, "You dress like a goth gypsy most of the time."

"It's called Bohemian. Gypsy is an unacceptable term these days. Besides, I don't have the money to waste on shiny clothes. Thrift stores are fine for me."

The secretary escorted them to more gigantic doors. "Thank you, Isolde. You're looking lovely today."

"Thank you, Dr. Chadwick. You're such a sweetheart."

Petra faked a cough, followed by a gag. She waved to Isolde, who appeared concerned. "I'm fine." Coughed a second time. "I'm fine. Really."

Once Petra and Chadwick entered the steam bath of an office, Mr. Janson rose from the mahogany desk and came around to shake their hands. He loved to dress as if he were going on safari and chewed on a cigar.

"Petra, you are looking the part today." He raised

his eyebrows and spoke around his obtuse cigar.

"And I see that you still have that monstrosity of a desk made of endangered mahogany. Shame on you."

"This is why I keep you on. I know you will make sure I don't break the law or—"

"Steal priceless antiquities that belong to another country?" She leaned in to level an innocent smile.

He let out a laugh, making his whole body jiggle. "That too, my dear Petra. However, as I told you many times before, the desk belonged to my grandfather, and mahogany wasn't endangered back then. I would never get anything made from it today. I'm crushed you haven't realized I am much more responsible than a furniture salesman."

"You're full of it."

Again, the laugh. He took his cigar out from the bulbous lips and pointed up and down at Petra's clothes. "The goth look actually becomes you. I may have a dog collar you can wear, somewhere around here. Has spikes and everything." He pretended to look around the office.

"Maybe it's with the whips and chains you keep for little Miss Dominatrix outside." She tilted her head and offered him one of the angelic tones that kept her from getting fired.

"Do I detect a twinge of jealousy?"

"I think you're experiencing gas."

Chadwick stepped forward and pulled her back next to him. "That's enough, Petra. Apologize."

"I'm sorry, Mr. Janson. I just love teasing you." She hoped batting her eyelashes at him helped.

He raised his chin and folded his lips together like a frog. "Now, who is full of it?" Mr. Janson walked to the refreshment cart and poured himself a cup of hot tea. He lifted the teapot toward them, but both waved it off. "I've finally got permission to go to Ethiopia and assist in the restoration of the churches of Lalibela."

Petra gasped and grabbed Chadwick's arm. "Oh. My. Gosh. This is amazing. We've been trying to get in there forever. How did you manage?"

Mr. Janson puffed out his chest at the nearest thing to a compliment he'd get from her. "I suppose it was a miracle. Divine intervention—"

"Good luck or you paid someone off," she interrupted.

"Not this time. We'd been told no so many times I'd given up. Then I met Father Novak. Just so happened, he'd served there for a while and is on friendly terms with the local government and people. He made a few calls for me, and here we are."

Decorum flew out the window as she clapped her hands in pure joy like a toddler. She even added the word "goody." She grabbed Mr. Janson's hands and forced him to dance in a circle with her. "When do I leave?"

"Yes, about that. I'm afraid you'll be partnering with Father Novak since he knows the ins and outs of the place."

"I work alone."

"Then I'll find someone else. Chadwick?"

"No," Petra shouted. "First time for everything. Poor old guy will probably stay put in a hotel or minister to the masses. I'm sure he'll be no problem."

Mr. Janson smirked as he laid his cigar across an ashtray atop his desk. "Yes. Again, about that, Petra."

"You keep saying that."

"He's a very hands-on kind of guy. Father Novak is running a little late. He stopped along the way to help out someone in need. Great guy. I think you'll like him." He buzzed Isolde. "Has Father Novak arrived yet?"

"Yes, sir. Just came in. I'll send him in."

Petra prepared herself to be polite and accommodating. After all, it would be worth it to finally get to visit the monolithic churches of Lalibela. If this old coot could get her there and inside to explore, then she'd stand on her head and spit nickels if that's what it took.

Mr. Janson moved toward the door as it opened.

"Father Novak. Thank you for coming." His wide body blocked a clear view of her new partner as they shook hands. "Come. I want you to meet two of the best archeologists in the country. Dr. Petra McGinnis and Dr. Thomas Chadwick. Meet Father Novak."

Petra straightened and blinked back her surprise. Father Novak stood relaxed, holding his bike helmet under one arm, glaring at her with hooded eyes that she knew were blue steel.

"You," she snapped.

One corner of his mouth turned up as he stepped forward and extended a hand. "We meet again."

Chadwick looked at Petra then the priest. "You know each other?"

"Yes, sir." Since Petra didn't accept his hand, he turned to Chadwick, who grabbed it immediately. "We met this morning over coffee and an unfortunate attempt at robbery."

Chadwick glanced her way, and she tried to hide her look of horror. "So, is this the hunk you were telling me about?" he quizzed in a calm voice.

Petra stuttered. "I-it most certainly is not."

"Oh, I'm pretty sure it was me," Mikhail offered cooly.

"You're kind of full of yourself. Besides, you aren't really my type," she said offhandedly.

He held up his palm and showed both men. "She wrote her number right here."

Chadwick peered closer. "Why would you give him my number, Petra?"

Novak glanced at his hand then dropped it to his side before sending a mischievous smile her way. "You lied to a priest?"

"If I knew you were a priest, I wouldn't have—" Petra stopped herself, seeing the immense pleasure in the eyes of Mr. Janson and Chadwick at her discomfort.

"I understand we're going to be partners. I'm sure I can be of great help." Mikhail cocked his head and let his gaze roam over her face then her body.

Petra could feel her eyebrow lift in irritation. "Let's not get ahead of yourself."

"I wish to be a fly on the wall," Mr. Janson quipped. "Seeing the two of you spar, even for a few minutes, gives me great joy. Father Novak has a degree in art history and a master's in cultural geography with an emphasis in world religions. And he has some medical training on top of that."

"Aren't you the bee's knees?" She couldn't help sounding flippant at the cocky priest's accomplishments.

"Yes, so I've been told," he admitted. "And you have degrees in anthropology and archelogy with a specialty in medieval and ancient biblical"—he paused and put his finger on his chin—"something or other. Sorry. I dozed off when I was reading your bio."

Petra waited for either of her bosses to speak up for her, but both just stood amused at the banter.

"Is it possible this will be a perfect match?" Chadwick whispered to Mr. Janson.

"Maybe even a match made in heaven," Mr. Janson responded, followed by a chuckle.

Both men turned to observe their not-so-perfect team players and wondered if they hadn't created a new atomic bomb.

Three

❖

Father Mikhail Novak returned to his church to find solace and communicate with God to soothe his troubled soul. The rush of anxiety and unworthiness washed over him after leaving the museum. He shouldn't wear a crucifix hidden in his clothes, preach forgiveness, or offer comfort when his inner turmoil often boiled over into a kind of chaos he found difficult to manage. Oftentimes his worldliness bathed him in irrational behavior, like today with Dr. Petra McGinnis.

He found her—enchanting. Pretty in an earthy, almost-magical way that kept him a little off-balance until she opened her mouth for verbal combat. It forced him to admit he wanted to spare and outsmart the obvious, archeological diva and darling of Mr. Janson. Her credentials indicated she came by the notoriety honestly. Her discoveries and acquisitions for the museum were nothing short of a miracle.

And he knew all about miracles.

When his lips stopped moving in prayer, Petra swam up to his consciousness and shattered any hope of continuing. He reflected back on the day and found his heart beat a little faster and his clothes grew tighter. But he let it happen. Once more, he played the conversation over again in his head.

"Let's get something straight, buddy—" Petra fumed.

"It's Father Novak, or Father Mikhail. Mike is also okay. But under no circumstance am I your 'buddy.'"

They had walked down to her lab, Chadwick left behind to firm up plans concerning Ethiopia. Although she continued to walk, more like a storm, her mouth stopped moving as she turned her face toward him and squinted her eyes.

"You're not a priest either, I suspect."

"Why would you say that? Because I drive a motorcycle and wear leather?"

"Because you took down that asshole at the coffee shop like you did that for a living."

"Your language is quite colorful, considering your extensive education. Where did you apprentice? On a river barge in the Congo?"

"Oh. I didn't mean to insult your sensibilities, Father Pretender."

"Let's try Father Mike."

"Whatever. Here we are." She opened the door and waved him inside. "And another thing, Mike. For a priest, you certainly were checking my backside out in the coffee shop."

He hoped his expression reflected contempt. "And

how do you know that?"

"There was a mirror on the wall under the menu board." She'd let her snarky attitude come out.

"Is that why you kept toying with your hair and making eye contact with me? Oh sorry. Let me put it in words you can understand. You were flirting with me."

Petra sucked in her breath and slammed the door shut. "Were you checking me out or not?"

"I was admiring God's creation. Nothing more. You think because I'm a priest I'm immune to a beautiful woman?" This took her aback, and she tightened her lips together so that they narrowed to a hard line. It was yet another habit causing his gaze to linger a little too long. "Are you going to give me the tour as Dr. Chadwick led me to believe you would do, or should I just leave until you feel less threatened?"

She tossed him a lab coat to wear and moved around the room explaining different artifacts under study or preservation. Her voice softened, and he felt like he'd fallen into a National Geographic journey with a master adventurer. Every word drew his undivided attention. When he had questions, she answered carefully and let him follow up with more questions if he didn't understand. All in all, it turned out to be a pleasant experience.

It neared two o'clock when Petra announced she had an appointment. They walked out in silence only to find another car had blocked her in.

"I'll call and cancel." She huffed her disappointment.

He noticed another biker arriving and went over to borrow his helmet for Petra. Since she was known around the museum, the biker gladly loaned it out.

"Here. Hop on. I'll take you to your lunch date. I need to finish up with your boyfriend too."

"He's not my boyfriend. Don't have time for romance." She didn't hesitate to slip on the helmet and climb on behind him. He could only imagine her pulling the tight skirt a little higher on her thighs. She wrapped her arms around him and squeezed.

Maybe he drove too fast to keep those arms tight around his waist. Maybe he was on one of the adrenaline highs he sometimes got. Maybe he liked feeling normal with a pretty woman on his bike and the sun in his face.

The police officer waiting at the café appeared a little disappointed when both of them entered. The obvious interest he showed in Petra was encouraged as she batted her long lashes at each question he asked. The officer picked up the tab, but Father Novak insisted on leaving a tip.

"I'll wait outside, Dr. McGinnis. Then I'll take you back to the museum." Father Novak laid some money on the table.

She nodded and kept talking to who must have been the president of her fan club. His mention that she needed to be careful and never try a stupid stunt like disarming a criminal because she could get hurt, said it all.

The drop-off was uneventful. She offered to take the helmet to the owner and pranced away without so much as a thanks for the ride. When she reached the back door, she turned to see if he was watching. He was. A smirk was all he could manage as he flipped down his visor and sped off.

Once again, here he was, lost in his own thoughts

and wondering why some days he just couldn't get his head on straight.

"Mikhail."

He turned to see his larger-than-life mentor standing in the shadows like a hulking monolith.

"I'm praying." Mikhail folded his hands together again. "Do you mind?"

"If you were really praying, I wouldn't have interrupted. I suspect you are thinking about other things, maybe Petra." He emerged into the dappled light streaming in through the stained glass windows. "You have nothing to fear from her."

"How would you know?" He rose from his knees and glared at a man who was something much different than what he once knew. It often frightened him. Maybe even terrified him.

"Do you need to ask me such a question, Mikhail?" Clothed in black, it was difficult to distinguish his mood or whether he'd come to taunt him into submission. "Answer me, Mikhail. We have had such conversations many times. I owe you much. I have not always wanted to believe it, of course."

"You owe me nothing. It was my job."

"You saved my life," the deep voice carried on the stillness of the sanctuary.

"I wish sometimes I hadn't," Mikhail admitted.

"Sometimes," he paused—"I do too. But we are far from being in control. And I am here to make sure you fulfill the will of God. Do you understand me?" Mikhail sought out the intricate stain glass windows above. "Mikhail?"

"I understand. But this woman—"

"This too is part of the will of God. I want you to

say the words with me, Mikhail."

"I can't. Not tonight."

"Say it." The man took a threatening step toward him.

"When I am afraid, I will trust in You. In God, whose word I praise, in God I trust, I will not be afraid. What can mortal man do to me? Psalm 56:3-4." He took a deep breath. "Thank you, Zane," he whispered. He kept his head bowed for a few more seconds.

When he lifted his chin, the man had disappeared—again.

He turned back to the altar and added a few prayer requests from people at the coffee shop earlier in the day. With his encouragement, they promised to attend services on Sunday.

The apartment over the garage behind the church was small; perhaps a thousand square feet. The furnishings were sparse, but it was enough. Any entertainment he did was held at the church banquet room, used for wedding receptions, showers, funeral dinners for a family in mourning, and classes for different ladies' groups. Living in close quarters suited him. At least the apartment boasted a view overlooking a small park with a walking trail leading to a farmer's market. Often times, he jogged around the pond when his brain twisted up with the past. The solitude of nature soothed his soul. If his mentor joined him, he was inclined to listen and learn. It grew easier to obey the words that often stuck in his craw. PTSD was a demon he often fought until Zane showed up.

Setting the tea kettle on the burner, he retrieved a chipped mug and a tea bag. While he waited, it suited him to observe the park bathed in twilight. He reflected back, as he often did, on those days when life took a dangerous turn in his life.

Years earlier in Afghanistan

Gunfire snapped around the Marines, pinning them down like cattle on their way to slaughter with no escape. A rocket launched, lobbing a missile toward them. The explosion rocked them, mixed with the death cries of men who would no longer experience the uncertainty of war. Mikhail knew he was almost out of ammunition as his feverish gaze went to his leg, covered in blood. All but four lay dead with horror-stricken faces. Sergeant Zane Spokane continued to fight to protect them until help came. The call for assistance had been made, but was it too late?

Mikhail staggered to position himself nearby and fired, just as a Taliban fighter leaped over the barricade and stabbed his rusty bayonet at his chest. The rifle dropped from his hands when he held it up to protect himself. Sergeant Spokane took his rifle and swung it like a club at the fighter's head, knocking him off Mikhail. The sergeant grabbed the bayonet and buried it in the man's chest whose face twisted in agony, knowing death was imminent. The sergeant watched with narrowed eyes until he died. Mikhail wondered if the sergeant took pleasure or revenge at the death. Either way, he was alive and grateful because of the sergeant's actions.

"Let's finish this, kid," the sergeant snapped.

Mikhail remembered later the odd order considering the sergeant was only about ten years older than himself. But he shook off what fear remained in his gut and jumped into action. Something about the man demanded respect and obedience. Was it the spark in his frosty gaze or the lack of fear he displayed that gave Mikhail the burst of courage needed to survive a surprise assault?

"We gotta pull back," Sergeant Zane shouted. "Go. I'll cover you. Our ride out of here should be on its way."

The other men rose carefully and took off running between discarded vehicles twisted from explosions and fire from other encounters. Mikhail hesitated until the sergeant turned an icy glare his way. "I said go!"

"Sarge, you'll die," he shouted as he hunkered down next to him.

"I'm already dead inside. Go."

More shots zinged overhead, along with the distant whop-whop sound of a helicopter. Mikhail would later remember it sounding like angel wings. He was easing out the back of their barricade, when he heard a grunt. Turning, he saw the sergeant fall and his rifle spiraling to the ground. Without another thought, Mikhail ran back, slung the rifle over his shoulder, and lifted the sergeant to his shoulder. He hadn't realized until that moment how big his sergeant was or if he would be able to carry him to the rescue helicopter. But at least he could get him to a safe place until help came.

Another shot whizzed over his head, and he instinctively knew the enemy had breached the makeshift wall they'd built. He could hear them yell words he didn't want to ever understand. The shouts of his fellow soldiers encouraged him on as bullets danced on the ground around his feet.

"Dear Jesus, save us," kept coming out of his mouth over and over until he felt something hard hit his leg. His forward motion caused the sergeant to hit the ground before he fell on top of him.

To his surprise, the sergeant was staring at him as their noses touched. "I told you to go."

Mikhail pushed himself up like a wobbly blow-up balloon people put in their yards at Christmas. Shots from the helicopter fired on the Taliban, slowing the enemy's progress. He took a second to glance over his shoulder, and they were still coming, even when others met their own death spiral.

In spite of the pain, he reached down and pulled the sergeant to his feet. Once more, he managed to balance him on his shoulder. Whether it was the adrenaline or God's grace, Mikhail limped forward, dragging the wounded leg at a snail's pace. He witnessed his friends running toward him to help, only to be cut down in their efforts.

"I'll come back for you!" Mikhail shouted to them as they tried to roll to their bellies and shoot at the enemy.

From out of nowhere, another soldier appeared. Lying down by the two on the ground, he put his hand upon them. When he staggered to the helicopter, a medic jumped out and helped with Sergeant Zane Spokane. Mikhail limped back to the men on the ground, firing at the oncoming Taliban. Without warning, they stopped as if trying to make sense of the confusion around them. Taking advantage of the chaos, Mikhail was able to slip behind them and retrieve the bodies of the fallen soldiers one at a time, in spite of a wounded leg.

Later, the medic admitted he'd never seen anything like it. The Taliban walked in circles as if disoriented, shooting in the wrong direction while Mikhail brought back the fallen.

Once more, he ran to the men who had tried to help him. He lifted one into his arms, and promised the last two he'd return.

"I'll wait with him. Hurry. The Taliban won't be confused for much longer, Mikhail," said the soldier he didn't recognize.

He returned in minutes for the last man and carried him to the helicopter as well.

"We're out of here!" shouted the pilot.

Mikhail tapped him on the shoulder. "What about the other guy?" he called out in panic. "Another man is out there."

The pilot shook his head. "You got them all, buddy. There wasn't anyone else."

"You saw him, right?" he asked the last two soldiers.

They shook their heads and fell back so the medic could assess their wounds as the chopper lifted to safety.

He felt a hand on his leg and noticed Sergeant Spokane watching him. "I saw him. He was no soldier."

"What? Then who?"

"An angel. I owe both of you."

Years later, Mikhail Novak had come to both appreciate and resent ever saving Sergeant Zane Spokane.

Four

The museum remained dark in the hall of displays. Lights would automatically come on around 8 a.m. In the wings, sensor lights detected heat and movements of the comings and goings of scientists, archeologists, anthropologists, botanists, and other technology-based geniuses who delved into the past. Most left between six and seven each day, especially those who were students or had families. A few classrooms provided stadium seating for evening classes attended by mostly graduate students. High-tech security kept tabs on these people and recorded on a twenty-four-hour loop, evaluated, then stored the information on servers kept at another location.

Depending on the instructor or speaker, the classroom seats were rarely more than half full. The exception was when Chadwick or Petra taught or spoke on a recent trip. When they teamed up, tickets were distributed by a lottery drawing unless you were already one of the accepted students working at the museum.

Chadwick came in early most mornings; somewhere around 5 a.m. He enjoyed the solitude and unearthly quiet of old things. He once declared it was the perfect time to listen to the whispers of the old ones. He would stroll through the darkened wings of new discoveries or restorations, knowing the twilight glows would brighten for a few minutes. It was enough to reassure himself all was well with the bygone eras.

Next, he would go to his office, make a pot of hot tea, study his schedule, and nibble on a bagel with cream cheese. After he finished cup number two of Earl Grey tea, he would slip into his lab coat and stroll to his lab he shared with Petra. The two of them were never far apart.

He retrieved the map Petra had been studying a few days earlier when they had been called to Mr. Janson's office. Spread out on a table the size of a double bed, it appeared small. Such a jewel of a find. Other than a few brittle tears from age and improper handling, the map was pristine. A chunk near the top where the title normally should be was one of those. He left it in the clear covering, concerned he might cause more damage.

Rolling the optical microscope over to explore the surface and project it onto a screen on the far side of the table a few feet away was much easier on his eyes. Currently, it wasn't clear where the map led or what it might reveal. He'd forgotten to ask Petra what she meant by thinking it was the clue they'd been looking for. That could have meant anything with her. Both of them usually had several projects, treasures, and mysteries they worked on at any given time.

Petra was one to flutter around the projects like a disoriented butterfly. Her mind was constantly twisting and turning ideas into adventurous possibilities until it made sense to approach Mr. Janson for funding. Chadwick, on the other hand, laid the groundwork for a project, researched it to death, then decided if it would be worth the time, money, and trouble to pursue it for the museum. His sweet Petra didn't care if the museum wanted it or not. She believed only they could preserve it for the world, insuring the educational value for future generations.

"Someone will want it," she'd say happily. "It's priceless," she'd declare with her hands on her hips and a mischievous glow on her freckled face.

"Then let them have it. We have three of those at this museum alone."

But the map intrigued both of them. Several things had escaped their grasp throughout their journeys. One of those was the Vessel of St. Mary where Petra had almost drowned. Chadwick attributed the discovery to Petra's overactive imagination after such a close call. Besides, after the cave flooded, there was no going back down with any hopes of finding it. Nothing had ever come of it by studying the map, which she believed was connected to the Vessel of St. Mary. In his mind, he wondered if the vessel existed.

He moved around the table to get a closer look. The eastern half of the map had two feeder rivers pouring into a larger river that flowed northward. He retrieved a transparency map of modern-day East Africa and laid it on this one under the microscope. Returning to his position in front of the screen, he squinted then rubbed his forehead.

The two rivers were the Blue and White Nile that fed into the larger Nile. He backtracked the rivers with his finger and realized most of the map was of Ethiopia. He noticed a tiny string of letters in Amharic as a whisper touched his ear.

"Tewahedo."

Chadwick rubbed his ear and glanced around him for another presence. He remained alone.

"Tewahedo. Lyesus." Was his mind playing tricks on him? This was a map of Ethiopia near the regions of Lalibela.

What secret could be kept there? An auspicious opportunity had just fallen into their laps to travel to Lalibela at this particular time. He decided to talk to Father Mikhail since he had served near the area. He glanced at his watch and secured the map in a tube container. Maybe the priest could make sense of it.

Before he left, he needed to write something to Petra to explain what he might be forced to do.

Morning prayers had concluded, Mikhail's favorite time of day. It meant a new beginning. The quiet always felt heavy but comforting to his troubled soul. The whispers of prayer throughout the Church of the Holy Trinity from the older members of the congregation never failed to give him the courage to move through another day.

The PTSD was getting better. Hard work, serving, therapy and, of course, prayer, pushed him to be normal again. He'd never mentioned to the therapist about the comings and goings of his mentor, Zane Spokane. There would always be the chance the suggestion of schizophrenia might be considered.

Those words might leak out and his lifeline at the church would be yanked away from him. Although men of God were supposed to believe angels moved among them, most had never been confronted by one. But Mikhail had on numerous occasions. The first time had been in battle. Then again when his wife died. Responsibilities piled up, along with the memories of being a soldier until he called out in God's name for help.

That's when Zane Spokane showed up. Although troubling, no one could see him, unless he chose for that to happen. Zane told Mikhail it was part of the process and not to worry. Healing took time.

It was hard to come to grips with Zane Spokane. He'd been his sergeant; a demanding one at that. The man had spiraled into madness after he returned home. Something happened to him in St. Louis, changing everything.

He'd gone to visit him while considering the solitary life of the priesthood. Seeing Zane, a tormented ex-soldier living among the homeless, drove a spike through his heart until the night he met a Watcher, or angel. His name was Rocco, and he took notice of Mikhail and confronted him about his own demons that plagued him. To be honest, Rocco scared the hell out of him.

Not long after their visit, Zane Spokane disappeared. His sister said he was officially a missing person, presumed dead. Then one day, he showed up to be his mentor—or tormentor. To this day, he wasn't sure which it was.

"Father Mikhail?" He recognized the voice of Dr. Thomas Chadwick from the museum. He held up a tube. "Have I come at a bad time? I know it's early."

The priest had moved to speak to an older couple edging out into the aisle. They were faithful and came each morning for prayers. After they waved him on to visit with someone else, Mikhail watched them until they reached the back of the church before turning to the unexpected guest.

"Dr. Chadwick. What a surprise." He extended his hand.

"Please. Just call me Chadwick. No need to stand on ceremony with me."

Father Mikhail motioned for the professor to follow. "Let's go to my office. I'm only an associate priest here, so my duties are finished for a few hours. How can I help you? Don't tell me you've come for confession. You strike me as a man who communes with God as he sees fit, without the use of a priest."

Chadwick chuckled softly. "No, nothing like that. I have something I want to show you."

The two men entered the small office. Mikhail quickly pushed over a padded chair for Chadwick. "Will this do? I'm not in here very much. I like to be out in the community serving." Mikhail sat on the edge of his empty desk and folded his hands in his lap.

"Not sure I've ever been to confession. Maybe I should give it a try." He held up the map tube for the second time. "This was recently found in our archives while trying to catalog decades of collections. Petra can't stop studying it because she thinks it is the key to some kind of treasure."

"Petra?" Mikhail hadn't seen her for a week. The arrangements were underway for their trip to Ethiopia. They would depart day after tomorrow. Except for a basic itinerary, Mikhail wasn't privy to what they'd be doing while there.

"Yes. Hasn't she been getting you up to speed on what she wants you to do? I will join you in a couple of weeks, at the end of the semester." He frowned. "Ah. I'm guessing she is trying to show you who's boss by leaving you out of the loop. Just a warning—she has no patience for anyone who pretends to know what they're doing."

"I assure you, Chadwick, I am well versed in the churches of Lalibela. It is a magical place. The people are loyal and protective of the site. And they are devout followers of Christ. Although their method of worship may deviate from what we experience in this country, their love of God and those monolithic structures are of utmost importance to them."

Chadwick bit his bottom lip then twisted his mouth as if to stop himself from speaking. Silence filled the room for a few seconds before he uncapped the map tube. "May I?"

Mikhail slid off the desk and helped him spread out the map. He accepted a pair of clear gloves and allowed the priest to retrieve four stacks of sticky notes, still in their packing, to place on the corners to keep it from rolling back up.

"The map has been a bundle of questions. Up until this morning, parts were missing, but it may be a map of what is currently Sudan and Ethiopia. It was like," he smiled, then continued, "you might laugh at this, but I felt like it magically added the missing parts."

Mikhail leaned in for closer examination and focused on the northwest corner. "Do you have any idea how this map came to be in the museum?" He couldn't take his eyes off the landforms and various symbols across the map.

"No. The last time we went through the contents of the archive room—maybe fifteen years ago—it wasn't there. Or at least, it wasn't mentioned or cataloged." He waved his hand over it. "It's in remarkable shape."

"Could it be a copy? Aged to trick a person without a trained eye?" He sniffed it. "It even smells old."

"I'm stumped. My first impression was maybe stored by mistake. We were shorthanded at the time and enlisted a few trustworthy students to aid the team."

Mikhail took a second whiff. "It even smells like Lalibela." He couldn't keep from feeling charmed by the memory of the place.

"Lalibela? Are you sure?"

"Yes. I worked in an orphanage not far from there and would visit at least once a month, more if there were holy days or festivals. Several times, I was asked to take pilgrims there because of my familiarity with the churches." He pulled out the desk drawer and retrieved a square magnifying glass resembling a child's toy. Bending low over the yellowed paper, he caught the emblem he hoped to find. When he straightened, Chadwick waited in anticipation.

"What did you find?"

"It appears to be a holy treasure, lost to the world for centuries." He pointed to a small marking near a city. See the letters RA? I'm guessing it's in one of the Rock Hewn Churches of Lalibela or traditionally known as Roha that was founded by the Agew family, thus RA."

Chadwick took the magnifying glass to study the map. "And tradition also holds that prior to his accession to the throne, Gebre Meskel Lalibela was guided by Christ on a tour of Jerusalem and instructed to build a second Jerusalem in Ethiopia."

"According to legend, God requested the king of Ethiopia, Lalibela, to build the churches as a replica of Jerusalem. It is said that men and angels worked together to construct them; the men worked during the day, and the angels came at night to work. When I was there, the old ones spoke of a special gift the angels left to safeguard the structures." Father Mikhail shrugged.

"What was it?" Chadwick sounded breathless.

"They would never tell me." Mikhail put the magnifying glass back in the desk. "But several of these elders were over a hundred years old. Claimed to be the guardians of truth, good health, and longevity."

"Good genes maybe."

Mikhail nodded. "Maybe. But whatever it was, they had the stamina of men in their twenties, good teeth, and resisted local disease and common flu outbreaks."

"Was it everyone or just a few elders?"

"Only a few. They called themselves the Guardians of Tomorrow."

"Maybe you could visit them again. Sounds as if it would be an incredible discovery." Chadwick rolled up the map. "I had an inkling when we met that you were just what the museum needed. New blood is always a shot in the arm. Can you reach out to these Guardians?"

"I'm not sure. Only one remains. He may not remember me."

"What happened to the others?" Chadwick smirked. "Died of old age after all?"

"No. They were murdered."

Five

Mikhail arranged to be gone from the church the rest of the day. There were two other priests there to carry out the few duties he had been assigned. Most of the time, he was on his own anyway. He was the youngest and, at times, felt the other two benefitted from staying busy more than he did. The church was a place of healing for him. However, the thought of getting back out in the world again had triggered a much deeper desire inside him.

The morning was still on the cool side, and traffic remained congested. Mikhail found weaving in and out of the mayhem a welcome distraction from what he might find at the museum, or rather who he'd meet. Chadwick insisted he come and spend the day with Petra who would be sorting through things for the trip. In his words, "It will be an excellent way to get used to each other."

It vaguely sounded like he'd been paired with a pit bull assistance dog with rabies.

She had brought out the worst in him with their first interaction at the natural history museum. His tongue had easily offered stinging comebacks when challenged. Having her on the back of his Harley with those slender arms wrapped snugly around him left him anxious to try it again in the near future. Remembering how she'd surprised the coffee-shop robber with her cup of coffee to his face still amused him. She was a fighter. He found a woman who could take care of herself more than a little sexy.

"Petra?" Mikhail saw her standing outside of the lecture hall going over notes on a clipboard. He ran his hand through his hair. From the way her gaze traveled over his face then up to the top of his head, it was a sure bet the bike helmet had given him a roll-out-of-bed appearance.

"Father Mikhail. I wasn't expecting you." At least her voice was friendly enough. "I was on my way to the lab. Want to join me?"

She'd already headed in the opposite direction. Her tight jeans and Black Sabbath T-shirt gave her an almost-teen appearance. He wondered if she knew he was coming and wore this particular band's T-shirt to taunt him. She had knotted the thick red hair into a bun on her neck, but unruly strands had loosened to frame her delicate face. The white strands fell across one of her eyes. The purple ones appeared to be tied up in the bun. Those probing eyes appeared too big for her freckled face.

Before she had a chance to change her mind,

Mikhail followed, taking long strides that forced her to speed up. He realized it was yet another power play on his part, but she didn't appear to notice.

"I was wondering when you would come back around. Thought maybe you had changed your mind about going to Ethiopia with me. It's fine if you'd rather not. I imagine you must be busy, and—"

"I'm not. I've already given notice and packed my bag. I haven't been around because I was waiting for an invite."

She arched an eyebrow and batted her eyelashes. "I guess it's a good thing you didn't wait."

"Is there a reason you don't like me, Petra, or do you just not like men in general?"

They entered the lab, and she pointed at a white coat hanging on a metal coatrack.

"I don't like pretenders, Mike, I mean, Father Mikhail." She slipped into a lab coat with a skull and crossbones on the back. "I think that's what you are. I can smell it."

"Perhaps what you smell is the pan on your hot plate over there that is about to burst into flames." He hurried to the smoking plastic handle and shoved it off the burner with a hot pad lying nearby.

"I never turned it on, and I certainly didn't put a pan on there."

"Right," he said offhandedly, doubting she'd admit to it.

"No. Really." She used a potholder and picked it up. "I've never even seen this pan before."

"Maybe Chadwick left it on when he came to visit me earlier."

She blinked and set the pan down and unplugged

the hot plate. "Chadwick came to see you? What did he want?"

"Confession is good for the soul." He leveled a narrowed glare at her.

"Maybe you should take your own words of wisdom." Her brow creased in confusion. "Sorry. This is just disturbing about the hot plate. It could have burned the lab down. I was in here an hour ago. As I said, I never used it."

"Does anyone else have access to the lab?"

"Yes. But, like me, they weren't in here. We were all in a meeting together. Only Chadwick was missing. He left me a message he was running an errand and would catch up later. Besides, he wasn't supposed to be at the meeting today. It was just a bunch of grad students and myself catching up on work schedules and sharing their final projects. Boring stuff. I hate those, but it has to be done. Maybe he did it."

"I doubt it. He came to see me around eight. This place would have caught fire by now."

Petra shivered at his words. "Thank goodness you distracted me, or I might not have come back to the lab. The midtown library called to tell me they found the book I wanted. I was going to head over there. It's on Lalibela."

Mikhail surveyed the room and proceeded to walk around inspecting other things that caught his interest.

She followed him and took on a snarky tone. "Aren't you going to say something relevant like God works in mysterious ways?"

"Kind of hokey, don't you think?" Mikhail focused on her lips then slowly moved to her eyes.

"Is it?" She shifted her weight to one hip. "I'm a

bit territorial and this whole partner thing took me by surprise." She cleaned up the mess. "Why did Chadwick come to see you?"

"Had a map the two of you had been studying. He was convinced it might be one of what is currently Sudan and Ethiopia. He was right. Several symbols puzzled him. I was able to help him make sense of it."

"Seriously?" Her surprise bordered on effervescent and caused him to suppress his amusement at observing her childish delight. "Wonder where he is?"

"He left maybe twenty minutes before me. I thought he'd be here. Maybe he stopped for coffee."

"He doesn't drink coffee, and when I poked my head in his office this morning, I could see he'd already made a pot of tea." She phoned the parking garage to check if he'd returned. "They say he never came back." Her voice slowed at the same time her fingers tapped on the table. "I'll call him." After she punched in his number, Petra continued to talk. "We keep pretty close tabs on each other. He's my only family here in the big city." She clicked off and sent a text.

Mikhail felt a tickle on the back of his neck and wondered if it might be a warning. In spite of it being annoying, he'd learned to pay attention to such things.

"Oh. Finally," she groaned, opening up the return text. She paled and fell back against the metal table.

"Petra, what is it?" Mikhail took the phone.

A picture of Chadwick bound and gagged sitting in the back seat of what may have been a limo, appeared. The words across the bottom said: "Protect the map and bring it to me."

Six

Petra paced and alternated between rubbing her hands down the side of her white lab coat and pushing loose strands of hair behind her ears. She stopped several times to study Father Mikhail. He stood tall and lent his full attention to whatever Mr. Janson was saying. He had come to them, an unusual event in itself. Having him take interest in the sudden disappearance of Chadwick only added to the stress she experienced.

Remarkably, it was the priest who reassured her. His demeanor was strong and true. The words of comfort he offered covered her like a warm blanket right out of the dryer. Taking her phone, he tried to trace the picture by using her computer, with no luck. Often, he took deep breaths and appeared to scrutinize the picture and helped her see Chadwick was unharmed. Those piercing blue eyes mesmerized her with calm and something else. What was it?

From time to time, she caught him studying her. He did offer a thin smile to take the edge off. If anything, it intensified the desire to be near him, breathe his air, and feel the energy she sensed every time she was near him. Whatever he was—priest, pretender, historian, or demon—Father Mikhail touched an unsettling spot deep inside her.

"The police will be here shortly, Petra," Mr. Janson informed her.

"No," she fumed. "The second message said not to get the police involved and to wait for more instructions. Can you imagine the hoopla with the media if this gets out? Please. Just wait."

Mr. Janson's secretary, Isolde, opened the door and ushered in two men. One was the cop from the coffee shop. The other was a hulk of a man, dressed in black. Petra assumed he was a detective, but he stood next to the door and observed Father Mikhail who carefully positioned himself between him and her line of sight. She saw the man in black lift his hand toward Mr. Janson then Officer Hawi Mathias who switched his attention to her but spoke to her boss.

"Mr. Janson," Officer Mathias began, "there really isn't anything I can do unless he's missing for twenty-four hours."

"But the picture?" She took the phone back to scroll through her latest pictures. "Hawi, it's gone." She turned to Mr. Janson and realized he must have erased it. But why?

"Sorry, Petra," Officer Mathias offered. "He'll show up. All you archeologist and scientist types lose track of time. I'll check back later. I bet you'll find him somewhere in the museum."

"No. He isn't. I checked." Officer Mathias scribbled in a little notebook and acted as if he didn't hear her.

"I'll walk you out, Officer. Thank you for coming. You're probably right." Mr. Janson headed toward the door.

The other man remained until Petra turned away to fume. She doubled her fists and pounded them on the metal table in panic. When she leveled a hateful glare at the man left behind, she discovered he was gone.

"Who was the other guy with Officer Mathias?" she asked, flopping down on a rolling stool.

Father Mikhail appeared startled at her questions; he came around and laid a hand on the table as if to steady himself. "What guy?"

"The one in black. You know, the big guy. Looked more like a gangster than a detective."

"You could see him?" His brow creased as surprise made him come stand before her.

Petra tried to evaluate the confused expression on Mikhail's face, but all she could think about was how blue those hooded eyes were and how deep his voice sounded. Priests shouldn't be this attractive.

"He was pretty hard to miss. What a question. It was kind of rude of Officer Mathias not to introduce us, don't you think?" She walked casually to the door and peered out. "Where did he go? He was just here?"

"Heaven only knows."

Mikhail turned back to her and frowned.

The rest of the day was spent retracing Chadwick's steps. Mikhail remembered he'd seen a couple of stores in the background of the picture of Chadwick. It wasn't far from the church. They took his Harley, but he stopped at a sporting goods store along the way. Petra followed him in, scrolling through her phone to try and find the picture of Chadwick. After bumping into several people, Mikhail took her elbow and led her to the back and had her fitted for a helmet. It was basic black with a face shield.

"They act like they know you," she teased. "Bring many women here for a helmet? Guess it can be a real turn-on."

He couldn't help but squint at her and felt a rising irritation at the insinuation. "Are you turned on, Petra?" He forced his voice to be ice cold to discourage her flippant attitude. "You know what they say, once you've had a holy man, you never go back."

"Eww," she said, wrinkling her nose. Slipping on the helmet, she stood in front of a mirror and modeled the addition. "Whoa. I look really badass. Oh sorry. I mean I look really tough."

Mikhail paid for the helmet and headed for the front door, leaving her to hurry after him. He pushed through the exterior doors, letting it close on her.

"Hey, that wasn't very nice," she fumed.

"Guess that makes me a badass too."

"I think I'm going to like you, Mikhail."

"Thanks for the warning."

Her light laughter touched his ear as she slipped on behind him and tapped him on the back of the helmet.

"Let's go, hot stuff."

Father Mikhail didn't appreciate being flirted with or called hot stuff. He was a priest, after all. Having her sit behind him forced him to harden his heart and sensibilities. Many of the priests he knew in the Eastern Orthodox Church were married and had children. Even he had been married for a time. His wife's death tore him apart, and it wasn't something he ever wanted to experience again. It set off his PTSD and forced him to remember Afghanistan. But the church provided a safe haven for his soul and his brain.

After weaving in and out of traffic at a dangerous speed, he hoped Petra would get her wisecracks under control when they stopped. That didn't happen.

"From what I remember of the picture"—he outstretched his hand for her to hand it over—"this cupcake shop was showing through the back window of the car."

"The picture is gone. Remember?"

He scrolled anyway, guessing his mentor, Zane, made it unavailable to the police and Mr. Janson. When he found it, he examined it closely and quickly discovered what he searched for down the street. "There." He pointed.

"Let me see that," she ordered. "It's here. How could I have missed it?"

Mikhail shrugged and walked back toward the cupcake shop with windows decorated with purple swirls and fairies. "Do you have a picture of Chadwick without the gag?"

"I think so."

When they entered the shop, two ladies behind the counter recognized him right away.

"Father Mikhail," the gray-haired lady chirped happily. "You've never been to our little shop?"

He laid a hand on his heart and frowned. "No. I don't believe I have." He leaned in and whispered, "I could no longer resist you two or your cupcakes. If I have to jog a couple more miles each day because of these tasty treats, so be it." The two women giggled and a rosy blush matched the roses on the cupcakes. "Now that I see all the beautiful creations you've made, I'm thinking it just might be worth it stopping on my way back each day. Is this shop yours?"

"Yes. Have you come to order cupcakes for the Holy Trinity Orphanage auction?" the shorter of the two ladies asked.

"Of course. How many would you suggest?" He took his wallet from inside his leather jacket.

They agreed upon a quantity, and the ladies offered each of them a free one.

"Oh, I almost forgot. I'm looking for a friend of mine. He came by earlier today."

"He's not answering his phone and, since he has a heart condition, I want to make sure I find him." Petra held up her phone to show Chadwick standing with his graduate students at his last birthday party.

"Oh, lordy me. You got me so flustered when you walked in, I almost forgot. Yes. I did," the lady with gray hair admitted. "He ran in here for us to hold something for him. Said you'd be by later to pick it up. When he left, a couple of guys dressed in suits escorted him to their big, honkin' limo. Whew. It was a beauty. Another man drove off in your friend's car."

The shorter of the two ladies wiped her hands on her purple apron and held up a finger. "I put it in the back. Just a second."

Petra and Mikhail exchanged glances of hope.

When she returned, she held a map tube and extended her hand. Petra reached for it, but the woman snatched it back and leveled a suspicious gaze at her. "The gentleman said to give it to no one but Father Mikhail. And that's what I intend to do." She tilted her head at the priest and gave him an endearing gaze.

Mikhail held out his hand and continued to smile at both the smitten ladies old enough to be his mother.

She gently placed the tube in his hand. "There ya go, Father. We'll deliver those cupcakes Saturday morning for the auction."

He leaned in and kissed the lady on the cheek. "What would the church do without you two? God bless you both."

To her credit, Petra resisted grabbing the tube from him. He pictured the protective ladies running out to drag her off the bike and club her with an icing-coated spatula. Once again, the image of his partner being a pit bull with rabies came to mind.

Once on the bike, he handed her the map tube. She held on to Mikhail with one hand and wedged the tube between them, making sure she kept her free hand pressed on top.

Since they weren't far from Church of the Holy Trinity, he drove them there and led her to his office through a back entrance. One of the senior priests stopped them for small talk and wanted to be introduced to Petra. To her credit, she remained polite and studious, mentioning how excited the museum was to be able to convince Father Mikhail to assist them in Ethiopia.

She held up the tube. "We're going to go over some maps. The good father was afraid he might be needed, so I insisted we come here to go over last-minute details. I hope you don't mind."

"Of course not," he said enthusiastically. "Father Mikhail is devoted to our congregation and seldom goes out. Because of his work, our congregation continues to grow. I'm glad he has a new project that will take him away for a while. It is hard to find things for him to do. His volunteer work puts the rest of us to shame." He chuckled and strolled away. "Nice to have met you, Dr. McGinnis."

"Ditto, Father."

Once inside the office, he relieved her of the map tube. "Do you always make a habit of lying, Petra?"

"Lying?" She moved around the office as if on some kind of exploration. "Oh, you mean about Chadwick having a heart condition and I needed to find him? Or maybe that I was excited you could help us out?"

"Just want to make sure I don't stand next to you in a lightning storm. Keep your friends close and your enemies closer kind of thing."

She laid a hand on her heart. "I'm crushed. And I thought we were becoming friends. I said those things about Chadwick because I thought it would get us the heck out of there. They were looking at you like a dying calf in a hailstorm, and it was making me nauseous."

The comparison made him chuckle under his breath.

She continued, "As to me being excited about you coming along to Ethiopia, yeah, that was a stretch, I guess. But I'm not your enemy—yet." Stopping at his bookcase, she eyed the vast collection of volumes on Lalibela before coming to stand a few feet away from him. "I'm guessing the increase in the congregation is mostly female since you seem to be a smooth talker."

He felt annoyed at her constant chatter and inappropriate ideas of who he was. Gritting his teeth, he resisted an obnoxious retort. "Actually it's mostly families. It is a sick world, Petra. People are searching for something bigger than themselves." He sighed as he sent her a narrowed gaze. "Sorry to disappoint you. Can we get down to business? I sense this conversation is going to get ugly."

"Roll that puppy out." She chuckled softly and pointed to the cap he lifted on the end.

Gently, he tilted the tube, and the yellowed paper slipped out onto the desk. Petra lifted her bare hands just as Mikhail pulled out a drawer and laid out clear gloves for both of them. He felt relief when she slipped into scholar mode.

When both of them were gloved, Petra carefully unrolled the map, with Mikhail holding down the edges. She caught her breath in her throat and stared wide-eyed at him.

The map was now blank.

SEVEN

❖

Both stared at the blank map. The yellowed paper, compass rose, and the outline around the edges remained the same. Petra lifted it to sniff then wrinkled her nose. The musty fragrance caused her to walk away and sneeze into her sleeve. Mikhail watched her as she inspected the inside of the tube, perhaps in case they'd missed the real map. She tapped both her middle fingers to her thumbs while she appeared to be lost in thought.

"How can this be?" she asked with irritation. "What are we supposed to do now? We've got to call the police again."

The landline phone rang on Mikhail's desk. He waited until the third ring to pick it up. He used the number three for many things, reminding him of the Trinity at every opportunity.

"Father Mikhail speaking."

"Dr. Chadwick came willingly but lacks the knowledge we seek." The voice, a deep Eastern European accent, spoke with a calm tone.

Mikhail quickly tapped the speaker button.

The speaker went on. "Only Petra can secure the clue you require to find Dr. Chadwick. But you must guide her to seek the future of tomorrow. It takes two to decide the meaning and location. If one is absent, I will know, and all will be lost. He is not a well man."

"Why didn't you just take the map and find this relic?" asked Mikhail.

"It holds clues for the worthy. Dr. Chadwick insists he has the answers we seek. It is doubtful. If he does not, then we will come for Petra and the map."

"Why me?" Petra leaned in to speak in the phone.

"Petra." There was a pause. "They wait for only you, as do others. Keep your phone on. The map is key. Will you trade it for Dr. Chadwick's life?"

"Who are 'they' you're talking about?" Mikhail could feel his patience stretched to the max. "Sounds like you're threatening Petra."

"I am." The voice clicked off.

"Mikhail, look at this." Petra lifted the map from the desk. She didn't miss a beat. The threat apparently didn't faze her. "The map has a riddle or poem that just appeared." She read it out loud.

> A parchment wet, with edges torn,
> Its surface empty, with angel scorn.
> Beneath the ink, a hidden hue,
> The map reveals a sacred clue.
> The winding lines, the symbols etched,
> A tale of wonders lies outstretched.

A path through forests, mountains, steep,
To secrets only angels keep.
A holy relic lost in time,
Awaits beneath the ancient grime.
Follow the map, its whispered song,
To find the place where she belongs.

Mikhail took a picture with his phone as it started to fade. "Maybe this isn't even the map. Is that possible?"

She rolled up the map and carefully slipped it into the tube. "Something isn't right, but I know this is the map." She pointed to a small scratch on the back before slipping it inside the tube. "See this? It's a tiny scratch I noticed when it was first discovered. Looks like a crease but, if you touch it, you can feel the perforation. It's been folded. Not as fragile as an old map should be."

Mikhail dared touch it and noticed the roughness.

"Only I knew about it," she said. "I didn't even tell Chadwick. Unfortunately, the picture of the map has vanished."

"Could it have been because it was exposed to the environment and accelerated the deterioration of the ink?"

"I don't see how. We would have seen a gradual breakdown. Besides, the lab is a controlled environment for that very reason. For it to be perfectly fine this morning when you saw it and for it to be void of any markings now is..." Her voice faded.

"Suspicious?" Mikhail asked.

She shrugged then sighed. "I think we should head to my place and wait. Do you have a problem with that?" She capped the tube.

"Let's go. It's a good place to wait." He wondered if he'd looked surprised at the offer.

Father Mikhail left word he had to go out and might not return until later. Traffic slowed their progress in reaching the museum. He dropped Petra off to get her car and followed her to her place, a loft over what used to be a furniture store.

This part of the city was undergoing a revitalization and restoration movement. It was both chic and artsy. He enjoyed cities which made an effort to recapture the past and bring it up to date with art galleries, First Friday night walks each month, the numerous outdoor bistros, and mom-and-pop stores. It still had the old brick streets and gas streetlamps that had been updated to dusk to dawn activation. The smell of flowers in crowded window boxes and topiary trees planted in large clay pots became eye candy this time of year. Parking lots on the back side of apartment buildings and shops kept traffic to a minimum on the main street.

"Here we are," Petra announced after she parked in a gated lot behind the old furniture store called Bobbles. The downstairs was divided into an antique mall. "I'm on the third floor. Take the elevator if you like. I usually take the stairs to stay in shape."

The priest unzipped his leather jacket and walked alongside her as she lectured him on the history of the building and how it had come to be restored. The idea she could talk with such calm and energy was a testament to her fitness. He was glad he didn't have to respond.

"There are two lofts up here. Mine is the only one

finished and with access to a rooftop terrace." She unlocked the door and pushed it open with her foot.

Mikhail was immediately taken aback by the mess; piles of books, half-opened boxes, a sink full of dirty dishes, and dusty floors. It did nothing to impress him. It was a work in progress. From the looks of chaos, it hadn't been fully attended to in some time.

"It's my little slice of heaven." Her light laugh drew his attention back to her. "No pun intended." She frowned when he ran a finger across what looked to be an antique lamp table from the 1940s.

He lifted his finger coated in dust then slapped his hands together to remove it. "This place is a pigsty," he mumbled.

The snarky burst out of her mouth. "Between working fourteen-hour days, and travel, my inner HGTV maven has had to take a break. I got this place for a steal if I agreed to fix it up myself." She raised a stubborn chin and pointed toward another room. "My bedroom is finished, though," she said with pride. She waved him to follow.

Mikhail entered the bedroom and decided maybe she wasn't a packrat after all. Although it bordered on being a bohemian-style retreat, it matched her personality, or was she was revealing herself? He strolled across to the bathroom and peeked in to find an all-white-and-gray interior resembling a spa.

"I know it's a little over the top, but I work hard, and it helps me relax. The rain shower is to die for after a long dirty day."

"Did you do all this work yourself?"

"Most of it. I have a couple of students I tutor. Their parents bartered with me because my fee was steep. Worked out for all of us." She plopped on the bed and bounced childlike. "I didn't spare any expense on the bed, either. I need my beauty sleep."

Mikhail contained his reaction by holding his breath for a few seconds. The truth overwhelmed him when he found himself watching her intently. Did he convince her that this tour of her bedroom bored rather than interested him, in her provocative posture on the edge of the bed? He turned and left the room and heard her follow.

The open-concept room included a kitchen and, except for the mess, looked first class and the delight of any chef. Finally, a subject that interested him because he loved to cook. The wall of windows let in the fading light of the day, bathing the room in colors. A sudden realization washed over him that he felt safe and protected here with nothing to fear.

"Should we order dinner or"—he went to the refrigerator and opened the door—"I could cook."

"I don't have much in there, but I'm pretty sick of pizza and cashew chicken from the Asian-American buffet from across the street. Besides, I don't want to tie up my phone in case we get a call."

Mikhail pulled out a carton of eggs, butter, half a green pepper, and a bag of shredded cheese. "Why don't you go over any notes you have from inspecting the map while I fix dinner. Okay to explore your cabinets?"

She gave him the thumbs-up sign then removed a pile of folders, magazines, and clippings from the leather couch. After taking a moment to place a pillow behind her back, she opened a laptop on the coffee table. It looked like it might have been a kitchen table in another life and had suffered having its legs cut down to size. A perfect working space, Mikhail surmised.

He admired how she became lost in her work so easily. Maybe this was why she lived alone. What man could compete with hundred-year-old relics and a hard-work ethic? Clearly, her work came first. That would make working with her much easier and less of a distraction, although he wasn't sure why he considered her a distraction at this point. There had been no one in his life since his wife died, except for people of the church who required comfort and support. Those moments had been more than enough.

His phone vibrated in his pocket, and he snapped it up, drawing Petra's attention.

"Hello, Father Mikhail Novak."

He heard a familiar deep breathing and knew Zane, his mentor, was giving him a gentle tap even before he spoke. "Father Novak. That's a good one. Just a reminder. You're not really a priest." Mikhail gritted his teeth and refused to be baited. "Are things going well?" he asked in a rather glib tone.

Mikhail shrugged at Petra and shook his head to let her know it wasn't the call they'd been waiting for.

"I didn't know you had a phone," Mikhail commented off-handedly.

There was a chuckle on the other end. "I don't. You know I don't need one, Mikhail. I thought this would be better than just speaking to you out of nowhere, like I often do."

"What's up?" Mikhail tried to sound upbeat since Petra kept glancing his way.

"Eat your dinner on the terrace."

"Why? I'm not so sure about that." Mikhail

shrugged at Petra then rolled his eyes as if frustrated.

"Are you questioning my methods? Do it." Zane's tone had changed from pleasant to irritated.

There were times when Zane Spokane annoyed him immensely. "I'm wondering how our friend is doing." It was a subtle way to ask about Chadwick.

"The terrace, Mikhail. And you're about to burn those eggs."

EIGHT

Mikhail dropped the phone on the granite countertop and grabbed a spatula to stir the eggs. Although a little dry, no real damage done to his concoction. He turned the burner off and grabbed two bottles of water out of the refrigerator. After he spotted a tangerine, he divided it between both plates.

"Let's eat on the terrace." He lifted the plates after shoving his phone back in his jeans pocket.

Petra grabbed the water bottles and pointed him toward the glass door that led onto the terrace. As soon as she opened it, Mikhail was struck by the beauty of her rooftop garden. The area was filled with flowers, vegetables, and herbs. The sound of a fountain reached his ears as he spotted an iron table with mismatched patio chairs. Candles of all sizes were placed throughout the space. A string of white Christmas lights woven through the wooden pergola flickered on.

"My kind of place, Petra." After setting down their food and relieving her of the water bottles, he followed her and watched with a kind of reverence as she lit the numerous candles.

"Gardens are my thing. Some girls buy fancy clothes. I have a weakness for seeds, plants, and accessories for the garden."

"And where did this love come from?" He took one of the small candles and used it to light others along the brick wall.

"Grew up on my grandparents' farm. It was how they fed all of us."

"Big family?"

She waved the question off. "Then I read about the Hanging Gardens of Babylon, and the floating gardens of the Aztecs, which led me to studying cultures." Again, she waved him off. "You don't want to hear about that. Boring."

Mikhail nodded acceptance, sensing she didn't want him knowing too much about her. In a way, he felt relief because he didn't want her discovering too much about him either.

With the task of lighting candles completed, the two sat down. She ate hungrily and admitted it was the first time all day. He enjoyed watching her eat. Between bites, she would wave her fork and share what she'd done to the loft. "Chadwick helped with the down payment and a few of the renovations."

"He's pretty fond of you."

"Yes. Likewise," she spoke softly. "I owe him everything. When I say helped, I mean, he hired someone for me." She offered a laugh that sounded forced.

Was she letting down her guard? The sadness in those hazel-green eyes that were almost too wide for such a delicate face tugged at his common sense. *Don't get too close*, whispered in his ear. Unfortunately, the mood evaporated too soon.

"This was delicious. Where did you learn to cook?"

"Thank you." He laid a hand over his heart and bowed his head. "Hopefully, we won't get heartburn since I forgot to say grace."

This made her laugh out loud. She lifted her eyes to Heaven. "Thank you, Jesus, for the divine meal and your capable server to cook for me. Amen."

He couldn't help but smile and repeated, "Amen."

They stacked the dishes in a metal tub with HOME written on the side. He carried them inside and then joined her at the firepit where she'd lit pieces of kindling. After adding a small log to the fire, he moved to the chairs by the firepit. Darkness had fallen and the lights of the city created a restful ambience. The two fell into silence as Mikhail poked the fire and settled in to enjoy the flickering flames, but decided to check his phone. He noticed Petra did the same.

"I wish we would hear something," she said softly.

"Have faith."

"Easy for you to say."

"Because I'm a priest?"

"No." She hugged her arms against the cool breeze sweeping across the terrace. "Because I have very little faith in the things I can't see or explain."

"In one of the most widely known scriptures, Matthew 17:20, Jesus said, 'Truly I tell you, if you have faith like a grain of mustard seed, you can say to this mountain, "Move from here to there, and it will move. Nothing will be impossible for you.'"

She wrinkled her nose and tilted her head as a coy expression toyed with the corners of her mouth. "Are you always so optimistic?"

"Part of the job description."

Petra stood and diverted her attention to the inside of her loft. "That's strange. The lights inside just went out."

"Maybe a power surge." He glanced over the edge of the terrace at the city below where other lights still burned brightly. "I'll have a look." But he already knew it wasn't a power surge. He could see someone moving inside. "Petra, I want you to stay right here. We're not alone."

"I'll call the police." She pulled out her phone and fumbled it into the water fountain.

He tossed her his.

"Don't go in there," she warned. "They might have a gun."

"It might be who we've been waiting for." He rushed the door and held his hand back at her to not come closer. "We left the map inside."

He didn't wait to hear the protests of Petra before he stormed into the open area of the loft. A figure dressed in black jerked his head around when the wind blew the door shut. He had been riffling through the papers on the coffee table and clutched Petra's computer. Tossing it to the one upholstered accent chair, the figure crouched for mere seconds and then lunged toward Mikhail who sidestepped him easily enough.

The intruder whirled around in surprise, and, this

time, approached with caution. With only his fingers twitching, Mikhail stood still with his hands down at his side. The dangerous side of him kicked in, along with a rush of adrenaline pumping toward his brain and heart. Feeling a surge of euphoria, he lowered his head and leveled a deadly gaze.

"Come on," Mikhail growled through gritted teeth. He grabbed a Samurai sword he'd spotted resting in an open box, which may have held long-stemmed roses from an admirer. He twirled it around, just like Zane had taught him during their frequent workouts.

"You are a priest," the stunned intruder laughed. "You are no match for me."

The man charged then slid down on his hip and swiped his foot under Mikhail who landed on the coffee table. He rolled off and jumped to his feet with the sword held out before him. Once more, the intruder attacked, only to feel the brunt of Mikhail's weapon smack across his back. He twirled the sword again, exhilaration pumping through his veins.

The intruder expelled a groan of pain as he stumbled then turned to grab the map tube he spotted on the couch. He ran toward the terrace door where Petra stood in shock. Before she could move, the man had his arm around her neck, dragging her backward.

For a split second, Mikhail experienced a sense of panic, similar to what he felt in Afghanistan. But like then, he tucked it away to deal with later, and marched forward, causing the intruder to continue pulling Petra backward and awkwardly tried to keep from dropping the map tube.

When he neared the three-foot wall that surrounded the rooftop terrace, he shoved Petra at Mikhail who caught her by the arm and slowed the momentum as she hit the ground. The dark-clad man jumped on top of the wall and jammed the tube into a quiver. He removed a piece of equipment from his belt, shot it toward the building across the street, and secured it to a piece of iron attached at his feet.

Mikhail leaped onto the wall and rushed him. He didn't have time to look down and be afraid. The intruder pulled out a knife resembling a weapon a martial artist uses. He jabbed it toward Mikhail only to have him knock it out of his hand to the street below with a swipe of the sword. The man in black landed a side kick at the sword held toward him, causing Mikhail to lose his balance.

He managed to use the weapon to right himself, in spite of having to wobble on one leg, his bad leg. The intruder glowered at him, when Mikhail didn't fall to his death, but stepped back to take deep breaths. Could the man sense he was unafraid?

The intruder let a look of satisfaction come to his narrow lips when he reached inside his black covering to pull out a red throwing star. He launched it so fast Mikhail almost didn't see it in time to raise the sword that bounced the deadly spike away but did manage to clip his hand. The man in black hooked onto the zipline he'd created just as Mikhail rushed him with the sword. The intruder had managed to nick the sword, causing it to fly out of Mikhail's hand as he disappeared into the night, along with the sword. Mikhail picked up the spiked star and hurled it at the figure he could no longer see.

He watched him disappear onto the roof of a two-story building then hopped down to see Petra standing wide-eyed and stunned. With great reserve and fake concern, he moved with a kind of stealth he forgot he possessed.

"Are you all right, Petra?" he asked, reaching down and pulling her up to stand a couple of inches from him. Her lips parted, trying to speak, but nothing came out. "Are. You. Hurt?"

She gulped and ran over to the edge then turned on him. "What in the hell was that?"

"I think he fancied himself a ninja or something." He shrugged.

The incredulous gaze she shot him amused him. But he picked up his phone dropped in the mayhem, to calm himself down and return to normal.

She buried her face in her hands and wept. "The map. Chadwick."

When she passed him, he reached out and grabbed her hand. Immediately, he noticed it wasn't soft like a lot of women he knew. These hands were used to hard work. "No worries."

He pulled her inside after him and found the circuit panel. Opening it, he located the problem and switched the lever so it would operate perfectly again. He dared put his hands on her shoulders and pushed her toward the kitchen. Reaching under the counter, he pulled out the map.

Petra gasped as she quickly unrolled it only to find that part of the northeast corner had filled in again. "Father Mikhail," she bubbled. "Look. The map is coming back to life." Before he could step away, she let the map roll back up, and grabbed him around the neck to show appreciation.

With a great deal of hesitation, he patted her back

lightly, as if she might have a contagious virus.

"When did you make the switch?"

"I brought our dishes in and noticed the map on the coffee table with a lot of other papers. The tube was close by. Since we didn't know who would contact us, I thought I should hide it just in case. That call we got earlier in the afternoon could have been a trap." He carefully removed her arms from around his neck and walked back into the living area.

"Do you think that was our contact to find Chadwick?"

"Hard to say. But when they find out the map tube is empty, they are going to want to make a deal."

"So, we wait." Tears had been replaced with pure glee. She danced around in a circle and clapped her hands. "It's almost eleven. You should stay here tonight."

A wave of panic washed over him. "Here? I'm not sure that's a good idea." What would his church say? What would Zane say?

"Besides, my phone isn't working, and you may be the one to get the call. Remember earlier, we were supposed to stay together."

She hurried into the bedroom and returned with a sheet, blanket, and a pillow. She made up the couch for him after clearing it off.

"Where did you learn to fight like that? You didn't bat an eye?"

"Seminary."

Petra gave him a bewildered expression then burst out laughing. "A priest who can fight and has a sense of humor, be it rather dry." She patted the couch. "There ya go. There's a roughed-in powder room over there next to another bedroom. Both a work in progress."

Morphing into his cold, dark self-felt a lot safer than verbally sparring with her. All he could manage was, "Thanks."

"I'm beat. See you in the morning." She pivoted to leave then faced him again. She grinned mischievously. "I don't think I've ever spent the night with a priest."

"I don't think I've ever spent the night with a pompous archeologist," he said a little harsher than he wanted. Her good-natured banter evaporated as she hurried into the bedroom, slamming the door. The lock clicked. The dark side of him felt amusement, knowing a lock couldn't stop him if he wanted to go in.

NINE

Petra slept fitfully for most of the night. After showering and slipping into clean clothes, she decided to try out the new coffeemaker whether Father Mikhail or Mike or whatever he called himself was up or not. One glance out her windows at the morning sky revealed dappled light with streaks of pink and gold welcoming the day.

The thought of Chadwick in danger removed the beauty of the moment. He'd been there for her since she was a little girl. Without him, her life would have been very different. Never would she be able to repay him for saving her life the day when her future turned a corner into being lost in a world of darkness and slavery to fear. Her hand went to her heart. She decided to follow his advice and "just shake it off." It gave her courage to face the day. No matter what, Petra promised to bring him home.

When she opened the bedroom door, the smell of coffee enticed her to ignore whether the priest might still be asleep. She hurried barefoot to the kitchen to find a pot full of black brew, a coffee mug, creamer, and sugar waiting for her. Doctoring her hot beverage and holding it in her hands for a few seconds for the heat to permeate her skin felt like heaven, an odd thought, considering. Turning to face the room, the transformation to her loft hit her.

The loft had been cleaned and organized. The haphazard piles of books on the floor had found a home in several of the makeshift bookcases she'd secured from the antique mall downstairs. The bedding was folded and placed on one end of the couch. The clutter she never had time to sort had been done for her. The faint smell of paint touched her nose, drawing her to the closed door of the second bedroom. When she entered, much to her delight, the entire room was painted white, extra paint cans stacked in the corner. Even the wood floor was void of dust and appeared to have been mopped. She backed out and dared peek inside the unfinished bathroom. It too was clean and smelled disinfected.

Still carrying her cup of mood-stabilizer juice, she moved lazily toward the terrace doors, having noticed movement. Carefully, she propped it open to watch the shirtless priest doing tai chi, appearing oblivious to the world.

The taut muscles across his back flexed over and over as he moved gracefully in the open space. Tattoos of angelic beings and fire covered his back in a macabre dance, fascinating her with uneasy curiosity. What kind of priest was Mikhail Novak?

Last night, she'd been shocked and unable to respond when he displayed fighting skills of a martial arts expert. He revealed an unflappable demeanor that left her breathless. The way he swung the samurai sword was fluid and natural, as if he were used to fighting the demons of life. Gazing at him with a new appreciation, she guessed the man had a lot of secrets.

She leaned against the open door and held her coffee close to her face to feel the steam. The cool morning air was refreshing, but she wished she'd worn a warmer sweater. He stopped and lifted his arms up slightly from his side and tilted his head back like he gazed toward Heaven. Was he praying? Should she escape, thinking she'd intruded on his communion with God? But the spell had been cast and she continued to enjoy watching him.

When he stopped and turned to level a hard gaze at her, she straightened, spilling her coffee on her hand.

"Ouch," she complained, trying to sling the droplets off. A red spot appeared as Mikhail grabbed up a towel and approached her with a determined gait. He took her cup and set it down on a small metal table.

He grabbed up her hand and examined it quickly. "Let's run cold water on that." He entered the loft, leaving her to follow. In one swift move, he flipped on the faucet and retrieved a bowl of ice from the freezer.

Petra followed him and experienced confusion when he once more took her hand and forced it under the cold water. When she tried to pull away from his touch, his grasp increased. Trying to frown evaporated the moment she dared meet his ice-blue eyes, laser-focused on her.

"Better?" he asked as he pushed her hand into the bowl of ice. "Are you always so clumsy?"

She jerked her hand out of the bowl and purposedly flicked cold water in his face. "Your bedside manner stinks." One of his eyebrows arched on an otherwise solemn face. He handed her a towel, but she decided rather than take it, she'd rub them on her jeans.

"Really? I've never had any complaints before," he said drily.

"I'll bet," was the best retort she could stutter, letting memory of all those tattoos come to mind. Once again, she noticed how the loft had shaped up overnight. The various pictures, lamps, and mementos had been properly placed, exactly how she would have displayed them. "Sorry. I'm kind of a grouch in the morning." She fanned her damp hand out toward the room. "Did you sleep last night? This is beautiful." Her voice softened as he handed her another full cup of coffee, doctored exactly how she drank it. How did he know?

"I don't need much sleep. Couldn't turn my brain off anyway, thinking about Chadwick, the map, and our trip to Lalibela. Thought I might as well make myself useful. If I misplaced your—stuff, I will be happy to redo it."

"It was a nice gesture. Thank you."

"There is just so much clutter I can handle and, since you obviously are too busy to do it yourself, I thought I'd help."

"You know you just insulted a compliment. Right?"

His ice-blue eyes narrowed when his generous lips pooched slightly into a lopsided grin. "Sorry. I'm not used to such an intelligent woman giving me a hard time."

"Better get used to it, Father HGTV Ninja."

This made him chuckle then pointed to her bedroom. "Can I use your shower?"

"Please. I was afraid I'd soon have to open the room you painted to let in fresh air." She held her nose.

"Touché."

Hearing the water turn on in the bathroom, Petra finished her coffee and placed the cup in the dishwasher. Most of the time, the dishwasher got used once a week when it had begun to smell rank. None of last night's dishes or cutlery were in sight; they'd been cleaned and stacked on the open shelving. To prove she wasn't a total slob, she washed her cup and placed it next to the others. Having him around would either make her a victim of his behavior modification or turn her into a killer.

The map was neatly rolled out and secured on the coffee table. She was amazed at how part of the map had appeared. What would make it do that? Maybe Mikhail was right when he mentioned an environmental reaction. That didn't explain why the map was slowly being restored.

The doorbell chimed, causing her to uncurl her legs on the couch and pad across the floor in her bare feet. Looking through the peephole, she saw it was the young coffee-shop policeman.

"Officer Hawi Mathias." She read his name tag slowly. "Do you have any word on Chadwick yet? Oh. I guess I should file a missing person report, since it's been twenty-four hours."

"No need to be angry with me. I was just doing my

job, Petra." He took a deep breath as he glanced around the room. Thank goodness he didn't show up yesterday to see the true side of her.

The man had a crush on her, and she intended to work it for all it was worth. "Sorry," she huffed out quietly. "I tend to be saying that a lot lately."

"What?"

"Can I pour you a cup of coffee?"

"I thought you always bought your first cup at the coffee shop?"

"I got up early and made a pot," came a warm, deep voice from the direction of Petra's bedroom. Mikhail buttoned up his black shirt but left plenty of skin showing. His dark hair was slicked back from the shower and, for a fleeting second, Petra imagined him under the rain showerhead. "I'm an early riser." He smiled rather diabolically at the officer. He came to stand next to Petra and outstretched his hand. "Good to see you again. Thanks for swinging by." He was barefoot and his pant legs had been turned up like he was ready to walk along a beach.

The young officer inspected him with a case of mild shock. "Father Mikhail?"

Mikhail touched Petra's elbow, drawing her attention to him. "Have you seen my boots? I took them off last night."

"Oh. I think so. Maybe behind the end table." She went to check since it was beginning to smell like the beginning of a testosterone war. Mikhail prayerfully folded his hands in front of him and locked eyes with the confused officer. The boots weren't there.

"No. Not here," she admitted.

"I bet I left them in the bedroom," Mikhail said

good-naturedly then turned to narrow his gaze at Officer Mathias. Although he referred to the room he painted, Petra was aware the officer didn't know that. Mikhail shrugged. "Don't worry about it. I'll look later."

Her face grew hot. Whether the sensation was from embarrassment or that the priest was insinuating his appearance so early in the morning meant they had a carnal relationship, she was losing control of the situation. Men.

"I'm glad you're here, Hawie." She tried to sound helpless while making eye contact with him. "We had a visitor last night who stole—"

"A map tube?" he asked, shifting his attention from Mikhail to her.

"Yes. How did you know?"

"He was found dead an hour ago." The officer shifted his weight and put his hands on his hips like a gunslinger. If he was trying to intimidate Mikhail, it wasn't working. The priest stood tall and self-assured while remaining super focused on every word Officer Mathias had to say. As a matter of fact, he didn't bat an eye.

TEN

❖

The dead body lay sprawled on top of her examining table in the museum lab. Security had found the body after examining the record of heat sensors on the detectors the previous night. Since no alarm had been activated, and the hourly walk-throughs hadn't indicated any unlocked areas or concerns, the sensors weren't checked until the morning. Mr. Janson, in the middle of a meltdown, threatened the head of security with termination and to bury the others in a sand pit with nothing but their heads showing as he released hungry fire ants.

"Calm down, Mr. Janson." Petra decided to focus on the head of security. She stepped in front of him and laid a hand on his chest while casting an anxious glance toward Officer Mathias, who observed and took notes. "I'm sure you and Officer Mathias should have a chat.

I'll be over in a few seconds. Okay?"

When Mr. Janson remained, he patted her hand impatiently. "Worthless. All of them. Can you imagine what the press will do to us? Our benefactors will be outraged. Contributions will certainly be affected, not to mention we'll have to shut the museum down while an investigation proceeds. We count on admission tickets, the gift shop, and the café to help make ends meet. I'm livid."

"Have you taken your blood pressure meds today?" she asked, stroking his arm like a concerned parent. He huffed out a negative response. She quickly called his secretary and asked her to bring down his medication.

"I will pray over the museum, Mr. Janson." Father Mikhail led him to a chair and remained calm as he looked down at him. "I will pray that this incident will become a blessing."

Mr. Janson bowed his head, and the priest laid his hand upon his shoulder. He thanked God for this chance to make the museum better and even asked forgiveness for the dead man. For whatever reason, everyone else in the room stopped and listened to the prayer. Even Officer Mathias stood statue still with closed eyes.

When Mikhail finished, he outstretched his hand to the secretary who had walked up behind him. Petra wondered how he even knew she was there. As she handed him the medication then the water bottle she held, Mikhail lifted his hooded eyes to her. She felt frozen at the connection between them. The secretary pulled up a chair by Mr. Janson and assured the priest she'd take care of him.

"I know you will, Isolde. You are very kind."

The priest pivoted to turn his attention to Officer

Mathias who leveled a hard gaze his way, laced with suspicion and contempt. In the six months she'd known the officer, he had always reacted to situations in a calm, caring manner. During the coffee-shop robbery, he'd demonstrated concern for the customers and especially her. Not once had she ever seen him become dangerous and menacing. Something had changed in his approach today. His nostrils on his wide nose flared with a seething anger. His dark skin blushed with a hint of intolerance when interacting with Father Mikhail. A shiver ran up her spine as she tried to remember he was a police officer, not a social worker. But the obvious scorn showing in his normally handsome brown eyes gave her a new sense of caution.

She stepped into his line of sight to block his view of Father Mikhail.

"Hawie, will your detective be with you on this?" She looked around the room to locate the man who stood in the corner watching them just yesterday.

"My detective?" His brow wrinkled in bewilderment. "I'm not sure they assigned one, but if so, whoever it is will be here shortly. I didn't bring anyone with me yesterday. If you saw a stranger lurking around, maybe they were connected to this."

"Actually, I—" started Petra.

"Why exactly have you brought us here, Officer Mathias?" Father Mikhail walked up beside her.

The officer pointed to the body on the table then frowned at Mikhail. "Can you identify him?"

"His face was covered. He ran out onto the terrace and—" Petra tried to add clarity to the scene.

"Created a zipline then just spun off into the night," Mikhail interrupted.

Petra swallowed hard.

The officer cocked his head at her. "Petra? Did you have anything to add to that?"

"No. No, that pretty much sums it up," she said then moved toward the body. "Can we take a look?"

He signaled the paramedic who was ready to zip up the body bag. The ninja mask had been pulled up to his forehead. Father Mikhail laid his hand on the ninja's forehead before his lips moved in silent prayer. The paramedic waited for the priest to give him a nod before zipping it up.

"Can't say if it's him or not."

Petra shrugged. "I mean, it was dark in the loft, and just candlelight and the firepit outside."

Hawie frowned and shifted his attention to the priest. "Candlelight? Guess you two had a lot to talk about."

"Exactly. We've planned a trip together and—"

When the officer's brow furrowed, Petra spoke up. "What Father Mikhail is saying is that he has partnered with us, the museum, to do work in Ethiopia on the churches of Lalibela. We were pooling our information and discussing what we planned to do once there. We leave tomorrow."

"Does this have anything to do with Dr. Chadwick?" The officer's voice had turned icy.

"We don't know." Did she just use the word we? "The map tube was key. We were called yesterday to bring it for his release." Timidly she added, "We were told to stay together."

"And you didn't think about calling me?"

Father Mikhail sighed impatiently. "Considering your lack of interest earlier in the day—"

"It had to be twenty-four hours to file a report, but this information would have changed everything," he fumed.

The priest tilted his head and folded his hands in front of him. "I see. That is unfortunate. I apologize. This is my fault, not Petra's. She was so upset, I'm afraid I may have influenced her decision to wait and see."

Hawie shifted his focus back to her, and she batted her lashes after sneaking a wet finger under her eyes to fake a few tears.

"Okay. So, he isn't familiar?" He raised his chin toward the body. "Not been hanging around here? We can look through the security tapes to check if he's there, but these ninja types"—he rolled his eyes in disgust—"think they're in a video game most of the time."

"How did he die?" Petra asked as the body was wheeled away. Hawie walked over to an object being placed in a plastic bag. Another officer handed it to him. When he turned to show Petra, a knot formed in her stomach. It belonged to her.

"Your prints are all over this sword, Petra."

It was the one Mikhail used the night before when the two sparred on the terrace.

She cleared her throat and glanced at Mikhail for a split second. "This is my lab. Look around. I have a lot of weapons here."

"But this one"—he rolled it over in his hands then squinted suspiciously at her—"I remember seeing you take home two weeks ago."

"Oh?" She leaned in to get a better look as she shook her head. "Hmm. It does look similar."

"It's been engraved with your name right here." He ran his finger over the letters.

Chadwick bought it last year for her birthday. She'd taken samurai lessons when a guest lecturer visited the museum. The instructor was so impressed with her progress he allowed her to use a real sword instead of the wooden one given to the other students. From that point on, her lessons were private.

"Petra? The sword was used on the ninja. Any idea how it got here?"

She twisted her lips and rubbed her jaw with her index finger. "No idea."

He continued to observe her with suspicion.

"Do you think I did this? Hawie?"

Petra watched Father Mikhail try to take a closer look at the sword, but the officer handed it off.

"Officer Mathias, I assure you, Petra never left last night." He cast a beguiling expression at Petra, sending a tingle up her spine then soured as his attention switched to the officer. "We both were upset. I was glad I was there to offer—support. Surely, you can take the word of a priest."

Her new ally was taunting the officer. Why? Maybe he was trying to protect her. That sword made her look guilty of involvement. "You'll make sure I get it back?"

He pushed past her. "Don't leave town until we get this ironed out."

When he followed the gurney out, Petra unloaded on her new partner. "What are you doing?"

"Excuse me?" Mikhail tilted his head as if confused.

"You know you used that sword at my house last

night to battle it out with the guy. It's here with blood all over it. Hopefully, yours won't be found on it too. Or fingerprints!"

"So, you're accusing me, a priest, of taking the life of a child of God." It was an accusation, not a question.

"Oh please. Spare me. You were up prowling around all night. How do I know you didn't get a call and slip out to take care of business here?"

"You don't. Guess you'll just have to trust me." His amusement made him look more demonic than holy.

Those ice-blue eyes penetrated her soul and, just like earlier, it was a cross between feeling exhilarated and terrified. A kind of rage boiled in those blue depths of mystery.

She started around him, but he cut her off. The close proximity of his tall, lean body gave her a chance to explore the chiseled face outlined with a couple days' growth of beard. He tightened and released his jaw without showing an ounce of emotion. Neither of them spoke.

Their battle of wills must have been intuitively obvious to the casual observer. But everyone appeared to be busy securing the crime scene and paid them little notice.

Isolde joined them and handed Father her cell phone. "Father, you have a call."

"Hello?"

Isolde returned to help Mr. Janson stand then escorted him out of the lab.

"I don't know what you're up to, but the dead man in the lab wasn't sent from me." It was the same voice giving them instructions the day before.

"Who is this? Is Chadwick okay?"

Petra stepped in to listen on the phone as he held it out.

The male voice continued, "Bring the map."

"Where?"

"A plane waits for you at the airport. Be there in one hour, or you'll never see Dr. Chadwick again." The line went dead.

Father Mikhail reached out and touched her back. "We have to leave. Are you okay with that?"

She grabbed her helmet off the desk. "Better use your prayer line. I have the feeling we're going to need it."

ELEVEN

❖

The plane taxied down the runway as Mikhail buckled his seat belt. He and Petra were the only passengers at this out-of-the-way airport he didn't know existed. Fortunately, they'd brought the map along to the museum, fearful to leave it behind at the loft. By the time they rushed out of the museum to the street level, a limo waited at the curb. An unusually tall man stepped forward and bowed.

"I'm Sharif. I'll be your driver today, Father Novak. There is nothing to be concerned about. I'm here to see that things go smoothly."

Two others exited the back seat. One man dressed like a biker; the other a woman, wore jeans, a ragged denim jacket with ornate designs on the back, and a red wig.

"You look like us," Petra said in surprise.

The driver handed Mikhail an envelope containing a typed message informing them to turn over the keys to the Harley and loft. Everything would be taken care of.

Petra bristled while glaring angrily at the three strangers.

"Father Novak," the driver spoke calmly while his eyes darted around the area, "I understand the situation is unusual, but we must hurry. Time is of the utmost importance." The driver looked over his shoulder then back at Mikhail with narrowed eyes. "The messenger said to tell you, Luke 4:10." He lowered his chin to glare down at Mikhail. "I believe he is a friend of yours, Father."

"Get in the car, Petra. It's okay." Mikhail took her elbow firmly and pulled her toward the open back seat.

"I will not," she fumed even as he tossed his keys to the leather-clad stranger waiting patiently. He grabbed Petra by her knapsack and fished out her loft keys. She tried to intercept them when he handed those off as well. She jerked away, but he once more grabbed her arm and twisted it enough for her to yelp.

"Get in the car," he ordered through clenched teeth.

The ride had been awkward and the silence so thick he could slice it with a knife. Another woman waited at the bottom of the air stairway, dressed in a pale-blue suit. The dark skin and hair tied in a bun on her neck gave her a professional vibe Mikhail appreciated as he offered a nod of thanks.

"Father Novak, everything you and Dr. McGinnis will need for the trip has already been packed and loaded onto the plane. Your pilot is currently checking systems to prepare for takeoff." She handed him a manila envelope. "All your concerns and questions will be answered here."

"Won't you be going with us?" Petra's voice held a slight panic.

The assistant batted her thick lashes and waved for a utility golf cart used to ferry passengers around airports. She quickly boarded. "No, sorry. I will not be traveling with you, Dr. McGinnis. Once you are aboard, I will order the steps retracted. Buckle in, and the pilot will address you at that time. Have a safe and pleasant trip."

Twenty minutes later, the plane picked up speed and lifted. Mikhail closed his eyes, loving the feel of flight. The *clonk* of the landing gear being locked into place gave him reassurance all was as it should be. The sensation of climbing, followed by leveling off, caused him to take a deep breath as he stole a look across the aisle at Petra who stared out the window. The sun lit up her red hair like a halo and paled the soft skin he'd touched the day before. He admired the freckles and wondered if she'd been teased about them as a child.

"Welcome," came a familiar voice over the intercom system. Zane. "This is a long flight. I'll be out later to visit. I'll navigate us out of our current airspace and try to put distance between those determined to detain you. We'll make several stops, the first in the Cape Verde Islands off the coast of Africa."

Just the sound of Zane's voice gave him a subliminal message to rest. Soon, his eyelids were too heavy to fight off sleep. The night before had kept him busy. Maybe taking a catnap might help him gain a little clarity and strength. This would prepare him for any verbal attacks from Petra. He imagined her sitting quietly, stewing about how she planned to take over this escape and interject her own will. Of course, that wasn't going to happen. It was a good thing she didn't know who she was really dealing with.

But, when sleep overtook him, the nightmares of war returned, and not even Zane could stop them.

TWELVE

❖

The plane bounced when it passed between towering thunderheads. It was enough to shake Petra awake to realize where she was, which was nowhere. Or at least, she didn't know anything except she'd boarded this plane and, shortly after takeoff, a wave of exhaustion got the best of her. Taking a quick nap felt so good. But when she held up her watch, she noticed several hours had passed.

Father Mikhail slept across the aisle from her. The manila envelope remained in his grasp, even though the rest of his body appeared relaxed. How the last forty-eight hours had changed her life. She enjoyed admiring the hard profile of a man who was anything but a priest. He might be fooling the people at The Church of the Holy Trinity, but not her. There was something unholy and contemptuous about his demeanor.

The priest breathed harder.

What did he know about Lalibela that could possibly help her? Big deal if he'd lived there and could pull a few strings. Mr. Janson had reached out to many of his contacts around the world with no luck, then this guy shows up and, presto, they were invited to come? Maybe he was a fortune hunter.

His fingers twitched then his shoulders.

The resume provided to her appeared genuine. She'd even made a few calls to make sure it was real. There were references from teachers, charity organizers, and religious institutions, all bestowing glowing accolades on his work ethic and ability to reach the lost. However, there was nothing about his family, personal history, or friendships, other than the ones he'd encountered through his work.

Where was he born? What about his parents or siblings? Surely, somewhere there was a romantic entanglement, or maybe he preferred men. He certainly hadn't been swayed by her flirtation attempts. If anything, he had flirted with her, teasing and watching her with those ice-blue eyes that were more like lasers that could penetrate the soul. Had she imagined he wanted Officer Mathias to think something was going on between them? Was that a little kinky or what?

Father Mikhail sucked in his breath and shuddered in his seat then tossed his head to the side.

She wanted to see what happened, but it was clear the man was in pain with a nightmare. His breathing became more labored, and his body trembled slightly as she eased out into the aisle. In that instant, the cockpit door opened, and the pilot took long strides to push in front of her. He laid his hand on the priest's shoulder and squeezed.

The priest became still and breathed normally as his eyes fluttered open. He looked up at the pilot and nodded as he reached over with his hand and rested it on his.

"I'm good," Father Mikhail whispered. "Thanks."

The pilot withdrew his hand and turned to look intently at Petra who backed up immediately, having recognized him from the day she first called Officer Mathias to the museum.

"You."

He stuck his hand out and, when she didn't take it, he reached in and grabbed it anyway. "Dr. McGinnis. A pleasure to meet you. I'm"—he glanced toward the priest who raised his eyebrows—"your pilot. You can call me Captain Spokane." A thin line of amusement creased his mouth.

"You were at the museum the other day. Isn't this the same guy, Father Mikhail?" Petra said, watching the priest rise from his seat and squeeze out into the aisle in front of the pilot, forcing him to back away from her.

"Whoever that was, stood in the shadows. Remember when I went to get a closer look, he left."

Petra wondered if that was a veiled lie. The man was taller than Mikhail and broad shouldered. His aviator haircut revealed a thick neck. Although clean-cut, he seemed out of place in the airline uniform. Those strange eyes shifted to the priest just as he raised his chin and looked down his nose in a cynical expression.

"Father Novak. It is good to see you again."

"You know each other?" Petra blurted.

"We served in the military together," the pilot

announced. Petra gawked at the priest in bewilderment. How did this not show up in the bio? "Boy, those were the days, huh?"

"Were you a chaplain, Father?" Petra quizzed.

"No," the captain chuckled, but continued to focus on the priest. "But he was a godsend, nonetheless."

"I'm assuming your copilot will be out soon to introduce himself?" Petra asked.

"Copilot? No. I'm afraid I'm it for this trip."

"What?" Petra felt panic. Before she could start a rapid-fire question session, the pilot reached out and touched her upper arm.

"God is my copilot," he mused. This only managed to make her hold her breath. Then he elbowed the priest. "Just joking. No worries." He backed down the aisle, but not before he relieved the priest of the manila envelope and handed it to her. "Maybe you could go over this while I have a chat with Father Novak. Father, care to follow me?"

Her first inclination was to demand to know what was going on, but the envelope was too intriguing to ignore. It was enough to distract her, and she sat down as she watched the two men go toward the cockpit.

❖

THIRTEEN

Both men stood outside the cockpit with Zane resting his hand on the door latch. Mikhail followed his line of sight leading to Petra who was pulling out the contents of the envelope given to her by the flight attendant. As he tore his attention away from the woman, Mikhail saw Zane's focus shift to him with a narrowed observation.

"I noticed you gave yourself a promotion to captain," Mikhail said with a yawn.

"It is tradition to call your pilot captain. James 4:6 says, 'God opposes the proud but gives grace to the humble.'" He laid his hand over his heart. "I am but a servant of God. Nothing more."

"Nothing more? We both know that isn't true. What is going on? Who sent this plane for us? Surely not the museum."

"Parties interested in your search for the truth concerning Lalibela."

"Not interested in treasure?"

Zane once more offered a narrow smile that made his hollow eyes squint. "And what does the apostle Matthew say about such things?" When Mikhail hesitated and took a deep breath toward rebellion, Zane snapped, "Say it."

"Matthew 6:19 and 20 says 'Lay not up for yourselves treasures upon earth, where moth and rust doth corrupt, and where thieves break through and steal. But lay up for yourselves treasures in heaven, where neither moth nor rust doth corrupt, and where thieves do not break through nor steal.'"

Zane bowed his head for a moment of satisfaction. "You please me, Mikhail. The treasure is not the gold and silver many seek. I would not lead you on such a wild goose chase that has no meaning or the advancement of the Word of God."

"Then what? It is dangerous in parts of Ethiopia, and I don't want Petra to get hurt. And why couldn't I have done this alone? I'm more familiar with Lalibela than anyone. I understand the people and their needs. They trust me. If I bring a woman who searches for secrets they've kept hidden for hundreds of years, it could be a problem."

"Yes. It certainly could." Once more, he took a quick glance to where Petra studied the envelope contents. "It was necessary is all I have to say. I understand she values treasure only if it contributes to a culture's civilization. Money means nothing to her." Zane chuckled. Something he rarely heard the man do. "She is very strong-willed."

"Incredibly so," Mikhail sighed. "How come she could see you in the museum? No one else could."

Zane shrugged. "There are things even I cannot explain."

"How much do I tell her—about you?"

"Nothing that might give her pause concerning your ability to function mentally." He turned to gaze at Petra then chuckled for the second time, as he added a fist bump to Mikhail's shoulder. "Although I'm told she is a believer, her beliefs get twisted up in many cultures and experiences that come with the profession she has chosen. And"—he turned his full attention back to the priest—"she suffered as a child and is slow to trust. Some things are never far from the heart and the dark side of the mind."

"What does that even mean?" Mikhail snapped. "Was she abused?"

"Only in spirit. But perhaps you can help with that. Chadwick has tried with little success. Discover why she is distraught over him missing. Maybe that will help you with the answers you seek."

"Great. Are you trying to sound like Obi-Wan-Kenobi? And where is Chadwick? I am betting you know. Is he okay?"

"He is alive. For now." Zane opened his mouth to continue, but Mikhail held up his hand.

"Don't quote scripture to me about the things not seen or anything else. I have a feeling you take a lot of scripture out of context to keep me in line."

Zane glared at the priest for several seconds. "Careful how you speak to me, Father Novak. Don't forget what I am capable of if you do not follow my— directions."

"Orders is more like it."

"You say potato. I say potahto." He put both hands on the priest's shoulders and squeezed. "Luke 12:34 says, 'For where your treasure is, there will your heart be also.' Careful you do not forget who you are and where you are headed." Both men turned to focus on Petra who lifted her gaze to them and frowned. "Do you understand?"

"Yes."

"Then let me pray over you. You will soon need the strength. Don't worry about my advice, for I'm being carried in the palm of God's hand. You know this."

Mikhail closed his eyes as the muffled words in an angelic language crossed the lips of his friend. Strength and clarity surged through his veins. His own lips moved with each word spoken to him by God. A feeling of calm and relief washed over him, as it always did when in prayer. It helped to keep the past from taking over his common sense. He repeated over and over at the end, as did Zane.

"I am a child of God."

"I am a child of God."

"I am a child of God."

Mikhail remained standing by the closed cockpit door after Zane returned to his duties. In those few moments, he let himself stare into nothingness, letting his thoughts wander and his body adjust to being awake. Since the galley was at hand, he decided there was no reason why they shouldn't take advantage of the good smells coming from the small oven that beeped.

"Hey, are you hungry?" he called to Petra who

slowly made her way to his side. It was close quarters, so he tried to keep as much space as possible between them.

"Hmm. Smells wonderful. Did we eat today?"

Mikhail slipped on the oven mitts and retrieved two dishes of lasagna. "Check to see if we are lucky enough to have any vegetables."

"Yep. Looks like Caesar salad. Oh my gosh. I think this is tiramisu." She pulled a small pan of the dessert from the tiny refrigerator. "Maybe we should start with dessert and eat in reverse." She placed her finds on the two trays where the lasagna steamed. "Breadsticks too? I smell garlic. I've eaten better in the last two days than I have in a month. I wouldn't have avoided you if I'd known you'd feed me."

"Sorry. No wine."

"Guess you can't do any of that changing the water into wine trick, huh?"

This made him laugh out loud. "No. Sorry. My culinary skills are limited to eggs and heating up lasagna someone else prepared. I'll work on that, though. Just for you."

They carried their trays to a small table inside the passenger area. Mikhail found bottled water in a small cabinet and added it to their trays at the last minute.

"So, you and Captain America in there"—she pointed over her shoulder toward the cockpit—"served in the military together."

"How did you figure that out?" Unease came over him.

"I did a background search on you from the other day and that guy's picture came up. Why was he at the museum, and why did you pretend not to know him?"

"He shows up at the most inappropriate times and is often a pain in the neck. He's been my mentor for a number of years."

"Interesting. Your bio didn't mention you had a mentor."

"Did it mention I couldn't turn water into wine?"

"If it had, this whole partner thing could look totally different." Her soft laugh caused him to pause for a few seconds. "Besides, I'm not much of a drinker. Why a couple of months ago, Hawie and I were having dinner and—"

"Officer Hawie Mathias?" Mikhail found himself not only curious but more than a little irritated. "I didn't realize the two of you were dating."

"We're not," she insisted. "We just sort of ended up at the same restaurant on the same night at the same time." She twisted her lips to the side. "Now that I say it out loud, it sounds like we are. But we aren't." She pointed her fork at him. "Chadwick and I went for dinner—our once-a-week thing—he was called away and in walked larger-than-life-I'll-shoot-you-in-the-butt Officer Hawie Mathias. Both of us were stood up and starving." She shoved more food in her mouth.

Watching her eat was such a pleasure. Every bite appeared to be savored.

"Anyway. There we were, and he ordered a really expensive bottle of wine. I can't even tell you what it was, but I took like two sips and washed it down with water. He did not look pleased."

Mikhail continued to hang on her every excited word.

"I did try a little more, but, you know, I really don't like drinking around men."

"Why is that?" Could this be part of her dark past?

She chewed slower and started moving her food around with her fork, as if looking for an answer. Then she brightened. "Oh, because I have deep-seated angst I need to deal with." She dropped the fork onto the plate. "Anyway, he got over it when I let him take me home. We kind of became friends after that. He thinks he looks after me."

"From what I saw in the coffee shop that day, you don't really need looking after."

She threw her hands up. "Thank you! I keep telling people that. If you don't mind, I'm going to attack this beautiful tiramisu." When she finished hers, she pointed to Mikhail's piece. "Are you going to eat that?"

He shoved it her way. "Help yourself. Back to Officer Mathias."

"This is yum. Who says airline food is garbage?" She rolled her eyes then waved her fork in the air. "Okay. Maybe I have said that a time or two, but this is manna from heaven." She tilted her head coyly. "Thought maybe my description would impress you."

"Keep trying," he said slowly and lowered his chin as he couldn't resist wanting to connect with her hazel-green eyes. "I'm sure you'll think of something."

Her eyes widened then she choked on her last bite, only to have part of it dribble out the corner of her mouth. She grabbed a napkin to stop the mess then laughed out loud. "Are you flirting with me again?"

"I'm a priest. I don't flirt."

"Like hell." She leaned back against the back of the seat. "Oh. That was probably inappropriate. Sorry."

"I don't think you are—inappropriate. I think you want to make me feel uncomfortable because you feel that way toward me. You're used to men thinking you're fragile, and I don't. Therefore, you can't take advantage of me to get what you want."

"Is this therapy session going someplace, or are you just trying to show me who's boss?" She stood up and gathered their plates and trash. "I'll do the dishes," she snapped.

"You do the dishes? From what I saw at your loft, it should be a learning experience. Call if you get stuck. Oh, and that bottle of blue liquid by the sink is for washing dishes. Wait. You do know what a sink is used for, right?"

"Of course, it's where you stack the dirty dishes until you can throw them in a dishwasher. Duh," she smarted.

"This is going to be a long flight," he mumbled.

"Anyway," she said, peeking around the galley door, "what was your buddy doing at my lab?"

"I can answer that." Zane stood, larger than life behind her. Like he always did, he just appeared, but it didn't seem to frighten Petra.

The water continued to run over her hands as she eyed their pilot with a mix of curiosity and suspicion. Zane reached in and turned off the water then handed her a paper towel.

"We meet again." She dried her hands. "Rather, here you are again, since we didn't exactly get introduced."

"Petra, this is Zane Spokane. We served together." Mikhail decided he'd better join them once he noticed the cynical expression on her face about the same time Zane's face hardened into a mask of intimidation.

"I repeat, why were you in my lab?" She folded her

arms across her chest, a definite defense mechanism.

"Let me see." Zane's voice boomed inside Mikhail's brain. "I knew my buddy here was headed to the lab and—"

"How did you know that?"

"Is this an interrogation?" Zane's face turned into a mask of fake amusement. This worried Mikhail.

"I called to let him know I wouldn't be meeting him for breakfast," Mikhail offered hurriedly as they continued to focus on each other rather than him. "That I had to go with you to the lab for—well you know the rest." Mikhail stole a warning glance in Zane's direction.

"Mikhail, you pretended to not know him when I asked you who the gangster was," Petra reminded him.

"I'm crushed, Mikhail. After all we've been through? A gangster? Really?" Zane continued to grin, but it appeared sinister with a warning. "He doesn't like to introduce me to his new girlfriends. Thinks I'm trying to hound dog him to take his girl."

"For one thing, I'm not one of his girlfriends. Eww. And for another, I don't like to be put in the same sentence with a hunting dog. Eww, again!" She pushed past them and hurried to her seat, and flopped down.

"Probably a good thing her backside isn't a mirror or—"

"Shut up, Zane. Sometimes I wonder how you got this job of being a—"

Zane held up his hand toward Mikhail's mouth. It clamped shut, and he couldn't speak. "Careful, my friend. You go back in there and do the job you were assigned. Are we good?" He dropped his hand to his side.

Mikhail could feel his temper subside under the penetrating glare of his mentor. When he didn't speak, Zane tilted his head and glared at his friend.

"We're good," Mikhail snapped.

FOURTEEN

By the time they'd flown out over the ocean, darkness covered the night. Together, they pulled out the map and spread it on their small table. The western side of the map had now filled in with landforms, symbols, and trade routes denoted in pale colors of red and blue. Mikhail translated some of the words the best he could.

"As near as I can tell," Mikhail said, examining the map, "this is written in the ancient language of the Aksumite empire. It's used primarily for religious writings and worship in the Ethiopian Orthodox Church." He pointed to a few other words. "But these are written in Amharic, one of the country's principal languages. It is considered the working language, although the many languages spoken there are recognized by various population groups in Ethiopia."

"Wouldn't that be confusing? I mean, why two languages?" Petra took out a magnifying glass she'd found in their small package of essentials for the plane trip. "Or maybe it's to hide important information by using different meanings."

"I don't follow." Mikhail took out his own magnifying glass to get a better look.

"Remember when an uncle or other older person pretended to take your nose between the index and middle fingers, like he stole it?"

Mikhail nodded.

Petra explained. "In Turkey if you do that, it's an obscene gesture, which is the same as giving someone the middle finger. In Brazil, it's a good luck charm to ward off the evil eye or jealousy. Another one would be giving the thumbs-up in America. Good, right? But in Iraq and Iran, it's the same as saying, 'Up yours, buddy.'"

Mikhail raised his concentration from the map. "That could be it." He rubbed his eyes and yawned. "Sorry. I guess I overdid it last night."

"We never talked about how that sword got from my loft to the museum." The new cell phone provided in a welcome gift bag dinged on the seat next to Petra. She glanced at the incoming number in awe. "It's Hawie. How did he get this number?"

Mikhail grabbed up his new phone and scrolled through to find familiar contacts, including Petra's new number and Officer Hawie Mathias. "Put it on speaker."

She rejected the idea with a wave of stubbornness, but Mikhail grabbed it and hit the speaker button. That got him an if-looks-could-kill expression. "Hawie," she cooed in a pleasant tone. "What's up?"

"What's up is you and Father Novak are nowhere to be found. My contacts say you may have left the country. Any truth to that?"

"Why would I do such a thing?"

"Because our dead ninja had a drop of blood on the sword that didn't belong to him."

"Well, it wasn't my blood, Hawie."

"No. It was Father Novak's. If he is with you, I'm warning you to be careful. We have him on a traffic camera about 2 a.m. Two blocks from the museum."

Petra jerked her head up to glare at the emotionless face of Mikhail. "Seriously? How could you even tell? He drives a Harley and wears a helmet. Besides, I already told you he was with me. And on top of that, he's a priest. They're not allowed to kill people. You know that whole, 'thou shalt not kill' stuff."

"His DNA was in that drop of blood. He's very persuasive and a smooth talker. Has he convinced you to help him leave the country?"

"Ahh—maybe. Not sure. I'm working at the moment."

"I'm standing in the museum, and you are not working. There's an officer outside your building, and you aren't there, either. The two of you were spotted getting in a limo after I left you this morning. Tell me where you are, and I'll come get you."

Mikhail grabbed the phone from her and calmly spoke into the phone. "Goodbye, Officer Mathias." He hung up and handed the phone back to Petra. "I'm beat. I'm going to try and get some sleep. The agenda said we'd be in the Cape Verde Islands by sunrise. You probably should get some rest too."

"Your DNA was on my samurai sword." Her voice had turned icy.

"He nicked me during the—scuffle." Mikhail tilted his head as his chin lowered. "As to how the sword got to the museum…"

"You lying piece of—"

"Yes. I did go to the museum. I watched the intruder land on the roof of the other building. I watched him escape that building. He searched and found the sword and held it up toward me in a taunt or maybe it was a challenge. I had to find him. But I didn't kill him. When he entered the museum, I thought the alarms would go off. They didn't. A system failure."

"Shut up," she barked. "Just shut up."

Watching the wheels turn in that pretty head of hers caused him to be silent.

"Look me in the eye and tell me the truth. Did you kill that man in my lab?"

"No."

"I don't believe you."

"Violence is against everything I stand for. I want no part of it."

"Are you even a priest?"

"I'm going to sleep for a few hours. You should do the same. When you've calmed down, we'll discuss this further. In the meantime, don't be talking to your boyfriend about where we are or what we're doing. Understand?" He eased back in to his captain chair across the aisle and stretched out his long legs. Since he wasn't sure how to proceed, he concentrated on the large movie screen at the front showing the location of the plane on the map.

Petra stepped out from the table and moved down

the aisle, but Mikhail grabbed her by the hand and jerked her back. She shook him off, but he came out of the seat and took her arm.

"Where do you think you're going?"

"I'm going to question the pilot."

Mikhail could feel his frustration and anger begin to boil. "I would advise you not to do that."

She tried to jerk free, but he only tightened his grip. "Don't tell me what to do," she snapped.

Mikhail could feel a fire about to ignite inside him. He shoved her gently into a seat and quickly buckled her in. A part of him felt guilty for using his strength against her, but stubbornness would not get them where they needed to be. He leaned down close. She pushed her head back hard against the headrest. Staring into her eyes took the edge off his anger, and he knew the temptation to teach her a lesson was masked on his emotionless face as he'd practiced so many times.

He took one finger and moved the soft red hair that had fallen in her eyes away, only to have her recoil from his touch. This did not discourage him. It managed to make him want to ignite her anger more.

"Enough, Mikhail." He heard the whisper in his brain. He glanced over his shoulder at the cockpit door. It was open partway, and a shadow stood there. "Rest now. Remember who you are."

The priest straightened but continued to focus on the woman. "Hawie Mathias," he spoke calmly.

"Not my boyfriend, and you can bet the first chance I get, I will be calling him. You can't stay awake forever. I'm sorry you're jealous, but I don't care."

Once more, Mikhail leaned down close enough

their noses nearly touched. "His name is spelled Hawi, which is Ethiopian for I wish. I saw how he spelled it when he signed for the check the day he paid for our lunch." This caused her to sit up straight in the seat with a sparked interest. "Mathias is also an Ethiopian name meaning 'gift from God.'"

"What? Are you serious?"

"He looks Ethiopian. Has he ever said his family is from there?"

"Just that his family immigrated from East Africa a couple of generations ago." Her voice had turned to a whisper.

"He is the one you need to be concerned about. Not me," he growled quietly.

This time, he edged back toward his seat and sat down. Her seat belt could not be opened until he wished it to be so. Her phone rested on the table, and there was no need to retrieve it. After a few minutes of silent prayer for control of his inner beast, he dared glare over at Petra who watched him in curiosity. Once they locked gazes, she turned away to unfold the blanket next to her. Soon, she dozed off and posed no more of a threat. He needed to sleep. Things were going to happen soon.

FIFTEEN

❖

Mikhail slept peacefully. Those nights didn't happen often and when they did, he thanked God. Although it was true he'd discovered how to exist on little sleep, at times, his inner batteries needed charging. The smell of coffee teased him awake, his eyelids struggling to open. When they did, his head was turned toward the window, and streaks of color painted the sky.

He glanced over to where he'd buckled Petra in the night before they both fell asleep. She was gone. He quickly unfastened his own seat belt and peered up and down the aisle to find her with no luck. The phone was missing from the table, causing mild concern as to whether or not she'd been able to call Hawi Mathias. Since Petra was up and about, it must mean Zane found it in his tarnished heart to release the mechanism he'd subtly placed to keep it locked. She had no way of knowing it would open after she tried X-number of times, which he imagined she did often, given her tenacious personality.

Zane had either taken the phone or sabotaged any way to reach out to her friend. Once he absorbed both possibilities, he relaxed and stretched then eased out into the aisle. He saw movement in the galley and decided to investigate.

"Morning," he grunted to Petra who removed a couple of muffins from the tiny oven. She cocked a tepid gaze his way. She placed both muffins on a tray then pushed past him, sloshing a tiny bit of coffee on the tray. "One of those for me?"

No response.

"Do we need to kiss and make up?" he asked sarcastically.

This halted her. She spun around to face him and nearly dropped the tray. He tried to rescue it but spilled the coffee on his hand. He jerked back when the heat permeated his skin.

Petra gasped, set the tray on the tiny peninsula table, and grabbed his hand. She pulled him over to the sink and ran cold water over it. She grabbed ice out of the ice machine and dropped them in a bowl. She gently shoved his hand in it then added more water.

It had been a long time since a woman took care of him. He'd forgotten how therapeutic it could be for the soul. Her close proximity was comforting. He'd made it a point to be extremely careful and distant around women over the years since his wife died. In the ministry, you couldn't take chances someone would get the wrong impression. The wall he'd built around himself grew into an insulated fortress against emotional attachments. Petra McGinnis had thrown him a curve ball and it was unsettling, but in a good way—he guessed.

His gaze roamed over her profile and the loose ponytail with strands of red hair framing her face. A little mascara smudge under her eyes gave her skin a paler appearance. With most of her makeup gone, the freckles were more pronounced than he first thought. Funny how it made her appear more youthful.

She lifted his hand from the icy water and wrapped a towel around it to pat it dry. Suddenly she paused and studied his hand for a few seconds before tilting her head in his direction. He'd noticed how she often did this when he got too close. Was it a way for her to control the situation by flaunting her charm at him? She took a deep breath. "I suppose you want me to kiss it and make it all better now."

Mikhail pulled his hand back and removed the cloth, not quite ready to deal with the turbulent sensations running through his veins. He offered an emotionless expression he was so proficient at. Served him right for the kiss-and-make-up crack.

"Thank you. You've done enough." He poured coffee in a disposable cup and double-checked the lid to secure it before returning to the cabin.

He left Petra to clean up her mess. She then carried the two muffins in on a dry tray with a couple of bottles of water and a new cup of coffee. He leaned against the table they'd used the night before. When she stopped next to him, he dared level a sour gaze her way.

"I'm sorry." She handed him a muffin. When he hesitated, she continued, "I didn't inject poison or anything, if that's what you're thinking. I swear on a stack of Bibles," she teased.

Mikhail accepted the muffin and watched her take a position at the table. He pointed toward the virtual map on the screen mounted at the front of the cabin. "Should be at the Cape Verde Islands soon."

"I could use a little exercise."

Mikhail finished his muffin between sips of coffee. "We'll probably be confined to the terminal while they fuel the plane. Last time I was here, it took an hour or so then we were on our way again. I went diving there once, though."

"Oh my gosh. Did you just tell me something personal about yourself?" The contempt was still in her voice, and her large eyes became hooded.

"I thought if I made something up and offered it as part of my profile, you would find it interesting enough to stop being an ass."

"An ass? Can a priest really call a person that?" She sounded bewildered.

"Only if they really mean it," he snapped. "And trust me when I say, I most definitely do." For whatever reason, this made her laugh out loud. The sound of it forced him to let down his guard. "About last night—"

She waved him off. "I managed to wander about after you went to sleep and had a nice chat with the pilot. I called Officer Mathias, and he convinced me he was only looking out for my best interests."

"Why, Pinocchio, what a big nose you have," Mikhail said sarcastically.

"What's that supposed to mean?" she asked through gritted teeth.

"It means"—Captain Zane Spokane handed her the

phone left on the table the night before—"Father Novak knows I'm not much of a talker, especially when I'm working. I came back to check on you guys several hours ago to find your phone blinking a low battery light. I took it with me to charge. Sorry if you missed it."

Petra twisted those pouty lips to the side but didn't apologize for lying. "Did you get any sleep?" she asked Zane.

"Yes. My copilot did a fine job." He yawned and cut his eyes to Mikhail.

"I guess you mean God, huh?" Petra mused.

"Of course." Zane shifted his attention to Mikhail. "Can we talk a minute?"

"Sure. Petra, let's have another look at the map before we pack it away. I don't think we should leave it on the plane."

"Twenty minutes, and we'll land," Zane added.

The priest followed a few steps behind his friend, and both stopped in the galley. Instinct kicked in as they both stopped to watch Petra shift her attention to the map rather than them.

"Officer Mathias tried several more times to reach Petra. I blocked all communications with him for the time being." Zane kept his eye on Petra.

"Who killed the man who came to her apartment and was found at the museum?"

Zane shrugged. "Difficult to say."

"Don't give me that. I saw you follow him inside that night."

"Doesn't mean I killed him."

"Doesn't mean you didn't."

"He was a bad player. That map cannot fall into the

wrong hands. It's more than a map. It will give Petra credibility to do what needs to be done if she plans to get Chadwick back."

"Are Mathias and Petra a couple?" It was a ridiculous question at this point in time, but he wanted to know.

"Would it matter to you?" Zane asked wickedly.

"I have sworn my allegiance to God and not myself."

"Then why haven't you taken your final steps to being ordained?"

Mikhail tried to present an emotionless face.

"Up until now, I actually believed you would become a full-fledged priest." Zane glanced toward Petra who continued to work. "I'm not so sure this is the path you should take."

"Many priests in the Eastern Orthodox Church have families."

"You have shown little interest in that until recently."

"I am content with my life, Zane. You of all people should know how difficult the PTSD road can be. Look at what you became to escape earthly pain."

"I have never regretted it, Father Novak. I really had no choice."

"Before you became a—"

Zane held up his hand to silence him.

"Before you chose this life, did you ever find someone—special?" Mikhail had always wondered.

"I did. But it was already too late for me, and I'd made promises I had to keep. This life is hard, but I welcome it compared to the hell I lived. I've never regretted the creature I've become." As was his usual gesture, he laid a large hand on Mikhail's shoulder, paralyzing him with anticipation and awe. "The days, and possibly years, ahead will be full of promise for you. Don't be afraid to heal from your past, and take risks that lead to a brighter tomorrow. Proverbs 3:5-6."

Say it with me, Mikhail."

"Trust in the Lord with all your heart, lean not on your own understanding; in all your ways submit to Him, and He will make your paths straight."

"Do you believe this?"

"Yes," Mikhail answered.

"Good. Allow me to pray over you. Do not question what is about to happen. I have everything prepared for you."

Mikhail closed his eyes and received the blessing.

SIXTEEN

❖

Petra tried to eavesdrop on the two men, but the map was much more interesting. The fact she had her phone and could call Hawie—or was it Hawi, like Mikhail had suggested—gave her an opportunity to dial while pretending to be absorbed in her work. When she got a busy signal the first time, she hit redial. The screen fizzed and went dark. Maybe there was no signal here. Could it be the pilot sabotaged it?

The guy acted very suspicious to her. Creepy may have been a better description. He looked normal enough, except for being a big guy with lots of hard angles on his face. His short hair was a blend of gray and brown. Those hooded eyes were hollow and dark and felt as if they pierced her soul. He reminded her of one of those questionable heroes from a video game. Yet, she'd watched him pray with Mikhail.

And why hadn't she seen the copilot this entire time? Didn't he need to stretch his legs, get a bite to eat, or at least use the restroom. Come to think of it, she'd not seen Zane do that either. She turned to casually check out the galley, only to find both men watching her. A chill ran up her back and she wondered if she'd made a pact with the wrong people.

Where was Chadwick? He had always been at her side or at least not far away. They'd talked every day since she was a little girl. Because of him, she was healthy and strong. She truly loved him like a father. The image of him bound and gagged, hungry and cold, in darkness, injured, alone, was too much for her to bear. Then a voice cut through her reverie.

"Plotting your next move?" Mikhail sat down across from her. He picked up her magnifying glass and twirled it between his long fingers.

"What was all that about?" she asked, turning to see Zane close the cockpit door.

"He told me I was a jerk to you last night, and I should make it up to you."

"How do you plan to do that?"

"I'm not sure. I'll think of something." He laid his hand on his heart. "I was rude, crude, and indifferent to your concerns. I apologize."

Petra raised her stubborn chin. "Fine. We're good." She pointed to the map. "Can you believe this? It's over halfway complete again. There have been changes, I think, to the area in the north."

"The area we need, though, is still missing. Any idea why Chadwick was taken? Did he find the map? He indicated a graduate student maybe discovered it in a vault or storeroom."

"Right. We were taking inventory of an old storage area that was all but forgotten. Besides the map, we found a few black-and-white photographs from the early 1900s and older drawings of Lalibela churches. None of them were labeled but there are current pictures that are."

"All of the churches were in the photographs?"

"Only three. Why?" Petra was bewildered.

"Could be the most important ones. I remembered Chadwick saying there were clues he hadn't remembered until we talked. He was going to meet me at the museum to show me. Could they have been the photographs?" Mikhail wondered.

"But he left me a message on my phone that he had those with him. Not to worry. He'd bring them back when he came to work. But he had already been in his office. I don't understand why he came to see you in the first place. So," Petra continued, "he had already left the photographs at the museum."

"Whatever is in those photographs may be the reason he was taken. If that is true, and they think you have them, I'm afraid you aren't safe either."

The captain announced over the intercom it was time to buckle up for landing.

Once the stairlift was released, an airport attendant escorted them inside. It was just past sunrise, and few people milled about the nondescript terminal. A military-style guard stood on the outside of each door while the plane was being refueled.

Petra and Mikhail strolled back and forth throughout the terminal to limber up, after having been confined for too long. They walked in awkward silence, but Mikhail knew from experience to stay alert as to if anyone paid them a little too much attention.

Another plane waited to be loaded with a cart of luggage. Petra paused at one of the large floor-to-ceiling windows. He stayed close to Petra as she watched the activities around the planes on the runway. Crossing his hands in front of him, he felt like a bodyguard as she managed to stretch, along with doing a few knee bends. Mikhail spotted unusual activity on the tarmac where a few men moved toward the plane, preparing to leave. Following his line of sight, Petra's breath caught in her throat.

A man paused and pointed back to where they stood inside the terminal. A taller, older gentleman pivoted and lifted a hand toward them. Mikhail recognized him the same time Petra slapped her hands against the glass.

"Chadwick!" she screamed. "Chadwick." She banged on the glass. "Chadwick," she continued as she ran to the double doors. Mikhail was on her heels and pulled her back when Chadwick lowered his fingertips to his lips to place a kiss. He then blew it her way. Chadwick turned to the others who appeared to be waiting patiently. Together, they boarded the plane.

"Stop him," she begged Mikhail.

The door guards turned around with deep scowls on their faces.

"Petra, he's gone."

She shook him off and raised her delicate chin in stubbornness. A solitary tear rolled down her cheek but was quickly wiped away with her sleeve. "I don't understand," she said with an icy calm that caused Mikhail to slip his arm through hers and pulled her away from the door. The two guards remained focused on her.

"At least we know he isn't hurt." Mikhail guided her to a refreshment stand where he purchased a bottle of water. "Drink this." When she didn't take the water but continued to watch the plane taxi out to the airstrip, he twisted the cap off and forced it into her hand. "We're going to figure this out. I promise."

Petra opened her mouth to speak, but nothing came out.

"Drink. Please."

She locked onto his eyes, and the toughness and bravado evaporated from her rigid stance. A kind of vulnerability flooded her eyes as if she was confused and heartbroken at the same time.

"You need to calm down." He watched her take a long drink of the water. "We cannot cause a scene. We don't know who is watching us."

"Dr. McGinnis? Dr. McGinnis?" came a voice over the PA system. "Please come to the information desk. Dr. McGinnis?"

Without warning, she grabbed his hand and squeezed. "Do you mind?"

"Not at all. We're partners. Remember?" This time, he felt warmer toward her, especially when there was a hint of a smile on her lips.

The information clerk handed her a legal-size envelope with her name written across the front. She read it then handed it to him.

Dearest Petra,

I'm sorry I had to deceive you. Do not worry about me. I will return soon enough. But, for now, you must return home. The job ahead of me will not be easy and is much too dangerous for you. If you insist on going to Lalibela, you put the whole operation in jeopardy. The treasure of a lifetime will be destroyed, as will the lives of many. I beg you. Go home. Trust the good Father Novak as I do. Do not trust what is easy or familiar. I've enclosed some photographs I promised to show you and Father Novak. They hold clues to this amazing discovery. My captors have allowed me to share them with you. They mean me no harm as long as I hold the key.

Your faithful servant,
Chadwick

"It doesn't make any sense. He must have been forced to write this." She sighed, rolling her eyes upward and blinking back pools of tears that threatened to escape. Her voice transitioned to being calm.

Mikhail could still see the hurt in her face.

"It's possible they did force him and that he also wants you to leave. What do you want to do, Petra? I'll support you, whatever you decide."

She thumbed through the pictures and handed them to him. "I see no clues."

He quickly sifted through the stack of pictures and agreed. "Let's wait and see if they are like the map and the clue materializes."

"I'm sorry I burned you earlier. You have a tendency to get my temper fired up. I should be more careful. Does it hurt?"

The woman could switch moods so fast it made his head spin. He glanced at his hand after slipping the pictures back in the envelope. "I was thinking maybe I'd take you up on your earlier suggestion to kiss it and make it better." He figured his voice sounded sarcastic even though he grinned in hopes it would lighten the burden she must feel. Petra appeared to tighten her lips together, but the corners of her mouth turned up ever so slightly.

Mikhail continued, "But in the meantime, I think we need a plan. Okay?"

"Okay." Her voice had grown so soft he found himself leaning in to hear her.

The guards unlocked the doors and motioned for them to return to their plane. It only took a few minutes for them to get comfortable and buckle up. Once in the air, they returned to the table to discuss their options. Petra was adamant about continuing to their destination, and Mikhail agreed.

"Chadwick would never do this to me. If he didn't want me to go, he would have said so once we got the go-ahead. We've worked together too long to not keep each other informed," she insisted.

"So, you think he was giving you a kind of message?" Mikhail sifted through the pictures again.

"I do. But, Mikhail, I don't want you to put your life in danger if you have a bad feeling about this or have decided you want to go back."

"I'm in. Besides, I know a lot about Ethiopia and how to get around. The people should remember me at Lalibela. Whatever the problem, we have to find out if Chadwick is safe. At this point, I think he may have been forced into helping do something against his will. That's my take on it, but you know him better than me."

"I agree."

They talked nonstop for several hours, and it wasn't all about work. Although the conversation didn't venture into personal things, they did talk about books, cultures, art, music, and began to create a bond of friendship.

When the plane hit turbulence and lost altitude, they both buckled up in their captain's chairs. The cockpit door opened, and a short man the color of obsidian ventured toward them, carrying a parachute. He had already slipped one on himself.

"Come. Let me help the two of you into this tandem chute."

"What? No," Petra balked. "Who are you? Where's Zane?"

"He did not return to the plane in the Cape Verde Islands. I was told to fly you to your destination. But the instruments are wrong. We are out of fuel." He ran to the back of the plane and prepared to open the door as the plane continued to lose altitude. "You're on your own," he said, ejecting the door, which sucked all the air out of the cabin.

Mikhail had just finished tying Petra into the harness with him and felt the pull toward freedom. They struggled to hold on until the cabin stabilized even though it felt nearly impossible. With Petra attached he forced himself to hobble to the open door to escape.

"Ready?" he yelled.

"Have you done this before?"

"No time like the present. Remember the Alamo," he yelled, more exhilarated than he thought possible. Then it was the wind beneath him as they plummeted toward the earth.

SEVENTEEN

The wind sounded hollow as it swept across the barren landscape. Shifting sand created patterns of light and shadow in the afternoon sun. The sand lifted and settled over and over. Only the flapping of an open parachute, fighting to be reined in, competed with the grunts of Father Mikhail Novak. He struggled to wad it into a lopsided ball that remained unruly in the gusts of wind sweeping across the Sahara.

Petra rushed to his side to assist, and, together, they managed to get the rainbow fabric under control. The bright colors appeared out of place in such a dry land. Together, they placed it on the ground to use as a seat.

"Where do you think we are?" asked Father Mikhail.

Beads of sweat dripping into her eyes, Petra surveyed the area around them. She'd always taught her graduate students who came and went at the museum to use the five themes of geography set forth by National Geographic years ago. It served her well many times. Location. Place. Human Environmental Interaction. Movement. Region.

The cell phone she'd secured in her jacket pocket after leaving the Cape Verde Islands pinpointed their location on the GPS map but showed little to identify the nearby towns. Even when she squeezed the map to reveal a wider version of where they were, nothing popped up.

"Lack of internet might be the problem." She shaded her eyes against the sun to get a better perspective. Place. What were things she could identify in the area to add clues to their whereabouts? Besides miles of sand, what stood out as unique? They were lost.

Human Environmental Interaction. Was there any indication how people survived here in such a harsh landscape? Without water, they would die soon enough. Could there be an oasis within walking distance? How would they find such a thing?

"Google, where is the nearest water supply?" She had to repeat it three times before her cell phone understood her question.

Father Mikhail came closer and listened to the directions.

"Father, if I were you, I'd say a prayer that we make it to this speck on the map, or we'll roast."

Two hours later, an image appeared in the distance in the form of hazy heat waves lifting from the desert floor. Putting one foot forward became more difficult with each minute. Once, Petra fell and Mikhail struggled to pull her to her feet.

"We're almost there. Keep going. Don't give up," he coaxed through parched lips.

Petra grabbed his forearm to steady herself until she could walk on her own. Thoughts swirled in her head about how she'd gotten here, where Chadwick was, and that she'd probably die without knowing love. The priest trudged onward, appearing more determined than her but also in bad shape from the looks of his sagging shoulders and eyes downturned away from the bright sun. He stopped every few steps to let her catch up and once took her hand to pull her along. She wanted to shake him off, to exert her will to survive. Instead, she clung to his sweaty hand.

When he stopped and squinted into the distance, she tried to follow his line of sight. Where were they? Had the blurry image faded into their imaginations? She wanted to speak, but he appeared dazed, dropped her hand, and pointed toward the horizon.

Did he try to smile? Lines deepened around his eyes, made worse by being peppered with sand. Why was he a blur? Why was... Petra sank to her knees. Nothing was left inside her except heat and despair. Would she finally be able to see her parents who died long ago? Chadwick couldn't save her this time.

She was barely aware of Mikhail who stumbled to her side and slipped to his knees as well. Was he praying for her?

"Dear merciful Lord..." Mikhail mumbled.

Darkness covered her fear of dying as she eased into a dimension of survival. Her body lifted, and the thought of fighting against the dark death evaporated, along with consciousness.

The smell of animals and the touch of folds of cloth covering her dragged her back to consciousness. Along with the sound of what reminded her of flapping fabric came the low murmurs of men's voices. It caused enough confusion to delay her opening her eyes as she tried to piece together her situation. *Hospital? Museum? Plane? No, this is the desert. Where in the desert? Did I die? Father Mikhail. Who is Father Mikhail? Friend. Parachute. Face in sand. Definitely dead. I'm dead. What, I'm dead?*

Something touched her face then pressed what felt like fingers to her neck.

"Pulse is strong," came a familiar voice. "Petra? Can you open your eyes?" The words were low and comforting. A damp cloth touched her forehead. "Wake up, Petra. I need you to drink this."

The smooth voice enticed her enough, her eyelids fluttered. Her tongue ran across her lips at the same moment she realized a real person spoke to her. With a sense of fear mixed with relief, she bolted upright to confront a man clothed in white squatting next to her. His head was wrapped in a dark-blue turban that, somehow, made his eyes appear softer. The lower part of his face was covered, but as she studied him, he removed it to reveal his identity.

"Petra." His wide smile was infectious. "Drink this."

He offered her a cup of water, but it tasted metallic with a side of chalk mixed in. Although it was body temperature, she gulped it nonetheless. A few drops spilled down her chin. She quickly rescued the drops with a finger and stuck it in her mouth. It was then she noticed another man stood behind Father Mikhail. Once they made eye contact, he squatted next to the priest as if to get a better look at her.

He dressed in blue robes and a navy turban, favored among the Tuareg of North Africa. He dropped his mouth covering and began an appreciative inspection as his gaze ran over her hair. His beautiful light-brown face was accented with a thin black mustache. Although the shape of his eyes was wide, he kept them half closed, making them appear sleepy. With chiseled cheekbones, he reminded her of a Hollywood heartthrob playing a desert bandit. Besides a wide ring on his pinkie finger, both wrists were adorned with bracelets.

"You have hair of fire." He created circles with his finger in the air then elbowed the priest. "Is she your woman?"

"We are"—Mikhail arched an eyebrow and raised his chin—"searching for a friend. He has disappeared. We need to find him."

She couldn't resist touching her hair since he had mentioned it, and pushed some strands behind her ears. But the white strip just wouldn't cooperate and fell down across her nose. Taking another sip of the reddish-brown water helped her gather her faculties about her, realizing she was dressed in robes too. Her other clothes were gone.

"Do you have a husband, Petra?" the man asked. His mischievous grin continued as he relieved her of the cup. "A woman in the desert, all alone, is not a good thing, especially one so beautiful."

Father Mikhail stood up and offered her a hand.

"Petra is her own woman. I am merely her spiritual advisor."

Petra flinched at his comment, knowing that might mean she'd get a visit from the Tuareg nomad in the middle of the night. Single Tuareg women had the freedom to take multiple lovers until they married. Even after they married, they remained in control of their own possessions. If they chose to divorce, they got to keep their wealth. The man must always be discreet when visiting a single woman and be gone by sunrise as to show respect. The women of the tribe were greatly respected.

Slipping her hand in Mikhail's, she allowed him to tug her up. The Tuareg stood at the same time, never letting his flirtatious interest fade. "I will leave you. Preparations are being made to feed you. When the sun sets deep into the night, we will head out to Mano Dayak. There, you can continue your journey by plane. My people are anxious to visit, so please"—he fanned his hand toward the open flap used as a door—"refresh and join us. I hope you and I can become better acquainted, Petra." His devilish grin widened as he bowed his head to take his leave and stopped to let his eyes run over her one more time.

"Thank you for your kindness—" She didn't know what to call him.

He laid a hand on his heart. "I am Reza Hama Ag Meslar."

There was magic in his charming expression, and this was exactly the kind of thing that had gotten her into trouble with men in the past. She was a sucker for fantasy romance, and Reza had that story written all over him.

"We won't be long, Reza." She couldn't resist a coy batting of the eyelashes as she tilted her head at the man who must have saved them.

As he disappeared out the door, Mikhail stepped in front of her, blocking her view of the Tuareg's exit. His expression of distaste mixed with unbelief showed on his pinched forehead.

"Are you flirting with him?"

"Of course not."

"I might be a priest, but I know flirting when I see it."

"Is that because all the cupcake moms hit on you, or are you speaking from experience?" she snapped.

"This isn't downtown USA, Petra. Things are different here. For all I know, you just indicated you wanted to have Reza's baby."

"Hmm. That's a pleasant thought," she cooed as she tapped her cheek with her index finger. When a look of horror crossed Mikhail's face, she chuckled and jabbed him where she thought his stomach might be under those white robes. "I'm kidding. Relax. Tuareg women are allowed to exert themselves as free thinkers."

"How did you know he was a Tuareg?"

"He's wearing blue. They're sometimes referred to as the Blue Men. It might be because some of the dye comes off on their faces, giving them a sheen. Kind of romantic, don't you think?"

"I wouldn't know." Mikhail's eyes became hooded and his lips puckered in a frown, causing his face to appear hard.

"Like hell. Oh sorry. My bad. Like whatever."

"You enjoy taunting me, don't you? I would think

a woman of your particular specialty could appreciate the spiritual realms of culture and history."

"Blah. Blah. Blah. You're only trying to put me in my place."

"I seriously doubt you even know your place. Why else would you be so irreverent and disrespectful?"

Petra paused to absorb his observation and realized everything he'd accused her of was true. "I apologize. You are right. I have not always been as polite and accommodating as I should have been with you. After all, you have put yourself in danger and—"

"Saved your scrawny neck. Just remember, I could have left you on the plane, let ninja man slice and dice you, not to mention the whole coffee-shop incident."

She opened her mouth to protest but bit her lip instead as she decided looking at him dressed like a Tuareg was a little more attractive than she'd noticed earlier. "Of course, you're right, Father Mikhail." Saying "Father" in front of his name took the edge off her sudden carnal image of him sprawled on a rug next to her under a Sahara moon.

"What?" he fumed. "Why are you looking at me that way?"

Eighteen

The Sahara moon loomed over the horizon like a giant white orb. The cool night air touched Petra's face as she watched the dancing flames of a small fire. The robes the women helped her change into earlier added a layer of warmth against the falling temperatures. They gossiped with coy glances in her direction.

Several had come to her with water to wash her face before dinner and pointed to her hair. She nodded and let them touch the dirty strands. One younger woman twirled her white forelock around her finger and laughed. In her youthful enthusiasm, she chatted happily to her as if she'd understood the entire conversation. Petra could only shrug and laugh too.

They led her outside and found her a place to sit. They seemed to argue who would get to sit next to her until Father Mikhail appeared. Then their attention shifted to him. When they started pointing to their eyes then his, Petra realized they must be smitten by the blue color. It wasn't hard to discern from their sudden tilted heads and shy expressions, the goal was to get his attention. She wanted to tell them they had a fat chance in hell making their dreams come true. Besides, she wasn't so sure she wanted to share. Then he disappeared with the man she'd met earlier, Reza.

Four men dressed in black marched out before the seated crowd and moved back and forth with music. Each held a three-foot-long stick in his right hand, using it to touch the ground as they swayed. With grace, the movements became more intense as their bodies bent forward and jabbed the stick into the ground.

Camels lined the edge of the camp, with several prepared to travel. A high-pitched horn was being played as drums hammered a rhythmic beat. The trill of the women's tongues lifted happily, as Petra experienced a thrill at what she was witnessing. She'd seen such displays on National Geographic films, but had never believed she'd get to see it in person.

Her heartbeat increased as her body moved beneath her robes to the beat of Tuareg music. The next group of dancers twirled their wooden swords, decorated with fringe and colored ropes. Two men split off and pretended to be opponents while twirling. The dancing never stopped. Their faces shrouded in black cloth from the nose down made Petra wonder how they managed to breathe and dance.

When the women began to sing, two more men dressed in black emerged from a tent. One wore a burgundy sash, and the second man wore a lime-green one. The sashes crisscrossed their chests and wrapped in a wide band around their waists. Each carried two swords: one of metal the other wood. They began a threatening dance, swinging the weapons and jabbing at each other, making contact from time to time.

It was beautiful.

The crowd cheered as they completed the routine just as the music stopped. The two men bowed to each other. Petra heard them laugh. She was overwhelmed with the sensation of being free from the trappings of civilization. What would it be like to travel with these people across the desert, not taking anything for granted and loving each moment that God granted you one more day to experience the raw beauty of this world?

Both men turned to stare at her as if they could read her mind. The shorter one elbowed the taller and pointed his sword her way. He pulled his shoulders back and handed the weapons to his opponent. A thrill raced up her spine as he stepped toward her. She did a quick visual search for Mikhail in case she required rescue, but he was gone. Did she even care?

The man in black approached her with slow determined steps as darkness fell all around them. The crackle of the fire and murmurs of the Tuareg people floated on the cool night air. Then he was in front of her. Only his eyes were visible, and even those were squinted in a serious kind of examination. She didn't waver in her own observation. He slowly lowered his body in a squatting position before her and removed his mask.

Petra sucked in her breath. "F-Father Mikhail," she stammered. The women near her giggled and quietly moved away, as if they were giving them a chance to get acquainted.

"Petra," he said matter-of-factly. His expression never changed. Those piercing eyes remained squinted, so the blue color was invisible. "You have caused quite a stir among the men with your flaming-red hair and pale skin. I suggest you choose me immediately, or you may have a number of interested visitors later. Reza being one of them."

Without hesitation, she extended her hand to him. It hung suspended in air as his appreciative expression raked over her face then slid down the front of her robes. He stood once more and reached down to take her hand. She suddenly comprehended his nearness when he jerked her to stand inches from him. The level of comfort evaporated when she became keenly aware of the secrets held in those piercing blue eyes that didn't shy away from penetrating her psyche. Her imagination had shifted into high gear with his firm grip on her hand. If he was really a priest, and she doubted it, then a lot of women at the church were going straight to Hell with their carnal thoughts, including her.

He dropped her hand and pivoted away. "Follow me," he ordered.

Petra adjusted her robes and pulled part of the head covering around her face. Focusing on the ground, she followed obediently until they entered the tent where she'd been earlier. Pushing the head covering completely away, she shoved her hands onto her waist. She watched Mikhail remove the black head dressing and loosen the burgundy sashes.

"What?" he asked flippantly. "You knew it was me out there dancing around like an idiot to impress you, right?"

"No. I had no idea," she confessed in a quiet voice. "You were trying to impress me?"

"I had to do something, the way you were mesmerized by those Tuareg men."

"It is merely a cultural fascination. It's what I do. Or have you forgotten?"

"That cultural fascination could have gotten you a lover if I hadn't stepped in to claim you."

"So, you're my lover for the night?" she teased, cocking her head.

"You're not my type. I'll stay here with you to make sure everyone knows we're together."

"What is your type, Father Mikhail?" she cooed playfully.

He straightened to his full height and raised his chin, as if finally picking up on her teasing. "I have pledged myself to God, Petra. I have no earthly desire to partner with you or anyone else."

"Partner? Is that what they're calling it in the church these days?"

"I resent that you always feel led to make fun of me or what I do for a living. And I certainly don't appreciate your constant flirting with me."

"Flirting with you," she gasped. "You've got to be kidding." She stormed up to him a little closer than she'd planned. He didn't budge but instead glared down at her with angry blue eyes that nearly made her forget what she'd plan to say. "You are a pompous ass. You know that, right?"

"Now that we both know your type of man, I'll be sure to not display that trait to tempt you." His voice was so unconcerned and cold, Petra stepped back and blinked with unbelief. "Do you have your other clothes on under those robes?" He started to touch her, but she jumped back.

Why did her breathing become labored and her heart pound? Was she angry that he put her in her place? She wasn't used to being stood up to and, when someone tried, there were a multitude of womanly charms and tricks she used to get what she wanted. Father Mikhail might as well have been a block of ice. This infuriated her to the point where she couldn't respond to his question.

"So, I get the silent treatment?" He lifted his eyes to Heaven. "Thank you, Jesus."

"Yes," she snarled. "I don't know why you've suddenly become irritated with me, nor do I care, but we've got to work together to find Chadwick. It's a wonder we're not dead after that jump into the desert. Lucky Reza found us."

Mikhail found a rug and spread it on the ground. When he sat down, he drew up his knees and once again eyed her like she was his property. "Luck had nothing to do with it."

"Let me guess. Divine intervention." She probably should find her own rug but found none. He patted a space next to him. With a huff of annoyance, she flopped down next to him, aware of his eyes still probing her body, head to toe. "Move over," she said, pointing to the end of the rug.

He attempted to scoot, but he still monopolized the area. "This is more than enough room for both of us to sleep. We should rest while we can. I think Reza wants to leave several hours before dawn. It will be cooler for us."

"Fine." She lay down then rolled to her side, away from him. "I'll warn you, I'm a bed hog and a very restless sleeper. So, give me plenty of room." The rug might have been big enough for two people, but having him this close unnerved her when she felt him lie down.

Flickering lights from outside seeped in enough to make patterns dance around the small tent. She hated sleeping on the ground but had endured uncomfortable accommodations on many a trip. This time, a new element added discomfort: having a self-absorbed priest on her backside. When his breathing had slowed, Petra rolled over just as Mikhail's eyes opened.

Those blue eyes were dark and pierced her usual self-confidence. He had tucked his arm under his head. "Do you want me to turn over? I don't mean to make you feel uncomfortable with me."

She was keenly aware of how low and calm his voice had become. "Ditto, Father Mikhail."

He grinned then chuckled. "I'll admit, it's been a long time since such a beautiful woman was in my bed."

"Guess you'll have an interesting tale to share at the next gospel retreat with the other fine shepherds of the flock."

He pursed his lips and narrowed those eyes that pierced her soul. "I think I'll keep this to myself."

"When was the last time you were with a woman?"

"When was the last time you were with a priest?" he responded immediately.

"Touché." She adjusted her robes to keep her warm against the night air. "I guess it's really none of your business."

"You took the words right out of my mouth."

There was no doubt the enjoyment on those firm lips indicated he was making fun of her.

Before she could think of a clever retort, Reza rushed in and loomed over them, causing Mikhail to scramble to his feet.

"My friend, we must leave. Boco Haram are coming. You will not be safe if found. Come. Everything has been prepared." Even before he finished speaking, Mikhail had reached down and pulled Petra to her feet.

Reza grabbed the small backpack Petra had managed to secure before jumping out of the plane. She wanted to protest, but Mikhail relieved him of the pack with their precious map. "Let's go."

NINETEEN

The moonlight provided a haunting trek across the desert. An urgency to escape caused Reza to push the camels harder than they were probably used to this time of day. The night temperature had fallen enough to make even Mikhail uncomfortable. He imagined Petra was also suffering, but didn't complain. He figured she was more concerned with Boko Haram finding them since she kept looking back toward the camp they'd escaped. Would they hole up in Reza's camp for the night or head out across the desert to find them?

"How do they know we're here?" Mikhail had asked as they mounted the camels in the rush to escape.

"I do not know. Perhaps they saw the plane go down or captured the pilot you told me about. They would have made him talk if he survived the jump. But if you were found, it would be trouble for my people and for you, especially your lady. Please. We must hurry."

They didn't speak for several hours. Riding in the desert was disorienting enough in the daylight, but at night, it was navigating a kind of hell Mikhail had never experienced. There were moments when fear whispered they were not safe, and perhaps Reza wasn't their friend.

Then he would pray for a comforting response, and a sense of protection flowed over him.

Where was Zane? Why hadn't he told him he wouldn't be their pilot after leaving the Cape Verde Islands? Had something prevented him from joining them? Zane was invincible since his spiritual transformation. He'd promised to protect them.

Perhaps this was a kind of test for him in his own spiritual growth. Self-doubt had plagued him over the last few years concerning the ministry: Was he good enough, did he possess the empathy required to walk in another man's shoes, or had his heart hardened to the extent he could no longer love as God commanded? Did he have the strength to resist the temptation of seeking out the solace from a warm touch in the middle of the night when loneliness drove him into depression?

Just when he believed those things were within his reach, in walked the very attractive Dr. Petra McGinnis, a stubborn and brilliant equal with a thirst for knowledge and adventure. She was fearless and stomped on any kind of social propriety. There had been no one special in his life for a long time. He'd forgotten what it felt like to be twisted with curiosity about someone other than himself or the needs of the people he tried to shepherd.

Zane was the only other one in his life who he tried to please or at least pause long enough to listen to. However, that had never really been his choice. He had been recruited. End of story.

"We will rest here. There is a well to refresh yourselves, and I'm sure your ride has made you sore. It is not an easy thing at first to ride these beasts."

Reza was the first to dismount and instructed Petra to wait then commanded Mikhail's camel to lie down as he held the bridle. The beast obeyed, and Mikhail slid out of the saddle and followed Reza to Petra's camel.

"Help your lady. Her legs may be weak," Reza said as he grabbed the reins to pull the animal's head down low enough to grab the bridle. This animal also obeyed.

Mikhail reached up to assist her, but she shooed him away. "I'm fine. I don't need any help," she insisted. He stepped back and watched.

Petra slung her leg over the saddle like a Montana ranch hand and practically jumped to the ground. Her legs gave way, and she crumpled into the sand with a loud, "Ouch." When she sheepishly looked up at him, Mikhail couldn't resist a told-you-so grin. He did not move to help her up, instead waited for her to ask him.

She tried several times, once getting her feet tangled in her robes and landing her face first in the sand. Mikhail crossed his arms across his chest and cocked his head to observe another desperate attempt at standing.

"Well, are you going to help me?" she growled.

"Of course. There is a sash hanging down from the horn of the saddle. See it?"

She turned slightly then glared back at him.

"Excellent. Grab it and pull yourself up." As her

eyes widened in fury, he pivoted and walked toward where Reza poured water into a small pot. He heard a lot of mumbling and possibly a great deal of inappropriate language for someone so educated. Although tempted to check her progress to make sure she actually rescued herself, he resisted and decided he enjoyed sparring with the woman.

When she managed to join them, her head was held high and she'd tied up her robe enough to walk without mixed messages with her body language and temper.

"You are a lucky man, Mikhail." He eyed Petra with his appreciative examination. "A fine strong woman to give you lots of sons." Reza called out to beware of the greenery because some plants were poisonous and caused blindness.

"I brought supplies to make tea. Then we will go. We will make it to the airport by sunrise if there is no trouble."

It didn't take long to prepare, and Petra joined them as they sat on the sandy ground. Reza poured small cups of the sweet tea and explained the meaning of tea for Saharan people.

"The first cup is really strong." He gulped his down and waited for them to savor theirs. "The second one is sweet like love, and the third will be weak because we are all weak and there isn't anything we can do about it." His mouth widened as his observation bounced between Petra and Mikhail.

"Delicious, Reza. Thank you," she said, lifting up her cup in a toast-like fashion. "The bouncing of the camel was hard on my…"

Mikhail noticed she paused as if realizing to be so frank around a Tuareg man might not be appropriate.

He didn't want things to go sideways before they reached the airport. Hopefully, Petra would rein herself in without sending a mixed message to Reza.

Mikhail reached over and took Petra's free hand. "Yes. I couldn't agree more."

Petra leveled a coy smirk at him as she tilted her head. "I can't wait to show you what you mean to me, Mikhail."

"Of that, I'm sure." One corner of his mouth lifted in sarcasm. She tried to wiggle her hand free. He tightened his grip, causing her to grit her teeth and narrow her eyes. She froze when he lifted her fingers to his lips. His low chuckle at her surprise definitely ended her smart mouth.

Reza slapped his hands together and proceeded to clear away any signs of their rest period. "Time to go. We have many more miles to cover before daylight."

The night dragged on and, at first, the show of stars moving across the sky, meteors, and the moon ever glowing like a giant orb kept Mikhail alert and impressed by God's handiwork. The quiet kept him oscillating between conversations with God and the problems that lay before them. Finding the solution to their quest, reaching Ethiopia, and why Chadwick had abandoned Petra were only a few of the issues at hand.

His attention shifted between these matters and Petra like the shifting sands. When he noticed Petra, ahead of him, dropping her head forward and swaying from time to time, he called to her.

"Petra." He rode up next to her. "Petra," he yelled, causing her to snap to attention and glance around in a dazed state. He reached the bridle of her camel and managed to stop its progress. Reza halted and turned back to them.

"She's exhausted. Is there any way I can ride with her? I'm afraid she'll fall out of the saddle."

"No. No. I'm fine." She yawned. She let her head fall back as if smelling the air, but her hands slipped off the bar of the saddle where she'd been holding on for dear life most of the night.

Reza and Mikhail dismounted and ordered the animal to kneel, which nearly sent Petra flying out of the saddle, but Mikhail caught her as she slipped toward him. Her eyes opened in a sleepy coma as she wrapped her arms around his neck then laid her head on his shoulder. "Thank you, Mikhail," she whispered.

The Tuareg helped him get her on the front of the camel and then assisted him onto the back. They were soon on their way with Mikhail holding her against him as they jogged along. It was uncomfortable and unsteady, especially with Petra's head bobbing against his shoulder. Gone were the serene moments of lumbering across the Sahara night. Holding a camel steady with a woman in his arms was both uncomfortable and amusing.

Several times, Petra roused and glanced around as if in confusion. She'd turned her head to find him behind her. In those moments, he had his hand on her midriff to make sure she was secure. He removed his touch and focused straight ahead, pretending she wasn't there. Once, she leaned back, and he decided she was snuggling tighter against him, perhaps for warmth. At times, her face rested against his cheek.

"Want me to drive for a while?" She reminded him of a drunk.

"Women drivers annoy me," he said off-handedly.

"Want to talk?"

"No. Go back to sleep."

A heavy sigh followed and, in seconds, she was asleep once more.

TWENTY

❖

The camels lumbered toward an old building the color of yellow sand on the horizon. At first, Mikhail thought he was hallucinating. He was sore and heavy with fatigue. Between holding Petra and controlling the camel, there wasn't much left of his stamina. Yet the building kept growing in size with each moment they progressed.

The structure had seen better days. It reminded him of adobe from the southwestern United States and was not much bigger than a gas station from the 1960s. Green shutters were used on the three doors. Part of the building appeared to be an air traffic control tower, although it was only a two-story structure. A barely hanging-on air conditioner had been attached on the front. The green tree in back looked out of place, as did the new pickup truck parked in its shade. The morning sun was already hot. There were no other vehicles, people, or activity. The land was flat enough, Mikhail wondered if he stood on the corrugated roof, he might be able to see for a hundred miles.

"This is Mano Dayak International Airport," Reza said, fanning out his hand in a kind of proud gesture. "It is named after our great Tuareg leader from many years ago during the rebellion. He was my grandfather's uncle's best friend's cousin." He laid his hand on his heart. "I am very proud."

"As you should be." Mikhail tried to sound impressed. He had no idea who this Mano Dayak was or what his importance was and made a mental note to check it out once they returned home.

Mikhail helped Petra off the camel. This time, she did not resist or spew a declaration of what an independent woman she was. She managed to say "thank you" and squeezed his upper arm as he stroked the head of his camel.

"I must go soon, my friend," Reza said. "I will rest the camels and get much-needed sleep before heading back tonight to my camp."

Mikhail extended his hand, only to have Reza place his hand over his own heart.

Petra turned her head and whispered, "Do the same. Muslims don't always shake hands."

"Oh," he said, repeating the gesture. "I hope we can meet again, Reza."

The Tuareg's eyes cut to Petra, who had shed her robes, her long red hair twisting in the wind. "As do I, Mikhail. And bring the woman. It is custom for them to choose another man for the night."

Petra jerked her chin up. "I—"

Before she could refuse, Reza pulled her into his arms and kissed her long and hard while she tried to push him away. Mikhail noticed the resistance subsided as the kiss lingered. Then she appeared to melt into the goodbye. The Tuareg released her and took a deep breath happily. "I think Western women enjoy this kind of farewell. I have read several American romance novels. Right?"

Petra staggered back next to Mikhail and made an effort to straighten her shoulders and run her hands down her vest, as if to smooth out wrinkles.

"How come you never kiss me like that?" Mikhail asked drily as he tilted his head.

"Maybe if you had let me drive last night…"

Reza laughed loudly. "Women. They are the same everywhere. They like to be in charge." He directed the comment to Mikhail even as he shifted his attention at movement on the horizon. "I think you may have company."

Following his line of sight, Mikhail spotted a plane on the runway, but beyond that, there was movement. At first, it appeared as wavy lines of heat rising from the desert floor. When Petra grabbed his forearm, they locked wide eyes of worry.

Reza raised his stubborn chin. "I think Boco Haram has located us. You better find your pilot and get out of here."

"I couldn't agree more," Mikhail said, pulling Petra after him toward the building.

Reza ran alongside them. "I will see you inside, then I must disappear."

Inside the nondescript terminal were about ten seats that could have been used in a baseball stadium from decades earlier. A chest-high counter that needed a fresh coat of paint was the only other furnishing. A small creature scampered across the floor and out the door, causing him to dodge to the right, nearly knocking Petra to the floor. As he caught her, she grabbed his hand.

"My pilot," he panted. "Can that plane take us?" He surveyed the room around him and noticed through the grimy window, a man had appeared near the plane. "Never mind. I see him. We don't care where he's going."

After dropping money onto the counter, Reza saluted him and hurried in the opposite direction. Mikhail hoped the Tuareg would be able to make his escape. His attention turned back to the plane on the runway. Petra motioned frantically for him to hurry. Together, they ran to the plane that had already taken on the high-pitched sound of the engine.

The passenger side door swung open just as the gunfire bounced off the ground. Puffs of sandy soil flew up. While Petra buckled up in the back seat and Mikhail positioned himself in the front next to the pilot, the plane slowly moved toward the runway. The pilot gave his instruments a knock with his fist, causing the priest to close his eyes and say a prayer of protection.

Opening one eye and stealing a nervous glance behind them, he saw two Jeeps full of men with machine guns speeding alongside them. A few waved the guns, while others slapped at the weapons angrily as if they suddenly stopped working.

"They're following us," Mikhail yelled above the roar of the noisy plane without taking his attention from impending doom. "Petra, keep your head down," he ordered.

She didn't respond.

With a jerk, he turned enough to notice her locked on the scene out the window, wide-eyed and pale. "Petra," he snapped.

As the plane lifted and tilted back and forth as if unsure of whether it wanted to leave the safety of gravity, Mikhail released the air in his lungs at the sight of the frustrated men yelling up at them. The Jeeps stopped and the men continued to beat their guns for failing them. Several men jumped out and kicked the tires while others pointed their weapons at them. Mikhail whispered a prayer of thanks and lifted his cross to kiss as he spotted the pilot grinning.

Since they were safely in the air, he gave the pilot his undivided attention. He was a big man, muscled and tall to the point of making Mikhail wonder if he'd been poured into the seat. He wore mirrored sunglasses and chewed gum. His safari hat was stained with sweat and dirt. Although he was clean-shaven, and the hair sticking out the back of the hat appeared clean, his jawline and flaring nostrils gave him a dangerous vibe. His long-sleeved shirt seemed out of place in such a hot climate. Without warning, the pilot jerked his head around to look at Petra then at him.

"Hello, Mikhail."

"Zane," the priest growled. "I should have known this was yours doing."

The pilot punched Mikhail in the arm with his fist and laughed. "Glad to see me?"

Petra pushed forward after releasing the seat belt and peered at their pilot. "Zane?" she gasped. "Where have you been? Why did you abandon us in Cape

Verde?" Her voice had taken on the uncomfortable sound of scraping a nail across a piece of slate.

"That is a long story. You'd better buckle back up."

"No. I want answers," she fumed.

Zane jerked the plane to an angle, throwing Petra into the window before he righted the plane. "Oops. Sorry about that." He turned and gave a diabolical I-warned-you expression. He continued to watch her until she eased back into her seat and buckled up. Once she had completed the task, he refocused on the instruments. "That's a good girl."

Mikhail twisted again to find her with arms crossed across her chest and sullen. He mouthed, "Are you okay?"

Without taking his eyes off the sky in front of them, Zane chuckled. "Of course, she is okay, Mikhail. Tough as nails, that one."

The priest eyed him then sighed. "I'm exhausted. I'm going to sleep." He leaned back against the headrest and closed his eyes.

"Go ahead. I'm sure having to balance Petra all night on a camel was no easy task."

He wanted to respond but knew it was useless. Besides, he could hear Petra suck in her breath and figured she would bombard Zane with enough questions, he would eventually cause her tongue to be silent. Such a thought made him want to chuckle and maybe rouse enough to watch what happened next, but he was just too tired. A heavy darkness fell over him as he felt her grab the back of his seat. Zane would protect them. There was nothing to worry about for a while. Whatever he'd done to cause this dangerous interlude for them would be revealed soon enough. Hopefully, Petra would know when to shut up. Zane could have a short fuse. Left over from his PTSD days, he figured. That was something he understood.

Breathe deep.

"Our Father which art in Heaven…" he chanted silently.

Breathe deep.

A voice whispered in his head, "That's right, Mikhail. Sleep. Fear not, for God carries you in the palm of his hand."

And then he relaxed, while the sound of Petra's voice teased his subconscious.

Zane laid a hand on the priest's shoulder and squeezed without taking his eyes off the windshield. When he slowly withdrew his hand, Mikhail's head fell to the side. He had been her protector all this time, and Petra had done her best to make his life miserable. He appeared to sleep, confident this Zane guy would get them to a safe place.

Who was this Zane character? He certainly was full of himself and a little bit too confident for her liking. And what was with the hair? When they started this trip, the guy had an aviator haircut. Now, he sported a style as if he belonged in a rock band or maybe that of an off-the-grid reject. Those mirrored sunglasses gave her the creeps, as did the whole Indiana Jones attire. There were tattoos on his neck and hands. Veins bulged on both places, and she swore she could see them pulse.

"It isn't polite to stare. If you have a question, ask

it." His voice could have been ice water. When she didn't respond, he turned his head only so far to look at Mikhail then forward again. "No? Good. You tend to…"

"Where did you go? And what were you thinking, letting someone else fly that plane? Did you even know there weren't enough parachutes? We could have died," she huffed. When he didn't answer, she continued, "Say something?"

"Like what?"

"You said to ask questions. That's what I'm doing. And, honestly, I don't trust you."

He turned enough for her to see him smirk. "Oh. You thought I would answer them. I just meant it was okay to ask, not that I would answer." The smirk continued. "As to you not trusting me, I'd be happy to push you out of the plane if you want out."

Petra sucked in her breath. "You wouldn't dare," she growled. "Mikhail would—"

"What? Save you? Don't count on it." Zane huffed.

"The two of you are pretty tight, huh?" This made him twist around enough to level an incredulous look at her.

"We have known each other a long time. Not always as friends, but our relationship evolved due to unexpected experiences." He continued to observe her. "And no, I won't elaborate. You are trouble. I warned him, but he didn't listen."

"Warned him? Against me? Just who do you think you are, and how do you even know anything about me? I think you're a pompous ass."

"Yes. Mikhail has often told me that. Maybe you should take a nap. Your voice is beginning to disturb me."

"La-di-dah. I'm sorry," she said flippantly.

"I didn't ask for a character reference, Petra. Sleep."

She wanted to respond, but her tongue grew thick and her eyes heavy. Fighting sleep was impossible. The last thing she heard was Zane's voice.

"No harm will come to you unless you betray God's servant. Rest."

Twenty-One

❖

Petra awoke to the men talking. She couldn't hear what they were saying because she wore headphones. How those got there was a mystery. She righted herself in the seat and discovered how refreshed she felt. Why had she fallen so deeply into a coma-like sleep? First, she stole a look out the window to gaze on the land below. They were flying over a magnificent waterfall. The mist created a smokey appearance.

She removed the headphones and yawned. "Where are we?"

Mikhail turned toward her. He wore sunglasses, similar to the mirrored ones worn by Zane. His five-o'clock shadow accented his hard jawline. For a few seconds, Petra thought he resembled a dangerous man, then she dismissed the notion, remembering he was a priest.

"We are over the falls on the Blue Nile River. It is known here in Ethiopia as Tis Abay in Amharic, meaning *great smoke*." His nostrils flared, and his eyebrows raised. "Feeling rested? You've been asleep for hours."

"Really? I never do that. I'm lucky to get five hours a night. I tend to stay up and work at home. But yes. I feel much better."

She thought it was curious both men locked gazes as the corner of Mikhail's mouth tilted up. If she didn't know better, she'd think they drugged her. Zane merely touched Mikhail's shoulder, and he fell asleep. Minutes later, he suggested she sleep. She checked her watch and was stunned at the time. Why did the priest appear to find this amusing? The sooner they were on the ground, the better.

"When do we land?"

"Soon," was the extent of Mikhail's answer before he turned back to look out the windshield.

An overpowering urge to stretch overwhelmed her. She raised her arms and fidgeted sideways to extend her legs. When Petra noticed a small mirror on the instrument panel, it became obvious Zane was watching her. He sent her an appreciative gaze that put her senses on high alert. Why did he make her feel so uncomfortable? There was definitively something off about him.

It was obvious their conversation stopped once they became aware she was awake. She wanted to drill them concerning the plan, like where were they going? It would be great to get more information on why Zane had abandoned them too. Why had he been waiting for them in Niger with a plane to escape Boka Haram. That was an enormous mystery. How did he know they'd be there? She and Mikhail definitely needed to have a come-to-Jesus talk about that guy.

The plane descended soon enough, and the men took their time unbuckling. They shared a joke she couldn't hear. Irritation got the best of her and she pounded on the back of Mikhail's seat to get his attention.

"And she's back," Mikhail grunted as he opened the door and slipped out, only to turn and reach in to assist her. "Petra." He cocked his head and frowned, giving her a glimpse of him being something other than what he pretended to be. That whole priest persona was getting a little old.

She could kick herself for not investigating him when her boss announced Father Novak would be tagging along on her journey. Maybe he wasn't a priest. Maybe he was a treasure hunter or a thief of antiquities. The man had smooth-talked his way into the good graces of everyone she'd relied on for years. It was like he cast a spell on people. And on top of that, the whole ninja fighting scene kept popping into her head. The relationship between him and the mystery man, Zane, was more than a little disturbing.

"Are you coming, or did you just want to annoy me with your rude behavior again?"

Petra snorted her displeasure at his comment and, when she reached for his hand, he withdrew and walked away toward the metal building that served as a waiting area. When she reached back to get her backpack then rose to ease out, Zane was waiting for her. She glared at him, but he continued to wait patiently.

"I see you aren't going to move so..." Before she

could ease out of an awkward position, Zane reached in and took her by the waist and lifted her out onto the ground like she was a rag doll. His touch sent an electric surge through her upper body for just a second. When she tried to withdraw, he squeezed tighter until she looked up into his eyes. Releasing her, Zane spun her around to help her position her backpack. "Thanks. I guess."

"Psalm 40:1 says, 'I waited patiently for the Lord; he inclined to and heard my cry.' The good news in this verse means when we listen intently for a sign from God, we will hear it." He raised his stubborn chin. "Are you a believer?"

"I imagine you already think you know the answer to that question."

His lips pressed tightly together, but his amusement still toyed with the edges of his mouth. "You remind me of my sister. She too was feisty and irresponsible." Zane's voice took on a softer tone.

She brushed past him with a haughty gait and snipped a retort. "Look, I don't know anything about you, but if you pull another stunt like back in Cape Verde, I'll…" She turned to glare at him, but Zane had disappeared. Pivoting in a complete circle, she found no sign of the man.

"Petra," Mikhail called from the doorway. His relaxed stance and dusty clothes did nothing to enhance the feeling he was a priest. "Are you coming?" He turned to disappear inside.

"I'm going to Hell," she mumbled, realizing her thoughts were anything but saintly.

Mikhail wasn't sure why Petra was dragging her feet at joining him. He pulled the map from his backpack and unfolded it on top of one of two card tables. Only a couple of mechanics stood drinking a soda and snacking on food that smelled like burritos. He shuddered to think what it might be out here in the middle of nowhere.

Glancing up, he spotted Petra standing in the doorway, looking behind her then surveying the interior like she was reluctant to enter. After the last few days, he didn't blame her. Most likely, her expeditions had always been well funded and planned out before she set foot into the unknown. It would have taken months of planning, with nothing left to chance. She would have been in control of everything, maybe even the weather.

In spite of the danger they'd faced, and the unexpected events, she'd been brave and never expressed a desire to turn back. Finding Chadwick in the care of someone else and leaving her behind puzzled him, so chances were, it must have disturbed her deeply. The look of betrayal on her face touched him. All he wanted to do was make it better, an emotion he rarely experienced. Wonder what Zane would have to say about that?

"Is Zane in here? He disappeared." Petra eased up next to him and leaned over the map.

"He does that a lot."

"I've noticed. Probably figuring out how to leave us behind again."

"We don't need him. If we do, then he'll be there."

Petra tilted her head at him. "What does that mean?"

Twenty-Two

❖

"Look at this." Mikhail pointed to the map. "It's completely filled in."

Petra took a closer look. "There is more on here than when it was taken."

"Are you sure? I only saw it for a short time."

"Yes." She waved her hand over several areas. "This is much more detailed. I don't understand why this would be important." She pulled out the pictures Chadwick had left behind. "See here at the edge of this Rock Hewn Church. A shadow. What is it? It wasn't on the map before."

Mikhail held the picture close to his face then laid it next to the map. "I can't believe it. It's an angel."

"What?" She leaned over the map. "Not one but maybe a dozen," she gasped. "I once saw a documentary where the images of angels in these churches were colorful and vibrant. But never did they appear all around the church like we see here."

"They're warrior angels protecting the holy site."

"Protecting from what?" Petra straightened and spoke softly. "What is happening? Maybe your spooky friend, Zane, would have some insight."

Mikhail folded the map after handing her the picture. "If he does, he'll let us find our own way. He doesn't like to make things easy."

"How is he on this trip? Did you enlist his help?" Petra continued to try and spot him.

"I don't control what Zane does or doesn't do. He's his own—man. I count on him for spiritual reassurance at times when I can't hear the voice of God."

"Oh. Silly me. That makes sense," she huffed. "You know, some would say if you're hearing voices, you might be on the verge of schizophrenia. I think there's a study someplace."

She tilted her head and taunted him with a slight smirk.

"You can take it up with Moses when you get to Heaven." He then shook his head. "Oh wait. He won't be the same place you're going. My bad." He carefully returned the map to his backpack.

"Funny. I was only making a joke." Her tone turned sour.

"Oh. Now I really feel bad."

"Why?"

"I wasn't making a joke." He swung the backpack to his shoulder then pointed to a café. "I'm starved."

Chadwick paced in straight lines, back and forth across the compacted dirt floor. Evidence of past human activity might reveal itself along the walls or foundations. The hope of discovering artifacts, or color changes in the soil, became challenging in candlelight. Hot wax dripped down on his scratched hand, but he focused on tiny clues and features rather than the pain. He wasn't sure what the search would reveal, since he wasn't given guidelines to what the treasure might entail. The promise was, if he came, a miracle would happen.

A couple of strangers had approached him that day after visiting Father Novak at his church. They presented evidence of how the Rock Hewn Churches were built by super humans. He rejected the idea of Petra getting involved. The stranger promised he would be the one to oversee a miracle. The promise most likely was a lie. Something else was needed of him, but what?

Something pulled him forward; a smell, a whisper, a gossamer touch from an invisible force. A looming shadow rose up before him from the dirt floor, cloaked in robes the color of freshly fallen snow. The shimmer of its purity momentarily blinded him as he stumbled backward only to be caught in the arms of another— what? An unknown being of questionable origin? The arms that surrounded him held him erect, as if making sure he could stand alone. Once he pulled his shoulders back in fake confidence, the hands withdrew, but the form did not. He could feel the presence a breath away.

The One before him continued to observe him then

turned away. The opening in the white hood revealed only a dark hole, creating the impression it was empty. Standing at least eight feet tall, the One moved slowly down a dark corridor. A bony finger pressed in the middle of his back, causing him to hurry his first few steps forward. He dared glance behind him, and the second One groaned. Chadwick wondered if it was a reflection of pain, speech, or a possible threat. Either way, he decided not to tempt fate and followed. After all, what choice did he have?

The candlelight flickered just as a breath snuffed it out. The twirl of smoke caused Chadwick to sneeze. The One behind him reached around him like a sloth in slow motion and gently removed it from his tight grasp. To give it up was relinquishing the last bit of control over the situation. Not that it mattered, since the glow of the robes from the One in front glided onward, and he could do nothing but follow.

If his curiosity had not taken control of his common sense, he imagined he would be in the throes of a heart attack instead of wondering what lay beyond in this underground corridor of holy reckoning revealed to only a few. Details of such a place had not been mentioned in writings about the occupation of this Rock Hewn Church. It was forbidden. So why were these— whatever they were, here?

His heart couldn't keep up with the expectation, and he laid his wax-covered hand on his chest, trying to breathe the pain away. Would he die here? Would his rambunctious Petra grieve for him? Of course, she would. She loved him. He had been her absent father. Would the pain last for long, or would he just collapse into death at any second? Did death always smell like this? Why did his eyes burn?

Both the One before and the One behind him stopped. Relief washed over him because he understood that he faced death alone. He couldn't go on no matter if he wanted to. Somehow, they knew of his dilemma. The One behind him put a bony hand on each shoulder while the One before him reached down and grabbed his ankles. Two other Ones appeared and slipped their hands beneath him as his body lifted, and the world went dark.

Mikhail realized they were an unlikely pair, archeologist and priest. They rode across miles of road that felt like it led to nowhere. With Zane gone, their only transportation option he found turned out to be a pickup truck transporting workers to Addis Ababa, the capital of Ethiopia. The number of stops to pick up more workers at small villages lengthened the trip. The driver agreed to a price and invited Mikhail and Petra to ride in the cab with him. His mouth was too big for his narrow face. The wide nose and close-set eyes appeared comical.

Thankfully, he didn't talk much and, when he did, he leaned forward to talk around Petra. Mikhail engaged in conversation with him for a while in his native language then decided to take in the landscape. Once, when they stopped, the driver encouraged the two to use the restrooms and get a drink for the road. There wouldn't be another stop.

Petra didn't appear to be put off by the crude facilities and, after taking out her hand sanitizer, she accepted the cola and straw Mikhail offered her. She didn't even complain that it was warm. He figured this part of the experience wasn't all that much different than when she took other expeditions. When you were in the middle of nowhere, digging and exploring old ruins or graves, the nearest mini-mart could be a couple of hundred miles away.

An image of her working in the dirt, reading an ancient script off cave walls or exploring ruins holding a torch flashed through his mind.

He turned his attention out the window and tried to avoid thinking about her straight red hair with the white streak that strayed into her eyes from time to time. Even the couple of purple strands gave her a carefree vibe he admired. The woman was pretty, maybe even beautiful. Dwelling on her image distracted him, and she wasn't part of the plan. Women weren't supposed to have this effect on him since Zane had taken over his everyday life and training.

Instead, he replaced her image with the map and what it might be telling them. There were Aramaic symbols he didn't understand. How the churches were created from a scientific standpoint was the whole purpose of this quest originally. It was hoped that the study of the frescoes and written history would complete the story of how the churches were built.

The ongoing project to save the churches from environmental erosion and even destruction had been halted because of an ongoing war between factions who hadn't clearly defined their objectives. Chadwick hoped to find how the people of the region could possibly have built the churches of Lalibela with the technology and know-how of that time period. There had always been a lot of speculation how these spectacular structures were built. A great many mysteries persisted about giants walking the earth from before the time of Noah. The book of Genesis caused a great deal of debate.

His thoughts ran back to the clues he left. It was what made him believe that had to be where the kidnappers took him.

Was it proof of space aliens? Unlikely. Angels? He closed his eyes and tried to imagine those early days of life and creation. Who were those Sons of God? Once more, he reflected on the scripture.

Genesis 6:1-8 King James Version: And it came to pass, when men began to multiply on the face of the earth, and daughters were born unto them, that the sons of God saw the daughters of men that they were fair; and they took them wives of all which they chose.

Fair? Petra's head tilted to rest on his shoulder. Asleep. She was as fair as they came. Those rough edges she flaunted were fake. He could smell her hair as the air from the open window brushed the strands against his face. Whispers stroked his consciousness.

"Sleep, my friend. I got you. Sleep." The words whispered softly in his ears.

Mikhail straightened in his seat, causing Petra to try and sit up, so he relaxed and took his right hand to pull her head back to his shoulder.

"Sleep, Mikhail. Sleep."

His eyes widened then felt heavy as he fought sleep.

"Sleep, Mikhail."

He decided to just close his eyes for a few seconds. What could it hurt? Petra's hair, soft and fragrant against his head that touched hers, lulled him to forget the war, his wife's death, his demons, and his periodic desire to die.

"Sleep, Mikhail. I got you." His hand lifted out of his control. "Take her hand, Mikhail. She is frightened, and so are you. Let her nurse your soul. Sleep, Mikhail. Sleep."

Petra's fingers tightened around his as he let an unfamiliar warmth twist into his body.

"Good, Mikhail. Now sleep and dream of the words I gave to Chadwick."

A parchment wet, with edges torn,
Its surface empty, with angel scorn.
Beneath the ink, a hidden hue,
The map revels a sacred clue.
The winding lines, the symbols etched,
A tale of wonders lies outstretched.
A path through forests, mountains steep,
To secrets only angels, keep.
A holy relic lost in time,
Awaits beneath the ancient grime.
Follow the map, its whispered song,
To find the place where she belongs.

Twenty-Three

The truck rolled into Addis Ababa at what appeared to be a construction site. The men in the back quickly exited and disappeared into the early twilight shadows of the city. Thankfully, the driver drove them to the airport. Mikhail gave him enough money to make him happy in such turbulent times.

"Looks like plenty of armed guards here." Petra slung her backpack over her shoulder and yawned. "Guess we better get inside."

"Seems pretty calm right now, but I don't want to be in the open if trouble breaks out." Mikhail stepped toward the reenforced door opened by a muscled policeman. He decided to engage the guard by speaking the native language, which changed the steely eyed glare to one of curiosity. "Thank you." He tilted his head toward the inside, and Petra followed.

"What did you say to him? I thought for sure we'd have to pay to get in or show our passports. We aren't supposed to need visas here."

Mikhail pointed toward a ticket counter. "No visa necessary for short stays. I told him I was a priest on a pilgrimage to Lalibela. He said it was safe to travel there, but the rebels were edging closer week by week. The locals try to protect the churches."

"Maybe the rebels are afraid if they get too close, God will strike them dead," Petra said sarcastically and leaned against the ticket counter.

"I think it's something more than that. The situation is dire in Ethiopia. Millions are suffering from food insecurity here. This city is relatively safe. Maybe safer than some cities in the US. But it's obvious we don't belong. Let caution be our mantra. The rebels are afraid of something else that keeps them out of Lalibela." Mikhail bought two one-way tickets to Lalibela and carried on a short conversation with the pretty young woman at the counter.

"I saw a coffee shop when we came in. Maybe they have food too." Petra moved in that direction without him, but Mikhail joined her after looking over their tickets. "What were you two talking about? She couldn't stop batting those eyelashes at you."

"People are friendly here."

"Baloney. She was flirting with you."

"I didn't notice. I merely commented how much I enjoyed other stays in her country and said I would pray for her safety and happiness."

"I just bet you did," she said with an exasperated sigh. "I watched how you leaned in and grinned while you were talking. You were conning her into giving you information, so spill it." They stopped in front of the coffee shop. "Fingers crossed there is something to eat. I'm starved."

"I'll check. Get us a table where we can watch the comings and goings. There does appear to be a large military presence or police force here. Hard to tell the difference these days."

Petra agreed and let him go to the counter. She wasn't sure why she resented the ticket agent flirting with Mikhail. Was she feeling protective? He could certainly take care of himself. Waking up against his shoulder embarrassed her. Why were her fingers woven with his, and yet he hadn't removed them?

Discovering his head against hers startled her at first and, when she tried to move, he leaned his head back. It had to be terribly uncomfortable. Rather than enjoy his profile in the fading light, she gave him an elbow to his side without releasing his hand. He did that on his own and immediatcly sat up straight. After rubbing his eyes, he glanced her way for just a few seconds, followed by shifting his attention out the windshield as if she'd become invisible.

He was annoying.

He pulled out a chair and handed her a bottle of water. "There's not much here at this time of day. But he said there are plenty of food options, including local cuisine. And"—he leaned forward and whispered as if he had a great secret—"they actually have a Pizza Hut here."

"What? Are you kidding? I'd kill for pizza."

He chuckled. "A better option might be the Ethiopian Skylight In-Terminal Hotel. Guests can check in airside at the hotel for a meal, shower, and a place to rest before continuing their journey. I mean, we're going to be here all night. I don't want to take a chance missing our flight tomorrow."

"I thought we had three options to fly to Lalibela in case we miss our flight?"

"Not anymore. Things are tight. The airport cut the number of flights because not as many tourists are coming. Probably because of the fighting going on in the countryside. People are afraid to travel. Our State Department had warnings out when I lived here. It's gotten worse."

"I could use some clean clothes. Maybe find a washer and dryer to clean these up." Petra smacked her chest, and dust flew up. "But you're not talking me out of pizza!"

"Deal."

By one o'clock in the morning, both were fed, clean, and stretched out on a couch in the VIP lounge. Since they were the only guests, they could have their pick of places to rest. They were not afraid of prying eyes here. Petra pulled out the map one more time and laid it between them as if they were looking at a tour agenda.

"The angels we saw earlier have surrounded the church." He pointed to several. "They're faint, but there."

"The number of them is increasing. Amazing." Petra leaned over to take a closer look but dared not remove it from the clear covering. "I can't believe the colors on the entire map. It was so faded when it was discovered in the archives. I assumed the pigment was gone because of light exposure at some point, leaving it just black and white. What could have made it do this?" Petra wasn't really asking Mikhail but rather thinking out loud.

"It's like it can finally breathe," he mumbled. "I wonder…"

"What?" Petra asked.

"In older maps, color was added by hand, kind of like when artists use watercolor techniques. The skill of the artist coloring the map might affect it. Not sure. I've seen a lot of old maps, even when I was in Afghanistan," Mikhail added as he took a closer look.

"You're right, but color wasn't added to maps at all until maybe the 16th century. The Rock Hewn Churches were built in the 12th or 13th century. One of the main clues showing if a map has the original colors is the evidence of oxidation on the verso, or back side. The bluish-green pigment we see here is a chemical reaction to being exposed to oxygen. This has occurred too quickly. The longer we have the map out of a controlled environment, the more it may worsen, and the paper will brown, grow brittle, and even disintegrate." Petra's voice held a tone of concern.

"The map is trying to tell us something. Our objective was to find evidence of how these churches were built in such a short period of time with the kinds of equipment available." Mikhail straightened and stretched, feeling the miles of travel making his muscles tight.

"You've been there, right?"

"Many times. It's a place of worship on most days, and there are hundreds of pilgrims there on sacred holidays. I never looked for the source of creation. My job was with international organizations who provided aid in food, immunizations, and other medical necessities. We also helped women start small businesses to help feed their families if the men were off fighting or had been killed by rebels. I really didn't have time to question the legends of how the churches were built."

"How long were you there?" Petra asked, hearing his voice take on a faraway tone.

"Off and on for three years. I had responsibilities stateside too. I finally decided to just—"

When he didn't finish the sentence, Petra turned her attention to him. He was staring down at the map in a hypnotic-like trance as if he might be thinking of other things. For a moment, he almost gave information away about himself. The man was definitely hiding secrets.

"To just what?" She spoke a little sharper than she intended, but it snapped him out of wherever he had drifted as he stood and rubbed his hands down the sides of his pants.

"I decided I needed a change." His voice had grown cold.

"Is that when you decided to go into the ministry?" Petra knew she was pushing him by the way his jaw tightened and released.

"I feel like a walk. I'll be back soon. I think you're safe in here. There's a guard outside this lobby if you want anything." He folded the map and placed it back in his backpack. "I'm leaving my things with you."

Confusion once again clouded her evaluation of the man. One minute, he was all talkative and almost normal, then when she asked a few simple questions, he froze up. She pulled her bare feet beneath her. "Sure. Knock yourself out," she snapped impatiently.

Mikhail narrowed his eyes as they fell on her. "Just need to think is all. Nothing to do with you." Pivoting, he strolled out into the corridor leading from their safe enclosure.

Unfolding her legs, she strolled to the double doors and watched him walk nonchalantly down the corridor—alone. At least until a large man exited a door in a pilot's uniform and followed him. He glanced back over his shoulder toward her and saluted.

Zane. What was he doing here, and why didn't he just fly them here? He caught up with Mikhail and slipped an arm over his shoulder. He faked a punch to his gut with his other hand. Laughter echoed down the corridor and, for just a second, she hoped it belonged to Mikhail.

She glanced back at the backpacks on the couch to reassure herself then returned her focus to the men. But there was only Mikhail, as if he'd always been alone. Had she imagined Zane being there? Maybe it was just another pilot who resembled him.

The coffee shop was still open, and the barista waved to Mikhail. Stepping inside, he asked if he still had any coffee. The answer was no, but he would be happy to make him a cup of tea. On the house. The water still rested on the burner behind the counter, and Mikhail was told to go pick the kind of tea he wanted.

"We have many good English teas."

He chose one without checking the label and quickly created a dark brew. The heat from the ceramic cup warmed his hands as he moved to a table near the door. The barista hummed a song and often took a little dance step with the mop he used across the floor. Maybe he'd transfer it to a to-go cup in a minute.

When the lights flickered, he rose slowly and glanced across the now-empty coffee shop. The barista had disappeared, putting Mikhail's brain on alert. He turned to leave, but a skinny man dressed in baggy clothing blocked his path. His zombie-like appearance, meant to frighten, only managed to irritate him.

"Excuse me." Mikhail sidestepped the man, but he mimicked the move. He guessed the man must be a rebel, considering the kind of pistol wedged in the side of his pants and had caught on his shirt. "Get out of my way," Mikhail snarled, feeling his body tighten and go on alert.

The lights flickered again as he noticed the heavy presence of soldiers were gone.

Petra. She was alone.

How many were there? Had they breached the entire terminal where he'd left her?

"You are my prisoner." The rebel's open mouth revealed yellow, chipped teeth. "Give me your money and come with me."

"Why in the world would I want to do that?"

"I will kill you if you don't." The rebel's voice took on an angry tone.

"In that case…" Mikhail threw the hot tea in the man's face. Before a scream could escape his mouth, he slugged him across the nose, sending a spray of blood over both of them. Grabbing the rebel's gun was child's play, since the other man was rubbing his face free of coffee and blood. This time, Mikhail swung the ceramic cup so hard at the rebel's head it shattered, sending him sprawling across the floor. He dragged him inside easily enough, since he weighed no more than a teenage boy. He stood over him and pointed the gun at his chest.

The dark demon of the soldier he once was kicked in as his finger slipped on the trigger. His pulse was calm. Hand steady. Breathing normal. Brain—raging. His eyes lifted to search the area outside the coffee shop. The lights blinked on and off then completely off.

He placed the gun in the waistband of his pants and bent down to check the man's pulse. Still alive. Feeling the unnatural strength bestowed upon him through Zane, he casually reached down and twisted the arm back, far enough he could feel the ligaments separate, and dislocated the elbow. The man wouldn't be able to carry a gun for a while, if ever.

The rebel cried out as Mikhail jammed the barrel of the gun in his mouth, stopping both the noise and his movements. Once more, his finger touched the trigger as the rebel's face twisted in horror. Mikhail tried to process what was happening in the terminal.

"How many others?" He removed the gun. "I won't ask again. You have another arm. This little peashooter you got here, at this range, might just blow it off. I haven't done that in a while." For some reason, this gave him pleasure, thinking how some things never changed, like his propensity to kill what he perceived as evil.

He jammed the gun in the rebel's mouth again.

"What the hell. I don't care how many there are."

The rebel used his good hand to hold up four fingers as tears ran down his cheeks.

"I want you to promise you'll not get up and tell the others about me."

The rebel nodded vigorously.

Mikhail's heartbeat pounded in his ears. "Now why don't I believe you?" He removed the gun from the man's mouth and pulled the trigger into his knee. "Night. Night." The rebel fell unconscious.

He stood and kept the gun down at his side. The smell of gunpowder teased his senses and for a few seconds, he had to remember who he was to transition to priest. "Petra," he mumbled then moved out into the dark corridor like a lion that stalked at night.

Twenty-Four

❖

Once Mikhail disappeared from sight, Petra sighed and turned back toward the couch where she'd left the backpacks. Suddenly overwhelmed with fatigue, she collapsed onto the very worn cushions then leaned against the backpacks, hoping her position would serve both as a pillow and protection from theft.

Sleep evaded her as her mind danced across the last few weeks. It lingered on Mikhail Novak longer than she thought wise, but the man was an enigma. At some point, she needed to do a deep dive into who the person he pretended to be was.

His identity of being a priest didn't match up with the special abilities he drew from at certain times. There was their first meeting at the coffee shop and how he disarmed the would-be robber, followed by the whole home invasion he thwarted without much difficulty.

Jumping out of an airplane didn't appear to faze him in the least, nor sword fighting in some kind of ritual with Tuareg men who should have won the challenge.

Yet the evidence kept mounting that he was indeed a priest until it crumbled at the most unexpected times. The prayers with Zane appeared real. The attention Mikhail gave people to secure information and trust, also genuine. It had to be more than those piercing blue eyes, high cheekbones, and a body used to physical work. His calm demeanor perturbed her, and no amount of insults, snarkiness, or obstinate attitude rattled him. He faced her rebellious personality with plenty of comebacks to let her know her place.

The holy priest façade with sly expressions and unabashed bravery meant he was either some kind of whack job with narcissistic tendencies or, dared she admit it? God really did have his hand upon his shoulder. He was just too good to be true.

And what was with that Zane character? No one at the museum remembered seeing him. She'd asked several people, including Chadwick. No one paid any attention to him, wherever they were when he showed up. Mikhail gave a number of flimsy reasons why the man had come along on this trip. She wasn't sure she liked him.

Zane, if that was his real name, was tall and fit, almost looked like he might lift weights. She'd noticed tattoos on his neck and arms once, but then they were gone when she tried to see them later. Hopefully, he wasn't one of those people who thought he'd just use fake tats to impress people, or maybe, in his case, intimidate them. Sometimes, he reminded her of a Hell's Angel from the biker group and then, like earlier when she thought she'd seen him, he took on the appearance of a well-groomed pilot. The man appeared to be a human watchdog for his friend Mikhail. Why?

When the lights flickered, she turned her attention to beyond the wall of glass separating her from the concourse that except, for a soldier staring down the area Mikhail had walked, no other people moved about. It was the middle of the night, after all. Why would there be people? Yet the soldier unshouldered his weapon and ran.

With the grace of a sloth, she lowered her legs to the floor and slipped on her hiker boots without taking her eyes off the concourse that just went dark.

Gunfire.

An inner voice whispered, "Lock the doors, Petra." She froze. "Do it now."

Fortunately, the lights, although dim, remained on in her enclosure with only an occasional flicker. She ran to the doors and grabbed the push bar to lock in place. When it wouldn't budge, she realized someone stood in the darkness on the other side of the door, watching her. He held the door bar on his side, making it impossible for her to lock.

A sinister chuckle escaped his thin lips then he jerked the door open. Although he wore some kind of uniform, it was not the same as the soldier who had recently disappeared. Taking a few steps backward, Petra heard more gunshots outside her enclosure. The man's eyes raked over her as another primal chuckle released from deep within his throat.

Was Mikhail dead? Captured? Wounded? Or maybe he was a prisoner.

"Who are you?" he demanded. "American?" When

she didn't answer, his eyes went to the backpacks on the couch. "Get your passport."

Swallowing hard, she obeyed and ran to the backpacks, feeling his slow march toward her. She reached in hers and felt for the small cannister she always carried along with the passport. Flipping the cap on the cannister, she pulled both from the backpack, handing him the passport first. When he took it, she sprayed the pepper spray into the man's face. He lunged at her, sending it flying out of her hands.

Although he groaned with great exaggeration and pain, the spray dripped from his cheek and one eye. But it was enough to let her grab her passport and kick him between the legs. Now his roar reminded her of a Halloween haunted house display. Then five more men entered through the back door to the hotel.

The man in charge wiped his face on his sleeve and pointed to her with the look of the devil on his face. She didn't have to speak the language to know what he said. "Get her!" He straightened his body but still caressed his privates where she'd assaulted him with full force of her boot.

She could hardly breathe. The men in the rear hurried her way as her attacker moved closer, spitting what she assumed were insults in a language she couldn't understand.

A choked sob escaped her mouth as the thought dawned on her that she was alone with no way out this time.

As the room dimmed even more, a dark figure slipped through the door so quickly, she sucked in her breath as he came up behind the attacker and circled his neck with his arm, choking off the man's ability to breathe.

"Are you all right, Petra?" Mikhail raised his other hand to hold a gun to the man's temple. When she didn't answer, he snapped at her. "Petra!"

"Yes. Yes, I'm okay."

"Get under that table. This will only take a minute. Take the backpacks with you."

"But…"

"Do it," he ordered, dragging the leader off to the side as the man tried to loosen the hold on his neck.

With a rush of adrenaline coursing through her veins, she cautiously edged in to grab the backpacks then ran to slide under the table. She felt like a small child escaping the boogeyman.

The soldiers, if that's what they were, focused on their leader. She figured they couldn't reach her anyway without going through Mikhail. Their bodies were hunched in alert and stalking Mikhail when one of them spoke in his language.

Mikhail growled in the leader's ear in English then in Ethiopian. "Tell them to put their weapons down, or this is going to get messy really fast." Mikhail squeezed a little tighter causing him to wave at the men and croak out his wishes. "Good boy."

Petra stared in disbelief watching Mikhail. He carried a rifle over one shoulder, an automatic weapon in the front of his belt, and held a pistol to the man's head. Blood was splattered on his neck and the front of his shirt.

But the most confusing thing was how his expression had changed from passive-uninterested to a dangerous rebel showing not an ounce of fear. Even from where she hid, she could see his jaw tighten and release. Those dreamy blue eyes had narrowed to slits of rage, and his nostrils flared every few seconds.

"Petra, I need you to be ready to run. Can you do that for me?" He remained focused on the rebels as he spoke.

"Yes!" There was plenty of room under the table to slip on her backpack and loop her arm through the second one. But her curiosity refused to stop watching what was unfolding.

The militants rushed forward, swinging their rifles around. Mikhail shoved his captive forward to protect himself, causing the rebels to shoot into the chest of their leader. While still in Mikhail's grasp, he managed to shield himself from another bullet before letting him slump to the floor. The look of surprise on their faces halted further action, giving Mikhail a split second to raise his pistol and storm toward them before shooting three of the five. When his gun clicked empty, he tossed it aside like a gum wrapper. The remaining two lifted their weapons to shoot, but Mikhail had already pulled his rifle off his shoulder as he walked with an unnerving calm. His aim was quick and deadly.

He slung the rifle and pivoted in her direction. Her body refused to move until he reached under the table and, with a surprising amount of strength, grabbed her by the collar and dragged her out.

"Get up. We need to go."

His gait never changed as he walked toward the doors. Petra smelled gunpowder, sweat, and couldn't help but see streaks of blood in the flickering light of what had become hell. Her attention refocused on the man ahead of her who moved like a panther with no remorse. Then, suddenly, he stopped and held the door for her by propping it open with his back, like this was no big deal.

She stopped and could see his face smudged with trails of sweat and blood. The sexy blue eyes simmering with anger, both frightened and captivated her. He blinked it away and transformed back into the priest he pretended to be.

"It will be okay, Petra. Trust me."

Petra watched him raise his chin and speak to someone else who had come to the door. "Zane." Her voice came out a whisper.

He ignored her, instead spoke to Mikhail. "There's a plane waiting for you. I'll clean this up. Go."

Mikhail never asked him anything. He just grabbed her arm to force her outside into the concourse. He never removed his grip as he navigated the various corridors to get outside. When they finally reached their gate to escape, the woman he spoke to when they first arrived was standing there as if nothing was wrong.

"I see you made it back, Messenger." She opened the door exposing the outside elements. "Good luck."

"Thank you for waiting, Seraph. Peace be unto you."

She bowed her head. "And also, with you."

Mikhail continued to hold her elbow, but she managed to look back at the woman he addressed as Seraph and realized the name meant angel. Seraph arched an eyebrow and tilted her head as if examining Petra for her worth. As she closed the door behind them, the woman pointed to her eyes with two fingers then turned them toward Petra. A chill ran up her back, knowing she had just been warned—but of what?

Even though Zane promised a flight out of hell, it didn't mean they should cast caution to the wind. Zane was notorious for testing him to see if Mikhail used the faith card. Part of him didn't trust the promise if it was too easy. The plane on the tarmac was a twin-engine jet. The window slid open and a familiar face appeared and waved him to hurry.

"You've got to be kidding me." Mikhail recognized the barista from the coffee shop who'd gotten him tea.

Petra leaned in closer. "What? More soldiers?"

"No. The pilot. Never mind. Let's go. I don't see any trouble, and the pilot seem to be in a hurry."

One more confusing twist to the journey he hadn't signed up for.

After checking for threats with a quick scan of the area, the two of them slinked forward, hunching their bodies to make them less visible. Although the runway lights still burned brightly, several of them flickered. Their pilot met them at the top of the steps to the plane and quickly closed the door once they had boarded.

"Fancy meeting you here." Mikhail couldn't restrain his sarcasm.

The pilot tipped his ball cap. "Buckle up. We have company coming toward us down the runway."

"Isn't that the barista guy we saw earlier?" Petra jerked off her backpack and threw it into a row of seats in back of them.

"It most certainly is. I'd like to know where he went when that rebel came in to hold me up."

When Petra fixated on him in disbelief instead of

buckling her seat belt, he reached over and did it for her. He cinched it tighter than necessary, resulting in her slapping at his hand before using her shoulder to shove him away.

"I can explain, Petra. I can see you're afraid of me."

"I'm not afraid of you. You're just another liar in my life. I don't know what you're after at the churches of Lalibela, and I really don't care anymore. I want to find Chadwick and bring him home where he belongs. Stop pretending to be something you're not. A priest doesn't do what you just managed to pull off back there with the stealth and calm of a hardened criminal."

"Petra—"

She folded her arms across her chest and opted to avoid those blue eyes that apparently had clouded her judgment.

The plane picked up speed. Mikhail could see the pilot and wondered if whoever was on the runway ahead of them would cause them to crash. He clicked opened his seat belt and hurried to drop into the seat opposite the pilot.

"What is it?"

"Rebels coming at us in a kind of armored vehicle, I think. Hard to tell with so few lights. They've stopped."

"I'm guessing they think we can't lift off," Mikhail said calmly.

"Can you help with that? We have heard you are a messenger." The barista glanced at his instruments then jutted out his jaw as if ready to pull the nose of the plane up. They barreled down the runway when the pilot spoke quietly. "Now would be a good time,

Messenger."

Mikhail reached over and put his hand on the pilot's shoulder before closing his eyes. Words from Psalm 23 rushed to his lips. As he uttered them, the sound of gunfire thunked off the nose of the plane. "Yea, though I walk through the valley of the shadow of death, I will fear no evil: for thou art with me; thy rod and thy staff, they comfort me." He repeated it over and over until he heard the pilot grunt and pulled back on the yoke. Mikhail's attention turned toward the vehicle looming on the runway, knowing they were feet from hitting it. "Pull harder."

The plane lifted, catching its wheels on the vehicle and flipping it over. Mikhail felt it slide away. As they lifted freely into the air, the vehicle burst into flames.

"Are you going to say a prayer for them, Father Mikhail?" the pilot asked drily as he checked his instruments.

"Only for the families they've left behind to starve and die of disease because of their actions."

"How is your woman in the back?"

Mikhail stood and patted him on the shoulder. "She is not my woman and, given her current state of mind, I'd better pray for the two of us."

This made the pilot chuckle. "Women are the same the world over."

"Yeah. I keep hearing that." He peeked out the cockpit and down the aisle where he could see Petra watching what must have been the burning vehicle on the ground. "I wouldn't know much about that, however. I do know this woman is unique and promises to be my undoing if I don't get my head on straight."

"Yep. The same the world over." He focused on

the night ahead of them. "We have a couple hours before landing. Going to take a little detour to make sure we do not get hit by ground fire."

Mikhail walked back to where Petra continued to avoid acknowledging his presence. Since she had retrieved her backpack, shoved it into the seat next to her, and tossed his on the floor, he took the hint. He picked it up, moved across the aisle, and buckled himself in. Resting his head back against the worn leather cushion, he felt satisfied and safe.

Sleep came on quickly, as he knew it would after such an encounter. It was a way for his brain to transition to being more human. But once he fell asleep, the nightmares of battle returned. This time, it wasn't a wounded Zane that needed rescuing but Petra. She was dying, and he had to reach her. Could that be the reason why she could see Zane and others could not?

He squeezed his eyes harder to force the picture to change. When the scene changed, it was Petra laughing and running across a field of flowers. Her red hair caught the light and nearly blinded him with its brilliance. Although her lips moved, the sound he heard was that of wind.

"Mikhail," came a distant voice. Then again, causing him to slowly open his eyes to see her standing over him. "We're getting ready to land."

He took a deep breath and rubbed his face, and finally noticed he still wore a blood-speckled shirt. He reached into his pack and pulled out a gray T-shirt. As he pulled off the soiled one, Petra watched him intently. She wasn't shy about exploring his body with those eyes that reminded him of an angry wolverine. Would lying with her be like that: tumultuous, dangerous, and breathtaking?

He decided to lock horns with her sooner rather than later as he pulled the shirt over his head then nonchalantly checked to see if the automatic weapon he'd taken off the dead man was secure in his pack. The plane came to a stop as he zipped the gun into an inner pocket.

"Planning on killing anyone else, Father Mikhail?" Petra rose from her seat and tilted her head at him as her voice dripped with venom.

He stepped out into the aisle and suddenly pushed his face into hers, causing her to almost fall back into her seat. Snaking an arm around her waist and pulling her closer, he offered a venomous smirk. "Every time you tick me off, you move up on my hit list."

Her eyes widened. Pulling his arm away, she fell back in her seat sideways, with her legs dangling in the air.

"Then explain yourself," she grumbled, trying to right herself.

"Later. But know this, you have nothing to fear from me."

"Said the spider to the fly," she retorted as she regained her footing.

"Good one. Let's go." Mikhail turned his back on her.

One thing for sure, she certainly was fearless. When she didn't budge, he turned to glare at her. "Are you trying to make me manhandle you because I'm almost there."

She huffed and leveled an if-looks-could-kill squint at him when brushing past him.

The pilot stood at the door, put a hand on his heart

at her thanks, then chuckled at Mikhail. "Good luck, my friend. She will test you in this journey if you want to remain a messenger of God."

"I'm beginning to think I'm doomed. She brings out the worst in me."

"It is but a way to shed the fire that burns within."

"Great. Another parable I have to figure out."

He extended his hand. "Do not be too hard on her or yourself. We are all pulling for you."

"Thanks again." He shook the man's hand.

He caught up with Petra at a booth just inside the airport terminal where she was skimming brochures on hotels. The desk clerk was on the phone. She handed Petra another brochure and pointed to what might have been a map on the inside. As he walked up, the clerk did a double take and ran around the counter to hug him.

"Father Mikhail. It is good to see you again. What brings you back?"

He stepped out of her young embrace and eyed her. "You have grown into a lovely woman since I was last here, Ayana. And how is your family?"

He listened intently as she went down the list of family members and their various ailments, jobs, and accomplishments while Petra propped herself against the counter and eyed him with contempt. Stealing an occasional glance her way, he could only imagine what might be going through her head as to his relationship to the lovely creature excited to see him.

"We are here to study the Rock Hewn Churches of Lalibela, of course. My colleague, Dr. Petra McGinnis, is a biblical archeologist."

"Among other things," she interjected.

"Many will be glad to see you, Father. You brought such hope to many of us who were struggling." She took the brochures from Petra. "Here, let me call them back and upgrade your accommodations."

"That won't be necessary—" Petra said, reaching to retrieve the brochures without any luck.

"I insist," Ayana said politely to Petra. "The Father is a friend to the people here. They will be pleased he has returned."

"Thank you, Ayana," he said. "We need rest and food before we begin our studies. Please give my love to your family."

She brightened even more at his words and finished upgrading the arrangements, followed by securing a taxi for them. "You will be only a quarter mile from the churches, and your suite has a lovely view of the mountains. The food is adequate, and the walk to the churches is pleasant enough. I'll contact my uncle who serves as the key holder."

"An honor for him."

"Yes. He is very proud. I will visit with him tonight."

"Thanks again, Ayana."s

The taxi to the hotel took twenty minutes. The road was tolerable and, with the windows rolled down, the heat was less oppressive. Although the car appeared to be a relic from the last century, it was clean and smelled of disinfectant. Heavy-duty tape concealed the rips in upholstery that had come with age. The driver talked nonstop and, once he discovered Mikhail could speak their language, he pummeled him with questions about America.

Once at the hotel, they were welcomed with open

arms and led to their suite. After the doors were closed, both dropped their backpacks on the floor and headed to the balcony.

"This is incredible. I have never been to Ethiopia," she said.

"I think this part of the country is the most beautiful. I love it here. The people are kind and eager to please. Their faith is real, and everyone is dedicated to the preservation of the Rock Hewn Churches. My years here were both therapeutic and gratifying." Petra turned away from the view and displayed a blank expression. He raised his chin then cleared his throat. "I'm going to take a shower." As he tried to walk away, he heard her haughty tone of voice.

"Want me to wash your back?"

Mikhail stopped short and paused a few seconds before facing her. "There you go again, taunting me with your sexuality and flippant remarks."

"It must be torture trying to be all holier than thou with all that pent-up rage." She sashayed within a few feet of his body and raised her eyebrows then tilted her head.

"I'd say I got rid of all that rage saving your ass—again. It's starting to be a full-time job."

"Just how many men did you kill back in Addis? My count was five, maybe six."

"Zero."

"I was there. Remember?"

"The guy who planned to ravage you, technically, was shot by his men. I just hid behind him to protect myself."

"What about the others?"

"Although it's true I shot them, I made sure I

merely disabled them." Petra opened her mouth to speak, but he held up his hand to stop her. "Yes, they went down, but were unconscious, not dead. If they bled out, that was on them. I'm a peaceful man."

"You showed up with blood on you. Where did that come from?"

He sighed. "Yes, I admit I had to shoot a rebel in his kneecaps. He was extremely rude and wouldn't move. He waved a gun around like it was some kind of flag, and I hate a bully. So—I disarmed him. To his credit, he let me know there were others, and I tried to get back to you as soon as I could. With your passive-aggressive personality disorder, I hoped you'd be able to bore them until I could save you. Apparently, that was the case."

"You are a narcissistic pig. Do you know that?" she fumed.

He grinned as he leaned toward her and spoke calmly. "Takes one to know one." He headed to the shower. "Don't go far. I might take you up on washing my back."

"Over my dead body."

"At the rate you're going, I fully expect that to be the case."

TWENTY-FIVE

❖

The suite, although bare bones, boasted two bedrooms with king-size beds and two bathrooms with decent-size showers. Towels were fresh and clean. She'd stayed in other African hotels in the past, where a guest was lucky to get a tiny bath towel and a washcloth. Didn't matter how many shared the room, that was all they got. This felt like luxury in comparison, and it came with a spectacular view.

If only she could tell Chadwick how she loved it. Hopefully, that would be soon. He was alive in the Cape Verde Islands. Whoever took him wanted him for something, and it involved the Rock Hewn Churches. The plan had always been to research the possibility of how they were built in such a short period of time. Find evidence of the truth behind each church constructed and pivot toward unraveling the legend of them having been built by angelic helpers.

Chadwick believed modern man just couldn't comprehend other beings—maybe angels, aliens, whatever—might have been present in those early days. Modern man required scientific proof of impossible things these days. Petra had to admit proof wasn't always the best thing. But since Chadwick was missing, she was going to be the scientist and find logical answers.

Unless Father Mikhail Novak got in the way. Had he become her watchdog to distract her from finding out any concrete information? Whatever she discovered, she could set it aside to take Chadwick home.

After taking a shower and slipping into a pair of clean khakis, her attitude toward Mikhail softened. When she threw open her door, she found him taking a tray of food from a waiter.

"I guessed what you might be hungry for. Thought this would hold us over. I'm about to crash. I desperately need a nap."

Petra surveyed the tray of spicy curry and flatbread. "Um. Looks delicious. What is this?" She pointed to a side dish.

"Sambusas. It's a popular appetizer served with coffee, soft drinks, even fresh fruit juice. I made coffee. I also left a message at the local police station to see if we could talk about Chadwick. I showed the waiter, who brought our food, his picture, and he thought he'd seen him several days ago. With any luck, the constable will come around after he gets off work. We can have dinner on the patio restaurant. I was told it is beautiful at night." He took a portion of the sambusas and smeared curry on it. "These are great. Try them."

Petra helped herself and carried her plate to the balcony where she set it down on the wide stone railing. Mikhail brought the tray out and set it on the table then poured two cups of coffee.

"I was rude earlier, Mikhail. I apologize. I appreciate you—saving my life. It was just a shock seeing you going all Rambo instead of the character from the Father Dowling Mysteries."

Mikhail chuckled. "Father Dowling I'm not. I guess you figured that out. Look, I know my actions are confusing. Before I became a priest, more of a priest in training, I was a soldier. Before that, I went to medical school and dropped out to be a medic in the Army Rangers. Uncle Sam was more than happy to promise me a free ride to college if I brought my knowledge to help them out in Afghanistan. I've had"—he sighed and rolled his eyes upward then down to meet hers—"some serious PTSD. It comes and goes. The only thing that has helped me is being in the ministry."

"I'm sorry. I had a brother killed over there. The last time he was home, he wasn't the same happy-go-lucky kid I knew. He never got a chance to start over. I'm glad you have something to hang on to."

"Last night just triggered that thing the US government trained me to do. It's the only way to survive over there."

"Where did you go after Afghanistan?"

"Home. For a while. Then Zane found me and knew I was having a rough time. Suggested the ministry and, next thing I knew, I was serving in another hellhole called Syria. But they needed me. When a group of Americans got trapped in pretty serious trouble, I ended up performing surgery on one of the guys and took care of him until help came. It was time to leave. I could feel myself sinking again."

"I shouldn't have called you a killer. So, you really are a priest?"

"Not officially. I haven't taken that last step toward ordination."

"Why not?"

"I ask myself that every day. Maybe because of all the things I did to survive in war or not feeling worthy." He shrugged. "But Zane says I'll know when the time is right. He is teaching me a lot."

Petra took a second serving of food but set the plate down on the table without touching it.

"Change of subject. I've been thinking, why take Chadwick? I've been racking my brain. Did he make a discovery that wasn't supposed to be revealed? Maybe he had information no one else understood and could be valuable? Maybe it's just a case of wanting the museum to pay a ransom for him? He is well-known in the biblical archaeology community and greatly respected." Petra threw her hands up in frustration.

"I'm thinking it's more than that."

"You mentioned that once before." Petra decided to taste her food.

"These people pride themselves on the Rock Hewn Churches. They've protected them for centuries, along with their history. They have strong beliefs in the creation of these structures."

"But the structures are decaying at an alarming rate. Environmental problems plague the exterior. Look at this." She grabbed her phone and showed him pictures of two years earlier and currently. "These were taken by a UNESCO representative not too long ago to check on things since the civil unrest might be a problem. These cracks across the front are big trouble."

"The gigantic metal roofs built to protect them from the rains have not proven to slow down the deterioration. I read where, when things settle down, the plan is to have architectural engineers remove them." Mikhail took a sip of coffee.

"Do you think opposing factions are trying to stop UNESCO from coming in because they want the churches to fall into such disrepair that nothing can be done to save them?"

"That would devastate these people," Mikhail admitted. "The warring forces aren't letting in the necessary experts in to do the restorations that can slow down the centuries of decay." He took the phone and scrolled through more of her pictures as she closed the gap between them and pointed to a few other things of concern.

The shoulder pressed against hers was hard as a rock and his body had suddenly become extremely still. His breathing grew slower, and he stopped talking. She stepped away and watched him relax. He passed the phone back to her.

"I'll think about this. I'm going to get a couple hours sleep. I'll leave the door open in case you need me." He headed through the living room then disappeared into his bedroom.

Petra didn't understand what came over him, but she had to wonder if sharing a suite with a man, even though a priest, was a good idea. Clearly, she made him feel uncomfortable at times. But then there were those few hours at the Tuareg camp where they had been forced to share a carpet on the ground for the night. She believed he wasn't as uncomfortable with her as she experienced.

The man hid personal secrets. But she was just too tired to process it. She cleaned up their empty dishes and serving tray after taking it inside. Maybe the lack of sleep played tricks on her and she'd imagined Mikhail's sudden desire to put distance between them. Taking a nap sounded like a great idea. She glanced toward his room and wondered what this trip would morph into if he weren't a priest. She shook it off and headed to her room.

"What are you doing here?" Mikhail asked when he saw Zane standing at the window, gazing out over the mountains.

"Enjoying the scenery. Got any of that curry left?"

"No. You should leave."

"Petra is out there cleaning up. I'm sure she'd wonder why I'm here," Zane insisted.

"Why are you here?" Mikhail asked, turning down the thin bedspread.

"What are you going to do about Petra?"

"There are moments I'd like to kill her. Why?"

Zane chuckled. "You're not a very good liar. You like her."

"I tolerate her. She gives as good as she gets. The mental combat is refreshing. I'm not used to being ignored, told no, or considered a jerk."

"You are a jerk and full of yourself," Zane reminded him.

Mikhail sighed. "What do you want to tell me? Get it over with so I can get some sleep."

"I cleaned up the mess at the airport." Zane turned away from the view.

"How many dead?" Mikhail wasn't sure he cared.

"More injured than dead. Those you shot will survive but, since the authorities in charge have them, it could go either way. The guards that tucked their tails and ran are taking credit for shutting the attack down. I understand you and the pilot got along."

"You could have warned me you have another protégé in the wings. No pun intended."

"I have several. Oh, and"—he moved away from the window and faced Mikhail squarely— "Chadwick is dead."

"What?" Mikhail snapped as he glanced toward the open door. "How?"

"All is not lost, however."

"Petra will be devastated." Mikhail's shoulders sagged.

"He is actually in a state of tranquility." Zane folded his hands together in front of him.

"Is this some kind of hocus-pocus angel stuff you want me to believe in?"

Zane arched an eyebrow. "I don't do hocus-pocus. That would be the other side. He appears to be dead because his captors wished it so. They want something from Petra that only she can give them. If she provides it, then Chadwick will resume a full life, at least after he recovers from being under so long, of course." Zane remained matter-of-fact.

"Who wants something from Petra, and what is it?"

"I didn't ask." Zane yawned. "I can't do everything

for you."

"I'm thinking you enjoy throwing obstacles in front of me to see how I'll react."

"Still glad you saved my life on the battlefield in Afghanistan?" Zane asked.

"I have my doubts about that," Mikhail admitted.

Zane placed a hand on his shoulder. "I know you do—about so many things. Don't shut Petra out. She's going to need you tonight when you tell her about Chadwick. I'll plant the details in your brain as you sleep. Tomorrow, you will see the body. Do not touch it. You will witness things that are unnerving and hard to believe. Rely on your faith."

"I'm running low on that." Mikhail yawned and eased down onto the bed.

"I will be nearby. Sleep, Mikhail," Zane whispered.

"Poor Petra," he mumbled as his eyes became heavy.

"She weeps even now. Feel her pain and give her comfort. Sleep, Mikhail."

"I don't want to be near her."

"I give you permission to comfort her. Sleep, Mikhail." Zane continued to soften his voice.

"Petra…"

"Sleep, Mikhail," he whispered.

His body relaxed into a dream world where life made sense.

Twenty-Six

Petra took a second shower when she woke up. One thing she never got used to in her line of work was being dirty from time to time. As long as she could get a shower most days, she could tolerate the sweat, body odor, and filthy clothes. But, at the end of the day, she wanted to be clean. Surprised at how long she slept, the sight of the sun hanging low in the sky painted a stunning picture adding to her peacefulness. Maybe Lalibela really was a magical place like the old ones had claimed when the Rock Hewn Churches were created.

A brown paper bag hung on the outside of the door she'd left cracked in case, like Mikhail, he needed her. Inside was a simple but pretty white and-yellow dress with a band of gold crosses on the white sections. The sweetheart neckline was a little daring but charming nonetheless. According to the attached label, it was an Ethiopian Habesha tibeb telet. She had a hard time imaging Mikhail picking it out for her.

Walking out into the living room, she found a note on the door instructing her to come downstairs when she was ready. He would order dinner when she arrived. Apparently, the constable arrived earlier than expected and only had a few minutes to visit.

Although disappointed she wouldn't get to hear what he had to say, this time, she expected Mikhail would ask all the right questions.

Grateful the outdoor patio would be empty when he told her about Chadwick, Mikhail couldn't help but marvel at how lovely Petra looked in the new dress. For the first time, he saw her hair down around her shoulders. A woman like that needed pretty things. Remembering her apartment, he suspected she spent little on herself and plenty on archeological finds, both real and fake. He couldn't help but remember how her hair had touched his face in the truck on their trip to Addis Abba.

"You clean up pretty good." He laughed lightly as she twirled around.

"Seriously? That's all you got? It's a good thing you're not dating anyone. But hey, if you are going to hang around me and I go to all this trouble wearing a dress, you should tell me I take your breath away."

"I didn't want to sound like everyone else in your circle of admirers."

"Ahh, about that, there aren't that many. Chadwick

says I intimidate men."

Mikhail laid his hand on his heart. "I can't imagine why. You're so genteel and soft spoken."

This made her laugh as he pulled a chair out for her. "Thanks for the dress. You have good taste."

"To be honest, a very nice lady in the gift shop helped me pick it out."

"I'm shocked. Another female who fell for your blue eyes. Hopefully, she wasn't jailbait."

He choked on his hot tea. "No. No. She was maybe in her seventies. When I described you, she insisted this would be perfect. Historically, it was used to refer to Semitic-speaking ethnicities and tribes in the highlands of Ethiopia and Eritrea, such as the Amhara, Tigray, and Tigrinya people. Since I told her why we're here, she thought this would be appropriate."

"Thank you. It's lovely. I don't have many dresses. My line of work isn't much on frilly." Food was set before them then they were left alone. "What did the constable have to say?"

"The people here are concerned about the safety and condition of the churches as we talked about earlier, along with the encroachment of the warring factors. The repairs that need to be done have to be approved by the elders, and that is not an easy process."

"Makes sense. Having outsiders, especially unbelievers or scientists, could appear to be a threat to their sacred churches. I get that." Petra leveled a coy expression toward him. "Do you think the churches were built by angels or heavenly beings? You can tell me."

"You'll have to admit, building them in such a short time frame with the kind of tools and equipment available at the time certainly opens the door for holy intervention."

"I think you avoided answering my question."

"Yes. I believe they had help. I don't know if it was angels or something else."

"You mean Nephilim? The giants among men? The offspring of angels and Earth women? Please." Petra rolled her eyes in disbelief.

"You can't totally rule it out as a biblical archeologist," Mikhail insisted.

"That's Chadwick's specialty. I'm more of an anthropological archaeologist who studies history through material culture."

"Sounds impressive."

She waved her fork at him. "That's why I said it that way. I study other people's junk basically." She pushed the plate away and sipped on her hot tea. "What else did the constable say? Has he seen Chadwick?"

The waiter removed their plates as Mikhail stood and led her to the balcony surrounding the patio. The breeze toyed with her hair, and she was quick to push one side behind her ear.

"Yes. He saw him several days ago, just like the waiter who came to our room earlier."

"Did he appear to be under duress, hurt, anything?" Petra's eyes widened in what he knew to be anticipating good news.

"No. He was with another man from the US at the time. However, he was Ethiopian. There didn't appear to be a problem, and he moved about on his own accord or so the constable believed."

"I don't understand. Why would he just leave me—us? He set this up for me to study and wanted you on board. This would have been exactly the kind of thing he would love, yet he passed it off to me. Then just disappeared? There's got to be a reason."

"Maybe we'll find out tomorrow. The bishop will escort us down to the churches in the morning. There were several men with Chadwick who he seemed to know and was comfortable with. His family is known around here."

"I doubt Chadwick knows anyone from here. It's been several decades since he visited."

"It was your admirer from the coffee shop."

"My admirer? You mean Hawi Mathias?"

Mikhail let the news sink in, as her expression morphed from confusion to anger.

"Are you saying Hawi kidnapped Chadwick? The constable could be wrong."

"I don't know if he actually kidnapped him, Petra. But he made sure nothing harmed him. Apparently, he arranged for Chadwick to have the escort we thought was a kidnapping. The constable knows Hawi's family who lived here for many years. They were among the protectors of the churches. The current bishop is also related to him."

"Are you saying he used me to gain Chadwick's confidence?" Petra's frown deepened.

"Looks that way. I'm sorry if you have feelings for him. He appeared to be genuinely taken with you." Mikhail stepped closer to her.

"What about Chadwick? That's who I care about. If he wasn't kidnapped, then who brought him here?"

"No one knows for sure. The constable believed it to be someone local since the gentleman was Ethiopian."

"Okay, then where is Chadwick? Is he okay?"

Mikhail laid a hand on her upper arm. "Petra, I…" His voice trailed off as she zeroed in on his face. "I have bad news about Chadwick."

She took a step back and pushed his hand from her arm. "No."

"It was his heart." He grabbed her hand. "We can see him tomorrow."

"I don't believe he's dead. No way. He was strong," she insisted.

"These things happen. If he had been home, maybe there would have been help."

"Fine," she huffed. "I'm going back to the room. I'll talk to you in the morning. Good night."

"Petra, let me help you."

She started to walk off then came back and jammed her finger in his chest. "If you hadn't gotten involved, I could have saved him. I would have been with him to help."

"I did not ask to be a part of this, Petra," he said calmly. "Chadwick sought me out the day he was kidnapped. Let me comfort you."

"I'm fine. I don't need one thing from you or anyone else. I'm going to do the job I came to do in his honor. Just stay out of my way."

"Petra…"

She stormed off.

He rubbed his face with one hand, trying to wipe away the frustration welling up inside him.

"Whew. That didn't go as I expected," Zane said, stepping out of the shadows. "Are you going to go after her?"

"No. I'm going to get a drink."

"Not a good idea."

"I don't remember asking your opinion," Mikhail huffed.

"I guess then you don't care someone is waiting up there for her. Wonder if it's our buddy, Hawi. I bet he knows how to comfort Petra."

"Great." He rushed out and found an out-of-order sign on the elevator. He rushed to the stairs and took them two at a time. Once on his floor, he watched as his suite's door closed. He checked the hall and saw nothing. Then it occurred to him the stranger must be inside. He pushed the door open so hard it banged against the wall, scaring Petra into letting out a yell.

"What are you doing?" she fumed.

"I-I thought I saw someone follow you up here."

"I didn't see anyone," she said firmly.

"Petra, are you all right?" He double-locked the door and went about checking the suite. He found nothing and realized Zane had just pulled a prank to get him to come upstairs. "Do you want to talk?"

"No." She turned away from him and headed to her room. He watched her freeze. "Mikhail?"

He rushed over to see her room tossed. "The map is in the safe. Anything missing?"

She ran to her backpack. "The pictures. They're gone." She collapsed on the bed. "How could I let that happen. I swear the door was locked when I came in."

"Maybe came in through the balcony. Let's take another look around." She sat still while he opened every drawer and emptied her backpack. Nothing. While he was checking, he put things right side up and straightened the mess. Petra's bottom lip trembled as she twisted part of the sheet between her fingers. He watched her look up at the ceiling then at the floor several times. She had fallen into despair.

"I know it's little comfort, Petra, but I took pictures of them with my phone." He took out this phone and scrolled through to find them then handed it over to her. "At least we have a copy."

He could have sworn she tried to smile at him and returned the phone. "Thank you, Mikhail." She refocused on her hands for a few seconds, wiped her eyes, then stood, pulling her brave shoulders back before meeting his eyes. "Where is he?"

"Chadwick lies in state at one of the Rock Hewn Churches."

She slowly turned and cocked her head in confusion. "Why isn't he at the morgue?"

"I'm not completely sure except the constable told me that since he is a foreigner, an American, someone from the embassy has to sign off on taking care of the body. And because it happened in the church, the priests also get involved."

"He deserves better. We'll end up burying him here." She sounded hopeless.

"I think a lot will be revealed to us tomorrow. You should prepare yourself."

"For what?"

"I don't know exactly. But the constable seemed to think you had answers to the problems the Rock Hewn Churches face. That could be a bargaining chip. I'll be right there with you."

She took a deep breath as if it were a dose of courage as tears pooled in the corners of her eyes. "I just want to go to bed, Mikhail."

"I'll sleep on the couch in case you need me."

"Thank you. You really are an angel sometimes." She reached out to touch his face then pulled away.

His heart caught in his throat so fast, he thought he might choke, but Petra was already moving toward the door. When her room went dark, he turned the rest of the lights out and lay down on the couch as he promised.

All that hurt and fear were pressing against a dam of emotions. He could feel it. Around midnight, he heard her moving around in her room. The sound of her French doors opening meant she might have stepped out onto her tiny balcony. In a few minutes, he could hear her muffled sobs.

He padded barefoot to the open door and saw her with her face in her hands. The moonlight was dim, but he could see she wore shorts and a T-shirt. The bed hinted she'd wrestled a crocodile. He approached and cleared his throat.

She lifted her face from her hands and stuttered through her grief. "I woke you. I'm sorry."

"I never went to sleep." He stood just a few steps from her. "Grief often visits during the night. I didn't want you to be alone when it hit."

This time, she stepped toward him. "I miss him, Mikhail. He helped raise me when my parents drowned. He saved me that day, and I never forgot it. He was my father, my mentor, my conscience, my inspiration. What am I going to do without him?"

Mikhail took her hands, pulled her into his arms, and held her quivering body tight against his chest. The tears flowed freely as her arms came up around his neck and she laid her cheek against his face. He remembered this kind of pain when his wife died. The thought she was experiencing such pain ruptured his heart.

After the tears stopped, she held on tight and breathed normally. She laid her head against his shoulder and placed a hand on his heart then moved it back and forth. "I'm so tired," she whispered as her body sagged against his. In one quick movement, he lifted her into his arms and carried her to the bed. Laying her down, he moved her tangled hair from her damp face before pulling up the sheet.

"Mikhail?" Her voice had lost its anger and was soft and inviting. "I don't want to be alone. Can you stay with me until I go to sleep? Please."

He moved to the other side of the bed and climbed on top of the covers as she rolled to face away from him. Petra linked her fingers through his that lay gently across her abdomen after he had pulled her into the curve of his body.

"Sleep, Mikhail," whispered in his ear as he stayed longer than he planned. But the sleep came heavy, and there were no nightmares. The rhythm of her breathing pulled him into a kind of peace he hadn't experienced in a long time.

Twenty-Seven

❖

The idea Ethiopia would be cool and wet in June was unexpected to Petra. This was her first trip to the African country. The continent of Africa remained an extremely diverse continent in all aspects of geography. With fifty-nine countries and 3,000 cultures, it stood to reason even an archeologist would never be able to study that many ethnic groups and traditions.

With the French doors open off the living room, she ventured out onto the balcony. The coffee she sipped took the edge off the chill that smacked bare arms. Holding the cup of warm brew in her cold hands, she decided to ponder the previous night wrapped in Mikhail's arms. She'd woken several times. The moment she rolled over to find herself nose to nose with Father Mikhail Novak with his arm still draped across her, a jolt of guilt hit her.

She had practically begged him to stay with her. The darkness of night and knowing she had lost the man who took the place of her father so long ago felt like she'd just been thrown into a river wearing concrete boots.

Mikhail slept peacefully and couldn't protest her as she studied him through shadows while the tumbling temperatures breezed in through the open balcony doors. Although fully dressed, she wondered if he was cold and respectfully avoided joining her under the covers. When she snuggled closer to warm him, his arm tightened to hold her.

Another man might have taken advantage of her weakness, and honestly, she would have succumbed to anyone else, to shake the brokenness coursing through her veins. What a waste, she thought, remembering how his embrace had given her comfort. When she awoke this morning, she discovered he'd moved back to the couch and slept soundly.

"Feels like rain." Mikhail joined her, carrying a mug of coffee and dressed like a backpacker from Colorado. "Most of their rain comes in June and July. The waiter last night said the rains were a little late this year. Global warming, I guess."

Petra turned to listen intently but mostly watched how he drank from the mug. His slow words resembled giving the stock market report to elderly investors. Moving to the railing along the balcony, he took in the landscape and avoided eye contact with her. Although innocent of carnal interaction, was he embarrassed he willingly slept with her?

"I could use another cup. Any left?" She moved

toward the inside.

"I could use a refill, too," he confessed.

"I'll bring the pot," Petra said anxiously.

"Are we still talking about coffee or an illegal habit you haven't disclosed?" he teased.

Petra stopped and burst out laughing. "And Mr. Snarky is back. I don't do drugs." Petra put her hands on her hips.

"Good to know. What do you do to take the edge off?" Mikhail tilted his head and let his narrowed eyes take her in, head to toe.

"I have sex with random strangers and drink way too much Jack Daniels."

"And lie. Don't forget that," he reminded her.

Taking a deep breath, she waved him off, still laughing, to retrieve the coffeepot. When she returned, she poured him the first cup then filled her own. He let one corner of his mouth tilt upward as she took a sip of her brew.

"What I do to take the edge off in real life is research, read, listen to music, ponder what my life would be like if my parents hadn't died, and where my next adventure will take me," she said.

"And I crochet, watch cooking shows, and play the French horn. Oh, and charm the ladies of the community to give their tithes and offerings to the church on a regular basis," Mikhail admitted seriously.

Once more, she couldn't help but laugh, nearly choking on her coffee. "Don't forget lying."

A slow smile spread across his mouth. "Are we good, Petra McGinnis?"

She tilted her head and eyed him. "We are good. If you need a reference in the future for the job of Knight in Shining Armor, I'm happy to give you a juicy letter of recommendation."

"Honestly, I have a number of parishioners who tell me that all the time. I'll put you on the list."

Silence sprang up between them for a few uncomfortable minutes, but Petra finally approached the elephant in the room. "Thanks for last night. I'm not used to being the helpless female unable to control my emotions."

"You had a right to be in distress. We'll see what unfolds today. Maybe we can claim Chadwick's body and get him back to the States. I'm hoping the bishop knows what to do. The constable acted like no matter what, the bishop had the last word."

"Maybe priest to priest, he'll listen to you," she suggested.

"One of the things I struggled with while living here was how gender roles were clearly defined. Women are considered to be subordinate to their husbands and fathers. There are laws to protect them from abuse, but I'm not sure how effective those are."

"So, what you're saying is, to keep my mouth shut."

"I would think in this case—definitely." He strode off to the living room, snatching up the coffeepot as he went. "Let's get a bite to eat downstairs before we head out. It's early, but the bishop I knew used to head out early."

When the bishop was a no-show, Mikhail decided to take a chance and hike the quarter mile to the Rock

Hewn Churches. The rugged, downward path to the structures made walking tricky since there were ruts from previous downpours and thousands of worshipers over the years. Thankfully he'd reminded Petra they might want to wear their windbreakers since the air remained cool with a light mist. Fog created what appeared to be ghostly apparitions floating above the treetops. The surreal absence of sound kept his neck on a swivel to check for trouble.

"There." Petra stepped up beside him and lifted her chin toward a statue-still figure ahead of them, dressed in white.

"I think he's waiting for us." Closing the gap between them, Mikhail recognized Bishop Bemnet. "Abun Bemnet, it gives me pleasure to see you again."

The fog lifted off the Rock Hewn Church where the bishop waited at the top of the trail leading downward.

"It has been a long time." The bishop shifted his attention to Petra.

"This is my friend, Dr. McGinnis. She is here to study the Rock Hewn Churches." Mikhail noticed the skepticism reflected in the bishop's refusal in speaking to her directly. "She is also here to worship, as I am. We are most thankful to be able to visit."

"Do you still know our language, Father Novak?"

"I do."

"Then I will speak to you in Amharic. What is the real reason you bring this woman to our holy churches?"

"At first, it was to study how these churches were created."

"We already know how they were created," the

bishop insisted.

"Yes. But she is a scientist and seeks to find proof to their beginnings. It will validate your traditions and beliefs."

"We do not follow what the world believes, Father Novak. It is not within us to want the world at our doorstep if they care nothing of why the churches exist. But I think there is something more this woman wants."

"True, Abun Bemnet. The man who also arrived to learn about the Rock Hewn Churches, and to find truth, is her guardian."

The bishop halted and turned to examine the woman following, but remained silent.

Mikhail dared continue. "We were told the man called Chadwick died while in one of the churches. She wishes to take his body home and bury him. Her heart is broken. Can you help us?"

"I know this man. He believes in the truth." The bishop laid his hand on his heart.

Mikhail hesitated before speaking. "You speak as if he lives."

"Follow me, Father Novak. There is still time to restore this man. But the woman must be willing to believe."

"Believe in what?" asked Mikhail.

"The impossible."

Together, the three took the winding path downward to one of the Rock Hewn Churches named Bete Mariam and sometimes St. Mary. Quietly, Mikhail shared the bishop's conversation with Petra. Navigating the steep ruts in the path, he reached back and took her hand. Several times, he felt her squeeze his fingers when she stumbled. Mikhail would halt suddenly to let her run into his body, which steadied her.

Once, he'd turned quickly to find her face near his own. He sucked in his breath at the smoothness of her skin and how the morning light touched her red hair. Both her hands went to his arm as if she were holding on for dear life. A tremble in her overconfident attitude touched deep inside him.

"Don't be afraid, Petra."

Her lips parted as if she wanted to speak, but shifted her attention to the magnificent Rock Hewn Church of St. Mary looming ahead like a monolithic giant.

"Are you ready to continue?" Mikhail asked her.

Petra slid one hand back down to tightly grasp his, while her other one crossed over to rest on his arm. It was as if her voice no longer existed, and her eyes glazed over as they got closer to the church. Her rigid body felt as if it had gone from human to zombie. Once they reached the interior of the canyon-like surface where St. Mary's stood, Petra leaned in to Mikhail.

"Petra," he snapped. Her eyelids didn't move, and her usually rosy face had grown ashen. "Petra." He pulled her around to face him. "What's wrong?"

The bishop eyed them straight-faced then stepped backward and motioned to them to follow. "She will be whole once we are in the holy place. Her spirit is overwhelmed. No harm will come to her."

A wave of comfort washed over him. Somehow, he knew they were in no danger and Petra needed to complete this journey, whatever that might be. Once more, he thought of the condition of Chadwick being in a state of tranquility. He should have asked more questions, but as usual, dismissed part of what Zane had shared.

The rock steps were steep and deep to climb. The obvious uneven surface had suffered from years of tourism and environmental challenges. Petra tried to step up but needed Mikhail to pull her up on each one. Once at the top, she fell into his arms like a helpless child requiring reassurance and comfort. He stood there with his arms around her, stroking her hair and whispering that they were almost ready to go inside.

The bishop stood at the door with an enormous key. "You must leave your shoes outside."

Mikhail bent down and helped her out of her boots then removed his own. The cool air of the morning was both refreshing and uncomfortable on bare feet. He observed that Petra was mesmerized by the enormity of the church. His first experience at seeing the magnificent structures of Lalibela had been similar. He'd been inside most of them, but never St. Mary's or the most impressive one, named St. George.

"Petra." Mikhail stood and gently took hold of her arms and blocked her focus on the church. "You have to wear a head covering." He slung off his backpack and pulled out a long white scarf with pale-blue embroidery along the fringe. It was an impulse buy from a vendor in the hotel. "Let me help you wrap it around your hair."

Petra made eye contact while he draped the scarf over her hair then around her neck and shoulders. "Women have to cover their head to enter the church."

"I remember," she said softly. "How could I have forgotten? What's wrong with me, Mikhail?"

"I don't know. This place has affected you. It's almost like you're under a spell. The bishop assured me you'd be okay once inside. Maybe the church is giving off a kind of energy or causing a chemical reaction in you."

"I feel so weak." Her speech slurred as she reached for his arm to steady her.

"The bishop is opening the door. Are you ready to do this?" asked Mikhail.

She bobbed her head and hugged his arm tighter.

TWENTY-EIGHT

❖

Petra halted and took a deep breath in a gigantic room filled with the subtle smell of incense and candle wax. Mikhail was forced to do the same but never dropped his attention to his surroundings. The faded frescos exposed the vulnerable volcanic basalt walls carved centuries ago. Filtered light highlighted the extensive artwork carved into the towering columns and arches.

"Astonishing," Petra spoke in her normal voice again. "I've never seen such beauty. It's incredible."

"Yes. It always takes my breath away." His attention turned from the painted ceiling to Petra. She no longer resembled a zombie. "The bishop is waiting."

"I hear chanting." She ventured forward without wobbling or fear. A good bet she was back to her tenacious self.

Several priests emerged from a side room carrying candles. Their Gregorian chants, soft and melodic, echoed off the rock-hewn walls. The farther they moved down the main corridor, the more white-clad priests emerged. Their voices remained quiet and reverent as they glided toward a set of twelve-foot-tall doors.

A movement in the shadows caught Mikhail's interest. A large winged creature clothed in black held a white sword and watched him with glowing yellow eyes. His vest opened to his waist revealing a muscled chest. Although he couldn't make them out, Mikhail knew there were intricate tattoo designs on his arms, composed of Celtic knots, a cross, and black roses twisted around a skull.

Mikhail kept walking, casting a glance toward the creature, checking to see if he stalked them for a reason. The first time he'd seen the creature, he'd fallen to his knees in fear. Gradually, Mikhail had realized the death angel meant him no harm. When the angel transformed to human, he recognized him as Zane, the man he saved on the battlefield in Afghanistan.

Time forced him to ignore Zane because part of him believed maybe he was going insane or suffered from schizophrenia. Eventually, he accepted Zane's friendship and counsel to help him with his own severe PTSD. The church helped him reach the point where he could maintain a calmness and a sense of being worthy while he served others. The rage evaporated with each day. He made promises for the healing, and now he wasn't so sure he would be willing to fulfill those obligations.

Zane remained invisible to humans unless they

were at death's door. Sometimes, the onlooker survived and other times, they succumbed to their illness or injuries. Petra was the first healthy person who could see him on a regular basis. Shocked at her snarky attitude and insults toward him, Mikhail feared Zane might reveal himself to shut her up. He soon realized the angel enjoyed the way she taunted Mikhail.

"Why do you keep looking over there?" Petra stretched her neck to get a glimpse, but Mikhail took a bigger step to cut off her line of sight.

"Just being cautious. You'll have to admit, this is all a bit organized and creepy."

"I think it's magnificent. I hope Chadwick feels how special he's been treated," Petra confessed.

"Oh, I'm pretty sure he does," he mumbled.

"What does that mean?" she asked.

"The bishop spoke in riddles I don't understand. He hinted he thought you held the answers."

"Whatever is going on, those giant statues standing on each side of the doors are alive."

Mikhail halted and pulled Petra back. "Those aren't statues. They're Nephilim."

"Aren't the Nephilim beings or people in the Bible? I remember, as a child, reading they were of great size and strength. Weren't they considered the offspring of the fallen ones?"

"Yes," Mikhail admitted. "In Genesis, it describes them as the sons of God and daughters of men. The fallen ones were—"

"Giants. Heavenly angels and Earth women bore their children. They really exist." Petra shifted her attention from Mikhail to the giants guarding the doors. "Incredible."

"Some believe the Nephilim still live among us, as do angels." Mikhail watched as the parade of priests divided themselves along each side of the colonnade and slowly turned their dark eyes toward them. "I think we should keep going. Maybe Chadwick is on the other side of those doors."

Petra jerked her stubborn chin higher and took a deep breath. "Are they dangerous? The Nephilim, I mean?"

"I've never seen them the many times I was here." Their steps were cautious, and each priest they passed, bowed their head as if in reverence. "The vote is out on whether the Nephilim were good or evil. The giant, Goliath, that the shepherd boy David killed in the Bible is thought to have been a Nephilim. What you don't hear about is Goliath had a bunch of ticked-off brothers."

"I bet they were pis—"

"Watch your language, Petra," he insisted.

"It's not like they speak English, right?" She stopped and spoke from the corner of her mouth. "Mikhail? Do they speak something other than Amharic?"

"I don't know. We may be among angels. Remember the pictures? The map?"

"You've got to be kidding me." She searched the area around her and elbowed Mikhail. "I saw something dark move over there behind that column. Have you ever seen an angel in your line of work?"

"Keep moving. Those Nephilim are opening the doors. These priests are watching you." He reached out and pulled her head covering down over the red hair that had found its way out onto her forehead. "Among these people, it might be taken as a sign of fire. Don't speak unless spoken to."

"Oh, you mean be all submissive and—"

"Remind me to buy duct tape next time we go anywhere together. Yes! Submissive. Do you want to find Chadwick or not?"

"I always get snarky when I'm nervous. I'm glad you're here."

Mikhail doubted that was true, but her hooded eyelids and pouty mouth indicated she just might be trying to make amends. He didn't want to feel sympathy for her. Didn't want to drown in those greenish-brown eyes or focus on her full lips that were slightly pink. Letting her know he was less than thrilled to be here could wait. The idea that Zane lurked in the shadows, eyeing them like he wanted to harvest a few bodies to toss into the pits of Hell, unnerved him for her safety.

"Remember, Petra. Submissive," he warned as they stood before the door fully open.

Petra lowered her eyes, letting Mikhail take her hand and lead her forward. Aware that she couldn't resist tilting her head slightly to catch glimpses of the ornate surroundings, he forced himself to focus on the bishop who stood rigid at yet another closed door.

No one else appeared to be aware that Zane, now in angel form, was parallel to them. His walk was confident as he moved his six-foot-seven body in the recesses of the new room. Trying to solve how he entered here without being seen was of little consequence, since no one noticed him. Once again, the sight of such a heavenly creature was both disturbing and a spiritual experience. He wanted to share it with

Petra, but it was forbidden.

"Petra McGinnis, daughter of William and Lydia McGinnis, come forward." The bishop held out his hand to her, but she stood steadfast as her eyes widened.

She spoke out of the corner of her mouth to Mikhail but focused on the bishop. "Why can I understand what he is saying? I don't speak Amharic."

"You are in a holy place where miracles happen every day," the bishop spoke in his gravelly voice. "Come. We shall see the man called Chadwick."

The second set of doors swung open from the inside. Candlelight filled the room, and a gentle stirring of air caused the flames to flicker, making the designs dance along the ancient walls. At times, the birds appeared to fly and the black lions shook their manes. The illusions captivated Petra's attention as the pictures moved around the room until they stopped behind a wall near a rock communion table.

Mikhail watched in awe as two more Nephilim approached the table and removed the white cloth that draped to the floor. Petra clutched his hand tighter as she met his gaze with wonder. When the Nephilim began to fold the cloth, he was reminded of the many flags he'd watched folded at military funerals. Like those, this cloth was handled with ceremony and respect.

The Nephilim slowly moved to each end of the table. The bishop held his hands upward and prayed for both help and forgiveness. He continued by asking for a special blessing upon the woman before him. As he lowered his hands then stretched them out over the table, the body of Chadwick appeared, first as a blur then completely visible.

Petra burst into tears and ran forward, only to have the two Nephilim block her advance.

Mikhail was quick to join her and circle her waist to pull her back at the moment he saw the angel appear behind the bishop. His jaw tightened and released. Mikhail could have sworn there was vapor escaping the angel's nostrils as his complexion turned red with anger.

"Petra, you must wait for the bishop to speak."

"But Chadwick… He looks alive. His coloring is clear, and he could be just sleeping."

The bishop came around the table and waved the Nephilim aside. "This man is both alive and dead."

"I want to touch him," she begged. "He is like a father to me."

The bishop stepped aside then reached out to take her hand. "We all know this. That is why he was allowed to enter our holy place, forbidden to the public. His heart suffered, but we caught him before he succumbed to this illness. The death angel circles even as we speak. He is here."

The bishop pulled Petra closer to view Chadwick's body.

"He isn't breathing. How can you say he is alive?" she whispered in misery. "Chadwick," she moaned. "My sweet Chadwick. I love you so much. Please wake up."

"He cannot. Only you can save him. Time is running out. The death angel is anxious to take him."

"Let me get him to a hospital."

"He will die if he leaves this chamber." The bishop shook his head.

"Then how can I save him—if he truly is alive?" Petra wiped her eyes on the sleeve of her shirt.

"You must return the Vessel of St. Mary to us."

"The Vessel of St. Mary? How can I possibly do that? It is in Turkey. The area is mountainous and the government requires a lot of paperwork to go in such a protected area. There is no way I can do that."

"You have done it before. That is why we took your Chadwick. He would never have allowed you to go. Now he can only survive if you bring it to us."

"Good Bishop, why the Vessel of St. Mary?" Mikhail shifted his attention from the angel who paced in the shadows behind the communion table opposite Petra, to the bishop. Mikhail stood behind her so close he could feel her reach back with her free hand to take his.

"Our churches are crumbling from decay, environmental exposure, and centuries of pilgrims using them. The UNESCO environmental architects have also made mistakes in trying to save our houses of worship." The bishop's voice grew melancholy.

"They have new plans that will help," Petra insisted.

"The wars among the people have kept them away. It has been deemed unsafe for them," the bishop informed her. "We do not have much time. The walls are cracking and jeopardize the people who come to worship. Soon, they will not be allowed to show their devotion and love for our Savior."

"Good bishop, they can do that anywhere," Petra pleaded.

"This place is difficult to reach. The pilgrims feel it shows their devotion by coming. It gives them happiness and fulfillment." The bishop took a deep breath. "The Vessel of St. Mary was a gift from the angels who helped King Gebre Meskel build these churches. It was to be a new Jerusalem. The angels left twelve vessels for us to call upon them to repair and worship as needed. The Vessel of St. Mary disappeared several centuries ago."

"What happened to the vessel?"

"We do not know," the bishop admitted. "Word of its power reached many who craved its gift. But it was meant for these holy structures. Nothing else. Angels will not return until it is opened within these walls."

"Why choose Petra?" asked Mikhail.

The bishop ignored her as he spoke to Mikhail. "She found it once before, as did her parents. They promised to return it if it was ever found." Finally, he addressed Petra. "You nearly drowned not so long ago, trying to take it. You must try again."

"How do you know that?" Petra appeared confused. "Only Chadwick knew about that."

"But you told someone else. And he has been shadowing you ever since. He is of our people and knew of the importance." The bishop raised his chin and turned to gaze at the creature who had come to take Chadwick.

"Hawi Mathis." Mikhail couldn't keep the sarcasm out of his voice. "What is his role in this?"

"It does not matter. What does matter is that you return the vessel within the next seventy-two hours, or Chadwick will die for eternity."

"Does he know I'm here?" There was a catch in Petra's voice.

"Yes. He knows. He hears your words and is

comforted by your presence. He is in no pain. We will see to him until the end if you are not successful."

"Thank you." Tears pooled in her eyes as she reached to touch Chadwick, only to be pushed away by the Nephilim.

"You must not interact with him in this state. He cannot survive with contact from this world. Only the Nephilim may care for him." The bishop made the sign of the cross as he faced her. "You possess a special power within you. This is why the church affected you when you approached. Father Mikhail Novak will see that you are protected. He, too, carries secrets that empower him." The bishop's attention refocused solely on Petra. "Petra, you must not be afraid. The life future of these Rock Hewn Churches rest in the palm of your hand. Leave us. Preparations have been arranged for you."

TWENTY-NINE

❖

Petra tried to piece together the last three days. None of it made sense. Or maybe it did, and her brain was just too addled to see a pattern. Although the whole experience at the Rock Hewn Churches still caused her head to spin, Father Mikhail Novak confused her the most. One minute, he was praying and listening patiently to one of his flock, and the next, he was brandishing weapons that would make the Terminator envious. His demeanor oscillated between caring and dangerous then spiritual and dancing on the fringes of darkness.

"I brought hot tea. No coffee available." Mikhail handed her the mug and eased down beside her.

She held it between her cold hands. "Thank you. I can't get warm. The church was cold. My feet are still freezing. Aren't you cold?"

"No. I'm pretty hot natured as a rule. But even I felt a little chilled once we were in the chamber with Chadwick. How are you doing anyway?" All the sympathy and understanding had left his voice. Petra wondered if he was tired of being her protector.

They hadn't had much time to talk about what happened at St. Mary's, one of the Rock Hewn Churches. Once they had climbed out of the deep pit where St. Mary's had been carved, a Jeep waited to take them to the airport in Lalibela. It was as if the ground crew knew they were coming and stood guard until they boarded the plane. There were a few other passengers, Ethiopians dressed in traditional clothing, and several others wore suits and carried briefcases.

"Was Chadwick dead or not?"

"More like he was in limbo. At least, that was what I gathered from the bishop's conversation."

Petra shivered at his words. "I don't understand any of this."

"Give me that," he said, taking the cup of tea and slipped it in a drink holder on the drop-down tray. "Give me your hands." He sucked in his breath as his fingers closed around hers. "You weren't kidding. Maybe the church had some kind of effect on your circulation." He closed his eyes then rubbed her hands vigorously.

A surge of warmth flowed through her fingers, hands, and up her arms until he opened his icy-blue eyes. She pulled them slowly out of his grasp that at first held on a little too tight.

"How did you do that?" Petra felt her body continue to warm.

He shrugged. "Just a gift I guess."

"Are you ever going to tell me who you really are, Father Mikhail Novak, the Imposter? Or do I want to know?"

"After this little adventure, you'll never see me again. I seriously doubt the museum will want my help, considering their two most renowned archaeologists are safely back home. Besides, I have a job, and you know everything you need to know about me." He handed her back the mug of tea. "I'm not that interesting."

"But you are mysterious."

"Let's talk about what we're going to do instead of me. I want to hear about the Vessel of St. Mary. Where did you find it, and why didn't you take it when you had the chance?"

Petra quickly told him about finding the vessel and nearly drowning in the process. "I panicked. I couldn't get out of there fast enough. Chadwick told me to wait, but when he got busy with something else, I slipped down in the cave. He managed to pull me out and was totally disgusted with me."

"Why were you so adamant about doing it yourself?"

"My parents searched for that vessel in those mountains many times. I remember hearing them talk about it around campfires and hoping they could return it to the rightful owners. I didn't know it belonged to the Rock Hewn Churches until today. There was no mention of the owner in any of my parents' journals."

"How did your parents die?"

Petra set the mug of tea on the tray and closed her eyes to remember. "I was eight years old. My parents usually dropped me off at my grandparents' farm when they went on an expedition. This time, they decided to take me with them. Chadwick warned them it wasn't a good idea, but they said I was a curious sprout and wanted to learn. They were sure that this time, they would find the Vessel of St. Mary. We were in Turkey for six weeks, and all went as planned until the rains came. It was a hundred-year flood. We were camped near a creek that turned into a river, washing away all their work and several workers."

"Were your parents washed away, too?"

"Not until they tried to save a few important artifacts that were thought to be stored in a safe place. They got to them in time, but the ground gave way beneath them, and they fell into the river that had been a gentle creek. I ran after them, screaming and I too slid into the water, but Chadwick dove in after me and managed to get us to shore."

"You must have been a terrified little girl."

"I was angry for a long time. I blamed myself. Bad luck and all that." She opened her eyes and was surprised how close Mikhail had leaned into her. "The one thing I wanted to do for a tribute to them was find the Vessel of St. Mary. And now I get another chance."

"Are you afraid?"

"Yes, I'm afraid I won't find it in time or get it back to save Chadwick."

He pulled out the map again. This time, the map area of Ethiopia had shrunk and included the countries touching the Red Sea plus the Middle Eastern countries on the western end of the Mediterranean Sea.

"We switch planes in Cairo then fly to Turkey." Mikhail held up the map for her to get a closer look.

"If I remember right, we can take a plane to Gazipasa Airport, which is about sixty miles from

Bucakkisla." Petra pointed to the map. "See here? We are pretty close to the Taurus Mountains. Remember Noah?"

"Is Mt. Ararat there?"

"Yes, and supposedly so is his beautiful ark. Too bad we can't hunt for it. That area is still covered in snow since it's the highest mountain in Turkey. We won't be going up that high. Besides, that's pretty close to some rough countries that don't necessarily like Turkey. Kind of a love-hate relationship. Hikers get kidnapped and robbed all the time too, so we'll need to steer clear of there. The mountain trails should still be open and easy to navigate. Not a lot of traffic this time of year. The Europeans come in another month or so." Petra drank the last of her tea.

"The Tigris River is pretty close." Mikhail continued to study the map.

"Exactly why the underground caves sometimes flood. The one where I saw the Vessel of St. Mary should have been dry. Chadwick tried to figure out why it suddenly flooded. If it is still full of water, we won't be able to get in there. And since the water is ice cold, we would need diving equipment to haul up there—what am I saying? It's not even available." Petra sighed, leaned her head back, and squeezed her eyes shut to think.

"Maybe I can reach out to Zane. He'll know if there's a place we can get that kind of equipment," Mikhail offered.

"How would he possibly know that? And why does he keep showing up everywhere we go? It's downright spooky."

"He's lived a colorful life."

"That means he's either has worked for the CIA or is some kind of angel." Petra jerked her head around. "He isn't some kind of angel, is he?"

Mikhail chuckled. "I can neither confirm nor deny that."

"Very funny. So, you two go way back, huh?"

"You might say that," Mikhail said cautiously.

"And you don't intend to tell me anything else, do you? And while I'm thinking about creepy things, did you see that shadow moving around the church? I could have sworn it was human—only bigger," Petra said excitedly.

"Maybe another Nephilim."

"I think it was something else. The bishop mentioned a death angel. Do you know anything about that?" Petra turned in her seat to lean in closer.

"Just because I'm a priest doesn't mean I know everything about the holy realm."

"And just because I'm not very well versed in the male psyche doesn't mean I can't recognize BS when I hear it from an oversexed priest."

Mikhail choked on his tea and spewed it back in his cup. His narrowed gaze caused her heart to jump into her throat. There was a mix of danger and sexual prowess for a few seconds before he blushed and looked away.

"I probably shouldn't have said that," she admitted.

"Ya think?" He gulped down the remaining tea before speaking. "We'll be landing at Cairo soon. I might take a nap."

"How can you sleep at a time like this?" Petra knew she came across as indignant, but her previous comments had embarrassed her and had clearly disrespected Mikhail. She felt more comfortable being snarky and hard to get along with than admitting she cared what he thought of her.

"If I sleep, I can dream about my next sexual conquest without anyone ever knowing." He tilted his head toward her and lifted one corner of his mouth. "Maybe it will even be you, Petra. You're wearing me down." His voice was deep and calm, unnerving Petra to her very core.

"Literally. In. Your. Dreams. Mikhail."

He turned away and closed his eyes with a devilish chuckle escaping his throat.

Petra grabbed the map to study it but couldn't focus on the task at hand. Instead, she replayed the morning over and over, trying to make sense of what she'd experienced. Was it possible Chadwick was actually alive and she held his fate in finding the Vessel of St. Mary?

THIRTY

Petra refused to surrender reins of the Jeep, claiming she knew the way. She'd experienced how recklessly Mikhail drove his motorcycle. This way, there was a certain amount of assurance they wouldn't drive off a ninety-degree turn on a one-way gravel road. Maybe she gasped, "Oops," a few too many times, causing him to grip the armrests like he had decided to ride the Screaming Eagle at Six Flags over America. He kept making the sign of the cross to add insult to injury.

"Are you driving like a maniac because you think God is my copilot, or I'll pray for safety?" Mikhail fumed.

"That's an excellent idea." Petra slowed the vehicle and enjoyed his disgruntled face.

"God is probably saying, 'Are you kidding me? You're on your own, you idiot,'" Mikhail fumed.

"No worries. This is as far as we can go." She jerked the steering wheel to the right and came to a sudden stop at the edge of a precarious overlook. "We hike the rest of the way." She released the seat belt and eyed Mikhail. "You're a lovely shade of green."

"I'm driving on the way down." He unbuckled and slid out, eyeing the position of the Jeep on the rocky edge. Reaching in the back, he pulled out the new backpacks prepared for camping and prospecting. There was also a supply of dried food and bottled water.

After securing the belt of the backpack around her waist, Petra took a deep breath. "Isn't it amazing here? Look at those mountains." She pointed. "Over to your north is probably the lake where all these creeks, drainage ditches, and springs end up. That's where we're headed. The trail is about five miles, only because there are so many switchbacks. We should be able to make it to the Whispering Caves by nightfall. You don't want to be fumbling around here in the dark. One step in the wrong direction, and you could be singing with the angels."

"Is that another dig because you're beginning to be obsessed with angels?" He moved toward the trailhead. "Let's go. You want the lead, or do you trust me? I was a Boy Scout."

"Of course you were. By all means, lead. The trail is well marked, and there are no forks to get us lost. You can set the pace. Wouldn't want you to tire out too soon following me."

Petra couldn't resist the snarky comment then regretted it when he arched an eyebrow and let a diabolical smirk play across those interesting lips. She realized too late that the comment may have triggered a response equivalent to throwing down a gauntlet to a Roman gladiator.

They made good time in spite of several washed-out places and having to navigate around gullies then back to the trail. They never lost sight of the trail. Both times, Mikhail suggested they stop and hydrate since the altitude had increased.

The irritating part was he hadn't broken a sweat, or bothered to look back to see if she was struggling to keep up. Perhaps the implication she could take whatever he dished out was taken to heart. Or maybe he decided to test her metal. No. Most likely he just wanted to exasperate her. Mission accomplished.

They emerged into a high mountain valley surrounded by boulders and trickling streams. The trail was crooked and cluttered with chunks of rocks and downed trees. Squeezing through narrow openings was easier than climbing at this point.

"According to the map, we should be just about be there," Mikhail said as he studied the map.

Petra came alongside him and he pointed to their destination. "Maybe another half mile or so. It will be dark soon. The mountains will block the setting sun. I think we'll still have time to set up camp. We've made good time."

"I'm impressed you could keep up. You look like such a fragile thing." He folded the map and returned it to one of the pockets on the backpack.

"Your compliments always sound like insults." Petra took the lead this time.

"And your perception of my intent is impressive."

Petra ignored the verbal confrontation and bristled when she heard him chuckle. Why did he exasperate her with whatever she said, and why did she care? Maybe when this was over, she'd get a therapist and explore her obsession to always be in control, admired, and loved. Mikhail shot her down at every turn and pulled the macho card to demonstrate her vulnerable side. Was this so he could swoop in and… She wasn't sure how to finish the thought.

The trail heading down to the caves was steep and smooth. Dust clouds lifted beneath their feet from the dry ground. Petra was able to find a flat area among some pines, with an outcropping of large rocks that would protect them from the wind.

"I'll gather kindling to build a fire." Mikhail propped his backpack against a rock and headed into a stand of trees. "I'll be back in a few minutes to set up."

Petra was beat, so she didn't protest. The outcropping was deep enough she was able to spread the barrier before setting up the two-man tent. Fortunately, both sleeping bags were heavy duty. At least the weather hadn't turned unfavorable.

Mikhail returned with an armful of kindling, dropping it near where she'd set up the tent. He cast a suspicious glance toward her efforts then to her. "I found a few small logs. Just couldn't carry it all. I'll get those, then when I get back, I'll start a fire." He turned to leave then pivoted. "Could you gather up those dry pine needles? Don't want to wait too long. The temperature is dropping fast."

Instead of answering him, she gave him a thumbs-up. As soon as he was out of earshot, she added, "I know how to do this, Mr. Boy Scout."

By the time he returned with the wood, Petra had a fire going, thanks to some fire-starter cubes she found in the backpack. The pine needles mixed with the dry kindling teased the tiny flames. Mikhail returned to squat down and placed the logs crisscross on her handiwork. It didn't take long to get a warm blaze going.

Petra found a foldable rack, in the supplies, to place on the fire after he stacked rocks around the perimeter. No words passed between them as she boiled water they'd brought to add to the powdered soup. With the hot tea and granola bars, she decided it was better than gourmet food from a swanky New York City restaurant. This was as good as it got on these kinds of trips. Thankfully, her partner didn't complain. He dragged his sleeve across his mouth then raised his tin cup up as if he were toasting her.

"My compliments to the cook," Mikhail said as he tossed a few more small sticks on the fire.

"And you thought I couldn't cook." She ate the last bite of her granola bar then threw the paper in the fire and watched it curl into black ashes. "There's enough for two more meals. Are you still hungry?" She dug in the backpack.

"Starved, but better save it in case we get stranded. Anything else in the supplies?"

"Not much. More granola and soup, a few tea bags and protein bars. It's enough. Hopefully, this time tomorrow, we'll be on our way back to Lalibela. We are cutting this close."

"How far are we from the actual site?" He pulled his backpack to retrieve the map. "Big surprise. It's changed again." He stood and came to sit on the ground next to her. "Does this red X mean anything to you?"

Darkness crashing around them caused her to lean

in over the map to get a better look by the flickering firelight. "Could be. Before we left, Chadwick insisted we cover the entrance along with the access point where I lowered myself into the interior. Not my finest moment. Lucky for us, Chadwick left the equipment to use again, if and when we came back. Wonder if that was foreshadowing?"

"There are times when a still, small voice whispers in our ears to be calm, give a warning, or even a promise of hope. Oftentimes, we call it common sense or a gut feeling," Mikhail said offhandedly.

"What do you call it?" she said softly as he folded the map and returned it to his backpack.

"What do you care what I call it? Clearly, we aren't on the same page when it comes to the spiritual realm. So, we'll just go with dumb luck." Mikhail wore a bored expression.

"Why are you doing this, Mikhail? I mean, really. You show up out of nowhere and next thing I know, you're helping the museum get an audience with the protectors of the Rock Hewn Churches. We have been trying to get in there for a good five years."

"I'm sure the wars raging around here, COVID and UNESCO restrictions, or anyone messing with what they believe to be their territory, had a lot to do with it. You know as well as I do that the State Department has had warnings against coming here for a long time. Your boss was introduced to me through a mutual friend."

"Who was the friend? Maybe I know him."

He tossed a few twigs in the fire but didn't answer her.

"Was it Zane?"

He chuckled. "I assure you; it wasn't Zane."

"I keep expecting him to appear out of nowhere. Where is he when we need him?"

"So, now it's we?" Standing, he dusted the gravel from the seat of his pants and glanced down at her for a few seconds then out into the darkness.

"I have to admit, without you, I would be in a heap of trouble. I don't mean to make you miserable or make fun of you. I'm just—not used to…"

"Sharing the limelight? Being told what to do? Not knowing everything about literally everything?" His tone was cool but not accusing. "And I'm also used to having my own way, being able to convince people what is best for them, and taking charge when those around me appear to be a flock of lost sheep. Putting the two of us together was like throwing gas on a fire."

Petra released a warm laugh as she also stood. "Maybe because we're both hardheaded, someone thought we'd be a good team."

His left cheek lifted in amusement. "Someone has a warped sense of humor." The gaze he leveled on her was penetrating and warm.

"You're staring." She dusted at her face, feeling a piece of granola on her lip.

"I'll get my sleeping bag and sleep by the fire." He moved toward the tent.

"We better hang our food packs either up in the trees or bury under some rocks. I've never seen any, but there are a few brown bears in these mountains."

He pivoted toward her. "Bears? What else?"

"Leopards, I think. Endangered. Probably one more thing we'll have to worry about. I think you better sleep in the tent with me. We both have a weapon in our packs and I mean…"

"I'll set up an alarm. If anything comes around, we'll be alerted. I'll fix the packs. The fire is almost out. Hopefully the smoke will discourage anything with four legs. Considering how you freaked out with me sharing a carpet with you in Niger, I figured we had other options here. I'll sleep outside."

"No, please. There's plenty of room. It will be safer. Besides, I'm safer with you than I would be with Hawi if he was here."

"Are you sure about that?" He didn't shy away from sending her another warm look of interest.

"I have a gun, a taser, and a bowie knife. I'm pretty sure."

"In that case, I would love sleeping with you."

"Ugh." Petra groaned then left him to take care of their cache. For a second, she thought she heard him laugh beneath his breath.

Thirty-One

❖

The display of stars in the heavens humbled Father Mikhail Novak as he sat next to the dying embers of the fire. It helped him delay slipping into the two-man tent where Petra slept. Waiting until she was asleep helped to remove his growing attraction to her. She gave as good as she got. It had been a long time since anyone had challenged who or what he was. Everyone was so accepting of his choice of profession. He was so adept at deception, he sometimes forgot there was another side of him, a darker, colder side that could be considered dangerous with zero empathy for mankind.

Petra was energetic, brilliant, and beautiful, although he wasn't sure she knew how her looks attracted attention. The woman was far from glamorous, but her underlying charisma and charm disturbed him to his very soul. The longer he lingered on certain aspects of their relationship, the more he wanted to explore the human side of himself that had vanished long ago. Even from here, he remembered the earthy fragrance of her hair. Except for the hard-work callouses on her hands, her skin was as soft as a baby's. The freckles on her face were few but gave her pale skin a little more color on her cheeks.

His senses grew dangerously overactive around her to the point he found himself walking away or being rude when all he wanted to do was take her. The more she fought him, the more the beast inside him tried to escape. Now, here he was, having once again to sleep in close proximity to her. This time, she wouldn't be grieving and need comfort. She would be helpless. Defenseless. Lonely. Worried about the future.

Mikhail stood and searched the heavens one more time. Should he say a prayer? No.

He kicked dirt on the last embers of the fire until only clouds of smoke curled upward, covering the smell of her. Slowly, he turned toward the tent and studied it for several minutes before approaching. Cautiously, he unzipped the tent and kneeled to crawl inside. He laid his hand on her sleeping bag where her legs were drawn up and could feel her warmth. Although surrounded by darkness, he could see her red hair had loosened from the ponytail she often wore, to spread out on her arm tucked beneath her head.

"Go to sleep, Mikhail." Zane's voice rang in his ear as clear as if he was standing next to him. "Remember what you are."

Mikhail didn't respond. Instead, he watched Petra in her peaceful slumber.

"Go to sleep, Mikhail. Have faith. You can do this. Do not be afraid."

Mikhail still refused to respond as he climbed into his sleeping bag and zipped it up to the top, although his body burned. He feared it would be another sleepless night.

"Go to sleep, Mikhail. I am on guard."

Mikhail tried to block the voice.

"Do not do that. It makes me angry. You must stay the course. Remember your promises. I stand between you and—"

"I know," Mikhail whispered in frustration. "I know."

"Go to sleep, Mikhail. Let me have my way tonight."

"But I want—"

"Yes. I know. Sleep."

Mikhail surrendered to Zane, understanding he would sleep soundly while Petra would be safe from outside elements and from him.

Sunrise took forever in this valley. Mikhail awakened early, like always, and unzipped his sleeping bag. Strangely enough, his body felt rested, and the soreness had left his limbs. Petra had rolled over toward him during the night and still slept soundly. Did Zane make her sleep, too, so she could face this day of discovery? It felt good to rest. He remained still and watched Petra breathe and occasionally smile in her sleep. What did people like her dream about?

Carefully, he managed to escape his sleeping bag and exit the tent without waking her. He built the fire back up with the still-smoldering embers from the night before. A nearby overlook beckoned him to watch the fog lift over the mountains as the sun climbed higher in the sky. Closing his eyes, he asked for forgiveness and a safe journey, success in the venture and protection from evil forces he felt stirring.

"Morning. I saw you over here and decided to make us some tea." Petra handed him a small tin cup. "I added a drop of honey since there was a small packet. Thought maybe it would be good for us."

He reached for the cup she held out. "Thank you. Did I wake you?"

"No. Considering I slept on the ground, I had a hard time waking up. You?"

"Slept like a rock. No pun intended."

"I've noticed you're not a morning person?" Petra carefully took a sip of her tea.

"I rarely have company first thing in the morning. It takes me a while. And I generally need three cups of coffee to stabilize my mood." He liked that she was interested in his habits. "I do like getting up early, however."

"Maybe when this is over, we can go into the coffee business together. Buy that little coffee shop where we met and call it The Mood Stabilizer Coffee Company." She took a deep breath and eyed the scenery.

"Kind of a catchy name. Guess if this priest stuff doesn't work out for me and you get tired of playing in the dirt or looking for junk, then I'm in." Mikhail stole a sideways glance at her. She clutched her cup with both hands.

"Honestly, sometimes I want to quit," she admitted softly and turned to face him. "I travel a lot. I hardly ever see my family. Most of my friends are old, stuffy professors who treat me like I'm too rambunctious and careless for this job."

"Get a dog. They like rambunctious."

She laughed, making him feel a little more lighthearted. "Do you care if I call him Novak, after you?"

"Knock yourself out. I was thinking something like Fluffy."

Now her laughter was loud and carefree. "Maybe Fluffy Novak."

"Perfect." He nodded and finished his tea.

"I'm starved." She turned back toward the campfire, and he followed. "I was thinking bacon, eggs, side order of country potatoes with biscuits and gravy. How does that sound?"

"I'd kill for some of that," he moaned.

"Ooo. Poor choice of words, but okay." She reached in her backpack and pulled out two MREs then read the label. "This says on the side that it is a 'self-contained operational ration consisting of a full meal contained in a flexible bag.'"

He took one and read the description. "Pretty high in calories. I've been trying to lose some weight."

She eyed him head to toe, making him feel a little exposed. "You look pretty good to me. Besides, there's no calories if you eat it standing up or are searching for lost treasure." She took a bite then grimaced. "I'm thinking you should have blessed this mess first."

"I had plenty of these when I was in the Rangers. You get used to them after a while."

"I'd like to hear about your experiences sometime."

"Sometime, maybe," he said off-handedly. *Too*

personal right now, he thought. "Let's pack everything up in case we're running short on time after we retrieve the Vessel of St. Mary. We don't want to miss our connections. Could be flying all night if flight crews don't show up on time."

"I never thought of that. Can't you pray that doesn't happen or voodoo?" She threw the remains of the MRE in the fire and stuck out her tongue. "I'm not that hungry," she confessed.

"Why don't you pray for it. My dog isn't in this fight. I'm just along for the free perks. Besides, if Hawi shows up, I might have to defend your honor. He seemed pretty smitten with you."

"He's bigger than you," she reminded him.

"The bigger they are, the harder they fall."

"Let me guess. You were a John Wayne fan as a kid." She rolled up the sleeping bags.

"That's right, pilgrim. Still am. You can learn a lot from the Duke."

The tent collapsed easy enough but took both of them to get folded so it would fit in the nylon case. He helped her with her backpack and bedroll then she did the same for him, finishing with attaching the tent and his bedroll.

They hiked almost thirty minutes before Petra had to stop and survey the surroundings to try and remember where the opening might be.

"Apparently, Chadwick did a good job of hiding the entrance." He pointed to several caves along the limestone bluff. "Any of those look familiar?"

"No. It was ground level. There are a number of them here."

Mikhail pulled the map from his inside jacket

pocket in hopes the map had changed once more. He was not disappointed.

Petra smiled at him. "Eureka! I remember where to go. See that lone pine next to the trickle of water cascading off the side of the boulder. It's behind that rock."

"Okay. Anything I should know before we go in there?"

Her devious chuckle did nothing to reassure him.

"Nothing a Boy Scout can't handle."

Thirty-Two

❖

The cave opening, the size of a king-sized bed, required brush and branches to be removed in order to enter. Once inside, Petra remembered the enormity of the first room. It tricked the sense of sight, considering she and Chadwick had almost missed it the first time. Geological maps and reports from hikers, spelunkers, and treasure hunters never indicated this particular cave.

Considering what Petra discovered, Chadwick wanted to keep the information secret. Unfortunately, their special permit had expired, and getting the Turkish Ministry of Culture and Tourism to issue a second one involved information on any archaeological activities, including surveys and research. Since those pieces of the puzzle had to be put in place, they returned home without the Vessel of St. Mary. No way would such a prize have gotten through customs without jail time.

"I'm not sure how we got all the permits this time, but it's a freakin' miracle." Petra placed her backpack against a wall. "I guess Chadwick started the process when we first returned home. His focus, for whatever reason, turned to the Rock Hewn Churches. Remind me to thank him when—I mean if..." Her voice faded as she dropped her hands to her sides and focused on the rock wall to compose herself.

A hand clamped on her shoulder, and a calming voice reached her. "Petra, let's just do what we can. You're trying. I'm betting Chadwick knows that. Maybe that's why I'm here. To make sure you don't have to do this alone—although I understand you're very capable without me."

Petra turned to face Mikhail, as he offered a narrowed look. "No. I couldn't. It's a dangerous place and I need backup. If I don't survive this, promise you'll get the vessel back to save Chadwick."

"Of course. Same goes for you. Whatever happens, get back to Ethiopia." He dropped his hands to his side, but they stood only a foot apart.

Their gazes lingered longer than normal, Petra exploring the deep connection between them. A sense of safety filled Petra as he stood there piercing her jumbled thoughts of doubt.

"You obviously haven't realized what a coward I am." She struggled to keep from choking up. The thought of lowering herself back down in the hole leading to the Vessel of St. Mary, terrified her.

"I'll be your guardian angel. How about that?"

Petra couldn't resist laying a hand on his cheek. Strangely enough, he didn't so much as blink when she did. But those piercing blue eyes turned navy, and his nostrils flared as if he were trying to contain any display of emotion. In a sudden move, he took her hand and placed her palm against his chest, sending a searing warmth deep inside her soul.

Mikhail whispered in a language she had never heard before as she fixated on his lips moving. The beat of his heart felt like thunder against her skin, and a surge of energy ran from his hand into hers then up her arm into her chest. She wanted to step away, but couldn't.

"Mikhail," she managed to say as he removed her hand.

"Trust in yourself. I'll be beside you the whole time. I won't let you fail."

His expression captivated her and she knew his words were true. It was one of those moments she wanted to remember when they parted ways. Then she realized losing Mikhail Novak was the last thing she wanted.

"Okay. I'm good to go." She slipped on her helmet and tossed one to Mikhail.

Petra rappelled down the hole leading to a series of tunnels and rooms that led to the Vessel of St. Mary. Mikhail followed like an experienced climber. For whatever reason, the man knew what he was doing. Was that one more thing he learned in the military?

"Last time, we had a rope ladder. It washed away." She couldn't help but survey the area in hopes she'd spot it. "Guess we'll have to climb out."

Mikhail patted the rocks then scanned them all the way to the top. "They're pretty dry so shouldn't be slick. There are plenty of jugs to help with stepping our way up." He turned to eye her. "Jugs are large holds you can grasp with your whole hand. Makes sense we could use them as steps if we need it."

"I know what a jug is. I'm just wondering how you know what it is. You also rappelled like you're used doing it."

"Kind of a hobby. I belong to a climbing gym." He walked around the area, feeling the other rocks and squatting down to touch the soil. "Good way to keep in shape."

She tucked her flashlight in a holster then flipped on her headlamp. Mikhail did the same. She'd wedged glow-in-the-dark trail markers between rocks, and they glowed as they proceeded down the first tunnel before entering a large open room where stalactites dripped into a skinny water stream emptying into a black pool. The temperature drop gave her a shiver as she zipped her jacket up over her chin.

Navigating through the large open area wasn't difficult in spite of stepping on a couple of slick rocks that may have been fallen stalactite chunks, broken off from the ceiling. The steady drip of icy water echoed throughout the room. Neither spoke. Petra glanced back at Mikhail only once after they'd been exploring for about fifteen minutes. He raised his chin in acknowledgement as if to reassure her. She was relieved he wasn't a complainer or required coaxing to enter a dark world with her.

She came to a sudden halt. The trail markers lit up like the sun had hit them. The room ahead appeared void of darkness.

"What just happened?" Mikhail asked, coming alongside her.

"I don't know. The last time I entered, I needed a nine-volt flashlight. They're pretty powerful. I didn't have a headlamp at the time. I think the ones in our holsters are almost as powerful. We should be fine."

"Were there booby traps?"

"No. Just fire and water. I don't understand why it isn't wetter here. Besides the stalactites, there's no sign of a flood. It's like I imagined it."

"How long has it been?"

"Maybe a year." Petra tilted her head toward the opening to the next room. "The only reason I made it out of here was because it wasn't far from where we entered. The water rose fast, and there was a strong current."

"It must empty out into the lake we saw in the distance." Mikhail let his headlamp beam land on the water. "Probably underground fissures from an extinct volcano. Good way to get rid of a lot of water."

"These volcanoes in Turkey don't erupt often. Maybe every 10,000 years or so, but they are still considered active. I did feel a rumble when I was here. Could have been a tremor. Plenty of active faults in Turkey.

They had a major quake not long after we left. A lot of damage and loss of life. Another reason we didn't return was because our State Department said it was too risky. Besides, Turkey is paranoid about Americans coming here and snooping around. They think we're all CIA agents." She chuckled.

He grinned. "Considering it looks like you described it with no damage, I guess that fault line didn't slip all that much."

"Could be why all that water was released, though.

I was just here at the wrong time."

Mikhail agreed. "You're lucky to be alive. Hopefully, the fault line, if there is one here, will behave itself."

Petra took a deep breath. "Okay. That's the room. I've got the inflatable bag in my pack." The smaller backpack she wore held a few tools, the inflatable container, and an extra flashlight in case she lost the two she carried.

Stepping behind her, he unzipped the pack and withdrew the inflatable bag for the transfer. "Did you get your hands on it when you were here the last time?"

"No. I was awestruck and couldn't believe I'd found it. Within seconds, everything started falling apart." She whirled around. "What if the flood took it? It might be gone." Panic gripped her chest.

"Listen to me." Mikhail's voice took on a serious note of authority. "The Nephelium and those other priests would not have sent us here if they didn't believe the vessel could be retrieved. They must know it still exists. All we can do is try and get it back. We'll never know if we don't go in there."

"You're probably right. It's a strange thing to say, but I almost wish your buddy Zane was here." She chuckled. "It would be just like him to show up at the end of the big show."

"That's Zane. I don't expect him. We're on our own. Ready?" He turned his attention toward the glowing opening in the cave.

"Ready."

Side by side, they moved with caution toward the room where the Vessel of St. Mary had been kept the last time Petra entered. Once inside, she gasped in disbelief at the mind-blowing frescos on the walls that, except for a few chipped places, appeared smooth and pristine.

"You never mentioned these," Mikhail said, walking over to get a closer inspection.

Petra followed. "That's because I never saw these. Remember I said I had to use my flashlight and only focused on the Vessel of St. Mary."

The paintings were of a mighty warrior slaying dragons and other creatures. "Could be St. George." Mikhail turned to her with amazement in his eyes.

"That story began circulating in the eleventh century so—" Petra said, wishing they had more time.

"And the Rock Hewn Churches were thought to have been built between the seventh and twelfth century." Mikhail moved to the next fresco. "Is it possible these were created by the Knights Templar?"

"They were also suspected of helping build the Rock Hewn Churches, not angels or Nephilim." Petra turned to search for the vessel. "Can you snap some pictures with your phone? I don't see the vessel. I'll look for it."

"Wait. You don't know if things changed down here. Holes may have opened up since the last time. We stick together."

As he snapped pictures of all the frescos, a recessed area oscillated between growing extremely bright then powering down to a dim shade of twilight.

"There. That's the vessel. It's still here," she said with excitement, starting in that direction.

"Stop!" Mikhail grabbed her arm and jerked her back just as flames of fire appeared from the mouths of a dragon head on each side of the insert where the vessel rested. She hadn't even noticed them.

"Yikes. Do I still have eyebrows?" she asked, trying to be funny while her heart thudded in her ears.

Mikhail gave her a disgruntled expression.

"Sorry. I forgot about those beasties being fire-breathers."

She spotted a painting of what she assumed were the apostles surrounding dragons. Just like before, their eyes were strange in that they moved with each step she took. A trick, like those pictures of Jesus in the cathedrals of Europe where no matter where you moved, His eyes followed.

"Kind of creepy, right?" She stood perfectly still, eyeing her surroundings, hoping to avoid any traps or more fire-breathing dragons. "Why do you think St. George and a dragon was such a big deal in the spread of Christianity?"

Like Petra, Mikhail surveyed the area with trepidation. "Since both characters were widely thought of as symbolic, representing good—enter St. George and then enter a dragon representing evil or darkness, good ole George embodies righteousness and faith, protecting God's children from demonic forces."

"I think I heard a flippant attitude. Not a fan of Saint George?" she asked calmly as her flashlight beam searched for problems. "I always loved that story as a kid. Didn't pick up the battling-sin part. I kind of felt sorry for the dragon. Guess I wanted one."

"I think it was a magnificent way to inspire the new converts. Symbolic as it was, it served a higher purpose. Over the years, people have turned it into something other than a spiritual awakening. Now the controversy is whether dragons were real, and why are we honoring a man who kills animals.”

“I see what you mean.” She took a deep breath as she gave the area one more inspection. “I don’t see any traps.”

“Me either. The Vessel of St. Mary isn’t as big as I expected,” Mikhail admitted.

“It looks like it is made of stone—like the Rock Hewn Churches.”

“Makes sense,” Mikhail agreed. “The rock there is porous basalt, a type of igneous rock made from the lava flows from the Northern Plateau. Not all that different than here with all the volcanoes.”

“A little convenient, don’t you think? I’m going to approach, one step at a time. If you think I should stop—”

“I’ll let you know,” he assured her.

One step. Two. Three. Nothing happened. As she extended her hand into the three-foot recessed area, the ground rumbled under her feet.

“Did you feel that?” she asked.

“Yes. Are there pressure plates or anything that looks like holes that would have darts or—”

“Oh, for heaven sakes, Mikhail,” she snapped. “This isn’t an Indiana Jones movie. No. There is nothing like that. Don’t be ridiculous.” She lowered her hand to the twelve-inch-high vessel. It was void of decoration, except for a small Star of David carved into the front. When she touched it, the vessel lit up and became ice cold to the touch.

“What’s wrong? Take it,” Mikhail insisted.

She turned to stare at him. “I can’t. My hand is stuck to the surface.”

A slight rumble caused dust to filter down from the

ceiling. And just like the first time, a voice whispered in her ear. "Run."

Thirty-Three

❖

Petra tried to pull her hand away, but it was stuck. Wrapping her other arm around the back of the vessel, she managed to jerk it out of the setback. Snuggling it against her chest, she jumped off the step. Mikhail caught her as she landed on unsteady feet. Once away from the stand, she easily pulled her hand free for him to drop it in the inflatable bag. It was padded enough she thought it would be safe.

"We've got to get moving, Petra. Look!" Mikhail grabbed her hand and tugged her forward as water trickled down the walls.

When they reached the entry arch to the room, the world shook violently. Both fell to the ground as they tried to push through the opening. Stalactites popped then broke off, only to drop like deadly missiles into the pool below.

Mikhail threw his arms out for balance as his feet slipped on the slick surface covered in ice chips. He managed to regain his footing as Petra toppled toward the ground. He caught her by the front of her jacket and jerked her up. She fumbled the vessel and almost lost control then slipped the bag under it and closed it as he widened his stance to stop the swaying of his body.

He fastened the bag around her shoulders and under her arms like a baby carrier. The shaking stopped, but the wet tenacles of revenge gushed through the vessel room and swirled around their knees.

"It's coming up fast," she cried in alarm. "Hurry. We don't have much time."

She led the way and felt as if the current was trying to sweep her feet out from under her. From behind her, Mikhail encouraged her to not stop, and reassured her he was fine. "Don't look back," he shouted.

By the time they reached the last room, the pool had risen to her chest. Her headlamp highlighted the ropes hanging from above. If they could hang onto them as they pulled themselves up high enough to reach the handholds that hadn't been submerged, they had a chance to escape.

Stepping on a ledge helped her propel herself up to grab a rope. A roaring wave knocked her off, but she held tight as her body twisted away from the rock wall. The angry torrents continued to rise, but she could see the lantern light they had left to help guide them in case they lost their way.

"Mikhail, we're almost there!"

No answer.

"Mikhail?" She tried her best to keep her head above water. Then she spotted him barreling toward her, clinging to the second rope.

"Keep climbing," he ordered. "The current is picking up speed."

Her arm muscles burned as she struggled to pull herself back toward the wall when Mikhail swung toward her, holding his rope. His hands grasped her belt, jerking her back to climb. Anxiety crashed in on her as memories flooded her with images of her parents being washed away. She clung to the wall and couldn't breathe. She wanted to scream but was frozen with fear, as she kept raising her head above the onslaught of powerful waves.

"Petra, I'm here. I'm going to swing behind you. Then I'm going to duck under you. I'll put my head between your legs and lift you. When you feel a handhold, you've got to pull yourself up enough to stand on my shoulders."

"You'll drown," she wept.

"No. I won't. I'm strong. Just like you. I'll come right back up. Ready?"

She nodded and watched him sink into the darkness. In seconds, his head was between her legs, lifting her up. One of his hands patted her leg. Awkwardly, she tried to stand on his shoulders when one foot slipped off. On the second attempt, she felt his hand on her lower leg holding tight until she managed to wiggle into place. It worked. Her shoulders came above the current. The climb remained tricky, but she grew confident with each second of progress. The exit hole became a beacon of light and a promise of survival when her rope broke, dropping her inches from her goal. But two sets of hands grabbed her harness and pulled her up onto dry ground. Two men dragged her away from the opening then fell back down on their stomachs to reach back down into the dark abyss of a turbulent death.

The men yelled into the cave over and over before pulling the rope completely free.

Mikhail was gone.

Petra stood at the window of her room where views of Lake Van could be enjoyed. A fire built in the stone fireplace warmed the small space, and a pot of tea rested on a tiny writing desk next to the bed. For the hundredth time, she glanced toward the upholstered chair she had dragged to the window and that now held her inflatable bag with the Vessel of St. Mary. It remained safe and secure.

The afternoon sun was trying to dip behind the mountains, and she had no idea how she would be able to leave. Once more, her thoughts turned to the Whispering Cave where two Kurdish men had pulled her from the jaws of death snapping at her heels. But they couldn't reach Mikhail in time. He had given his life for her.

She remembered crawling to the opening when the men stood up and shook their heads. Crawling to the hole, wet sprays splashed up onto her face as she screamed Mikhail's name until the men reached down and pulled her away. As they lifted her to her feet, their faces were sympathetic when a third man wrapped a blanket around her shoulders.

The rest was kind of a blur. There were snippets of walking then staggering to a horse, where they helped her mount. One of the men who had saved her, rode behind her on the trail until they reached their car. Others carefully put their equipment and supplies into the vehicle. The Kurd in charge asked her in English if he could remove the bag on her chest and promised not to look inside or harm it in anyway. Did she answer?

Whatever happened next was a blank slate. The next thing she knew, there was a church. One of the men told her it was the Holy Cross of Lake Van and she was safe. A woman escorted her to what she thought was a monastery or house where a hot bath was prepared and warm clothes provided several hours ago.

"Who are you?" she asked the woman attending her.

"We are Kurds. A small remnant of Christians who have been waiting for the one who would return the Vessel of St. Mary to its rightful place. We watched you the first time you came and knew you were not successful. Since then, like always, we have watched over the Whispering Cave to make sure it was not disturbed. You have cheated death twice."

"Are you Turkish?" It was a silly question, but her brain was still a little rattled.

The middle-aged woman continued. "Some say we are. Others say we are Armenian. We are Kurds. Turkey does not embrace our people. They hate us. There is a large presence of Kurds here. Even our religious beliefs are varied. The majority of Kurds are Sunni Muslim, but there are Jewish and Yezidi communities too. Then there is us. We stay to ourselves." She wrapped a warm blanket around her after she'd dressed in dry clothes. "We are happy to have you here."

"What about my friend? Please. I have to find him."

"They are out looking for him now. I am sorry. It is a dangerous cave and not a place to explore. You must prepare yourself."

She crumpled onto the floor, weeping for yet another mistake she'd made. The friend who tried to save her at the sacrifice of his own life and for Chadwick who would surely die, was gone because without Mikhail, she might not make it back in time. The woman touched the top of Petra's head before she removed herself and let her grieve.

Climbing onto the bed, she slipped between the faded covers and fell into a fitful sleep. A nap rested her enough to ponder what she planned to do next. What was the point? Although they knew the importance of the vessel, how would she make these people understand time was running out?

Twilight brought a red-and-pink sunset as if all was well with the world. A light tap at the door snapped her out of her dismal view of the future.

"Yes?"

"Cheshti kurdi is ready, Petra. The food is hot and will give your strength."

"I'll be down in a minute. Thank you."

She turned to stare out the window one more time, not quite ready to face a bunch of strangers, in spite of having saved her life. How would she secure the vessel? Could she hide it?

Another knock at the door.

"I'm coming," she snapped as the door squeaked open. She covered the bag with the vessel with her pillow when a male voice spoke.

"Do you really think a pillow will protect that blasted thing?"

Petra whirled around to see Mikhail standing in the doorway. Her hands went to her mouth as a gasp tried to explode from deep inside her. He shoved the door closed with his foot without taking his eyes off her.

"You're... You're alive," she whispered.

"Always a perceptive woman. I like that." He let a lopsided grin come to his mouth.

Then she was running to him. He caught her up in his arms as she buried her face in his neck. It was impossible to keep the tears from rolling down her cheeks onto his skin. She held on tight as he slowly let her feet touch the floor. She patted his shoulders then his chest and arms, causing him to grimace.

"Easy. I'm a bit beat up. That was quite a ride I took."

Petra couldn't help herself. She hugged him gently then stood back to gaze at him. Without thinking, she reached up and moved his unruly curly dark hair away from his forehead. "I'm so glad to see you. I thought I had lost you forever."

"I told you..." He was letting his eyes drink her in as if he wanted to say more but changed his mind. "The water took me down a tunnel. I fought the best I could until it opened up more and spread out where I could swim with my head above water. Turned out, one of those fissures we talked about emptied out into a stream outside the cave. I still couldn't get out of it, but I knew it was headed to the lake since I could see it. When I got there, several Kurds were waiting for me. Pretty amazing, isn't it?"

Afraid to believe her eyes, she continued to reach

out and touch him. At one point, he laid his hand on hers.

"I-I was about to give up when I saw them. I was pretty cold and could hardly move. They got me as warm as possible before bringing me here."

"How long have you been here?"

"A couple of hours. I came up here first thing, even though they told me I should get warm and have soup forced on me." He chuckled. "You were sleeping like a baby. They said you were having a hard time and I should let you rest."

She bit her bottom lip. "Mikhail," was all she could say as he stepped closer and pulled her into his arms.

"It's going to be okay. We've still got time to save Chadwick. With any luck, we'll make it by morning." He pushed her to arm's length. "Get the vessel, and let's get out of here."

Thirty-Four

Mikhail hurt over his entire body from being slammed against rock walls and crashing into boulders. The rushing water prevented him from putting his feet down to try and find the bottom of the tunnel. It had shot him out into a stream. The feeling of kicking air and falling at the same time caused him to hold his breath as he watched rapids tunneling between giant boulders. If he hit one, he'd be dead. If he hit the water at this speed, his body might explode in pain if not death. But at the last second, he heard a still, calm voice whisper in his consciousness.

"You're almost there. Focus on the lake."

The current swallowed him, tumbling his body over and over, allowing him mere seconds to lift his head above the surface. In those moments when the current slowed enough that he could float, he felt nothing. His body was numb, and his teeth chattered.

"You're almost there," the voice whispered again. "Others wait for you."

That's when he saw Petra standing on the shore waving to him. She was jumping up and down calling his name, telling him to fight. But he soon discovered it had been several men who waded out into the calm water to pull him to safety. She was nowhere to be found.

"Petra." He choked then expelled the liquid filling his lungs. "Petra?"

The Kurds quickly explained she was safe and they would take him to her. Relief washed over him like the fierce rapids that had tried to kill him. Only, this time, it soothed him more than he expected. He remembered seeing the rope break in her hand as she neared the top. He had grasped his own line, but something had hit him and shoved him into the darkness.

To reassure himself she was really alive, he just wanted to watch her sleep. His body rebelled against being cramped in a plane and unable to move around. He dozed awhile, but he rarely slept the entire night. Sitting across the aisle from her distracted him from the pain. Letting himself remember how it felt when she discovered he was alive, played over and over in his head.

"Careful, Mikhail," Zane whispered from afar. "Remember who you are."

"You're not likely to let me forget," he mumbled out loud.

"Did you say something?" Petra asked as she pulled the blanket up around her neck. "Is it cold in here?"

Mikhail stood and removed his blanket. Bending over her, he paused to drink in the exposed skin on her face. There were a couple of bruises, but nothing serious. Her red hair was once again tied in a messy bun that had become lopsided.

"Here. Take my blanket. It is a little chilly." The lights were dim in the cabin of the Learjet provided by an unknown benefactor.

She had pulled her knees up and sat sideways on her bench seat.

When he laid the blanket on her, he couldn't resist tucking it around her shoulders.

Her eyelids opened slightly then she smiled. "Aren't you cold?"

"I'll be fine."

She lowered her feet to the floor and scooted over. "Sit next to me. Please."

Normally, he would have given her a sharp retort to put her in her place, but they were both experiencing a little shell shock from the events over the last twenty-four hours. He joined her and allowed her to share the blanket as he laid his head back against the headrest.

"I'm glad you're not dead." She yawned and moved closer.

"Not as glad as I am," he mumbled as sleep closed in on him. He remembered hearing her soft chuckle.

The plane landed at 5 a.m. at the Lalibela. As they approached the terminal, shots pinged off the plane. One hit the window behind them. The pilot spoke over the loudspeaker, telling them to get down on the floor, that they were under attack by rebels.

Mikhail woke from a deep sleep and made a dive for the floor. The aisle was wide enough when Petra fell out of her seat, he could pull her to his side. Covering part of her body with his, he cradled her head in the bend of his elbow then draped his hand over the side of her face. He could feel the plane continuing to move, toward what he hoped was an enclosed jet bridge to allow them to exit. The plane swerved.

"Stay here. Something is wrong." He crawled to the cockpit, where the door stood ajar. He could still hear an occasional ping of a stray bullet. The pilot's arms were dangling at his sides, and blood soaked through his white shirt.

They were headed toward the terminal, but at a snail's pace. He could see concrete barriers near a jetway and several men on the ground motioning them to steer left. Mikhail recognized a tiller or steering wheel on the controls. He heard another ping of a bullet that shattered the window on the copilot side of the cockpit. Carefully, he pulled the pilot out of his seat onto the floor. The pilot stared at him in alarm.

"I'm going to navigate us away from the terminal and crash us into the pile of pallets and concrete barriers. Is that okay with you?"

Mikhail thought he grunted an okay as he took the controls and maneuvered the nose wheel closer to the building at an angle. The crunch of concrete against the jet reminded him of popcorn exploding. In seconds, the plane had come to a stop. He grabbed the radio transceiver to alert the control tower or whoever was listening, the pilot had been shot and required medical assistance. In less than a minute, resistance to the attack brought a military-style truck and plenty of men to fight off the attackers.

"Mikhail?" It was Petra holding onto the doorframe

of the cockpit.

He rolled out of the seat, jumped over the pilot, and hurried to push her back where there were no windows. "You shouldn't have come up here," he chastised. "There may still be rebels out there who can hit us."

Her attention went to the pilot on the floor. "Is he…"

"No. I've radioed for help."

"Mikhail, you're bleeding." Her eyes were full of terror as she turned his chin to see the side of his face. He reached up and felt wetness on his ear.

"A bullet hit the windshield. See? A shard of glass hit me. It's everywhere."

"I'll get a first aid kit."

Before she could turn around, an airport support team entered and worked on the pilot. They asked them to follow a guard to a safe place. After Mikhail insisted they carry their own backpacks and duffle bag, they proceeded under the protection of several dangerous-looking characters. He wasn't sure who the players were in all this, but he sensed they might all be on the shady side. For such a small airport in Lalibela, a lot of nervous energy and movement filled the air.

"We're running out of time, Mikhail." Petra pointed to her watch. "We've got to catch a ride. How far are we from the churches?"

"At least fourteen miles. We can try and catch a taxi or maybe a bus, but with the ruckus that just happened, a lot of people will have their heads down."

They exited the building, hoping they weren't stopped to give an account of the attack on the plane. They just didn't have time. No one bothered to pay much attention to them, especially outside where traffic had backed up. Horns were honking as a bus stalled. Tourists were screaming as they exited the bus and rushed into the airport to avoid being shot.

"There!" Petra pointed to a taxi where a man exited his vehicle. "Maybe he can take us."

They ran to the taxi, dodging frightened locals and tourists who pushed and shoved them in the opposite direction from where they wanted to go. When they finally reached the taxi, the driver eyed them suspiciously. Mikhail noticed his cross hanging over his white robe. A white turban indicated he might be a priest.

"This is Petra McGinnis. She has brought a special gift to the Church of St. Mary. They are waiting for her."

"I do not care." The driver leaned against the car and folded his arms across his chest. "Everyone is in a hurry."

"I carry the Vessel of St. Mary," Petra spoke with authority. "I demand you take us this instant, or you will be punished by the bishop and his legions of Nephilim."

Mikhail wasn't sure if he should laugh at the terrified expression on the driver's face or be impressed by Petra's brave gamble. The driver opened the back door for them and bowed his compliance, assuring them over and over how sorry he was.

The harrowing drive felt a little like the Baja Race 1000. They were thrown back and forth as the driver dodged animals crossing the road, a few potholes, and a number of sketchy men with guns trekking alongside the road. One dared to point his weapon at them. The driver swerved and knocked him off his feet.

Petra let out a scream as the driver turned to comfort her. "No worries, lady. All good. He okay. Just have a headache for a few days."

"Oh. My. Gosh." Petra hugged the front backpack against her chest.

"Almost there. No worries. Tell bishop I help you. Yes?"

"Then get us there in one piece." Mikhail leaned forward to read the dashboard as the taxi sputtered. "We're out of gas," he moaned.

"No. No. All is good. You see. I have more." He pulled over to the side of the road and hurried to the trunk where he took out a milk jug of gas. Lifting it for them to see, he revealed a toothless smile. "I told you."

In a couple of minutes, they were on their way again.

"We were riding on top of a potential disaster." Petra sighed and stroked the backpack with the vessel. She checked her watch and showed Mikhail.

When the taxi slammed on its brakes, a cloud of dust engulfed them and entered the windows. Both of them coughed and attempted to wave the air away from the back seat. Exiting the taxi, Mikhail tried to force money on the driver.

"No. No. My honor for the lady. We are here. Walk down the trail. Hurry. I saw rebels down the road. Please. Hurry. You'll be safe in the church."

Mikhail led Petra down the path leading to the Rock Hewn Church of St. Mary. Once again, she became dazed and confused. This time, he didn't wait. He had watched her pull the white scarf from her pack and place it around her neck. Even though the path was steep and lopsided from erosion, he forced her to move faster. Several times, she slipped, but he caught her without reminding her to be careful. At this point, she had no idea where she was.

The bishop waited for them at the giant doors of the church. Mikhail bent down and removed her shoes then his before pulling her scarf over her head. Another priest exited the church and brought white robes for both of them, along with a turban for Mikhail.

"You may enter."

Like before, the priests lined the corridor and chanted as they walked by. Nephilim pulled the double doors open for them to enter. This time, the outer room had what looked to be twenty Nephilim who stood at attention until Petra walked by. She had come to her senses again and watched the giants in awe.

Mikhail once again saw Zane lurking in the shadows, not as a human but an angelic creature he knew him to be. Then he disappeared; he guessed through the thick walls like the first time. He could feel him probing his brain, pushing on his chest to get his attention, checking to see what he'd been up to with Petra.

"I have done nothing," Mikhail told him in their silent language. "She found the vessel. Make them surrender Chadwick."

"Only she can do that. Tell her to believe." Then his voice went silent.

The second set of doors opened, and the bishop led them to the altar table where Chadwick's body lay, covered in a white sheet.

Mikhail glanced at Petra who had tears at the corner of her eyes. "Be brave. Don't hesitate. Offer the Vessel of St. Mary to the bishop. You must believe."

She stopped and focused on him with questions in her eyes. "Do you hear me? You must believe this will work."

She stepped within inches of the altar and looked longingly at Chadwick then over at the bishop.

"I have brought you the Vessel of St. Mary." She reached into the front bag and removed the vessel and offered it to the bishop.

"You must place it with the others."

"The others?" Petra's forehead creased in confusion.

"There. Behind the altar." A Nephilim pulled back a curtain revealing a gold case with other vessels. Each one was a little different. "You have brought the twelfth vessel, each representing one of the twelve tribes of Israel. This will allow our Rock Hewn Churches to be restored."

To Mikhail's horror, Zane appeared next to the case as she gently set the vessel in its place. Could she see him? Would she recognize him? Screaming at the sight of him would most likely undo everything they came to do. He watched her body stiffen and look up at the creature next to her. Even from where he stood, he knew her eyes had glazed over against recognition. Only he could see Zane as he put his hands on Petra's shoulders.

His voice filled the room as he turned Petra around to face the priests and Nephilim who crowded inside. "This woman has put her life in great danger to restore the Vessel of St. Mary's rightful place. The churches will be restored in the ancient tradition." He moved to the altar. "Chadwick, you must rise and let this woman take you to a place that can heal you."

To Mikhail's surprise, Chadwick began to move then pushed away the sheet.

"Chadwick," Petra cried. This time, no one stopped her from touching him. Mikhail also moved closer and helped him off the altar. He was confused and weak but alive.

"We are in danger," the bishop said hurriedly. "The rebels are here. They want our power."

Zane remained in angel form as he touched the other vessels and pointed toward the corridor. The wind created by wings filled the rooms tunneling toward the outside. The Nephilim ran after them.

"What is happening?" Petra said, slipping her arm around Chadwick's waist.

"They are protecting the churches—and us." Chadwick spoke with authority.

"Who is? They have no weapons," Petra insisted.

Mikhail put the man's arm around his shoulder. "Believe, Petra. And we'll be safe."

The priests hurried forward then out onto the veranda of the church. When the three exited the church, their eyes went to the top of the ridge above. They had been encircled with rebels aiming rifles at them. There was no way to escape.

Thirty-Five

❖

The Nephilim created a perimeter of defense on the ground level. They were dressed in crimson robes with hoods pulled up over their heads. In each hand, they carried a dagger. He couldn't imagine how that would protect them from rifle fire. The sun had risen above the treetops, causing a blinding light through the branches. What happened next would brand itself on his memory forever.

Wind gushed forth from the open doors of the church, nearly knocking them down. Chadwick wobbled slightly causing Petra to tighten her hold on him, even though she watched in awe at the army of creatures dressed like warriors who took their place between the Nephilim. Their black armor trimmed in silver reflected light back at the rebels. Helmets covered their heads, and giant dusty gray wings extended out six to eight feet on each side of their bodies.

He watched as each pulled a five-foot sword forged of silver and gold with ornate designs on the hilt. They were both spellbinding and terrifying. In front of all of them was Zane who glared ominously up at the rebels. He raised his sword toward a man who appeared to be in charge but said nothing.

"Are you seeing this, or am I tripping?" Petra mumbled. "Is this really happening?"

The rebels on the ridge dropped their weapons and backed up. Their eyes bulged with terror, and they cried out for protection. In that same instant, crowds of local people ran down the paths and along the ridge to chase the rebels away. They carried clubs, garden tools, anything that could be used as a weapon. The rebels turned and ran faster than Mikhail had ever seen anyone escape. Part of him wanted to laugh at their cowardice, but he knew they were unable to comprehend the miracle that protected all of the Rock Hewn Churches.

The locals jumped and danced along the ridge, proud of their ability to defend what they had loved for centuries. Singing broke out, and they swayed back and forth with joy.

"Where did they go?" Petra asked as she stepped away from Chadwick. The outside energy still affected her, from the way she struggled to get her speech from slurring.

Mikhail could still see the angelic creatures but realized she no longer could. He drank in the wonderous sight of them and watched as they faded away before causing the wind to return inside the Church of St. Mary. The Nephilim were also gone.

Only the bishop remained.

"Did I imagine that? What just happened?" She turned to the bishop, confused.

"The people of Lalibela have saved the churches from the rebels. And because you returned the Vessel of St. Mary, our restoration can begin without the interference of outsiders who know nothing of our ways. Thank you." He bowed his head toward her then made eye contact with Chadwick. "Thank you for bringing her to us. Once your health improves, I welcome you to come study and absorb the truth of our miracles."

Chadwick nodded. "It will be my honor."

The bishop took Petra's hands in his and spoke in Amharic, but this time, she couldn't understand. She looked to Mikhail to translate.

"He said you have brought honor and hope back to the Rock Hewn Churches. You are always welcome here."

"Thank you."

"Transportation has been provided for you, and my friends will see that Chadwick is carried to the top of the ridge." The bishop glanced over his shoulder toward the darkness of the church. They had started down the steps when the bishop grabbed Mikhail's arm. His eyes became dark and narrowed. "Do not be afraid of what is ahead for you. You are worthy."

Six Weeks Later

Mikhail parked his Harley outside Petra's apartment building. When he removed his helmet, he saw Zane leaning against the brick building enjoying the sunset. The surprise was more due to seeing him smoke a cigarette than waiting for him. They hadn't seen much of each other the last few weeks.

"Isn't smoking bad for your health?" Mikhail asked flippantly, knowing full well it made no difference.

Zane dropped the cigarette and rubbed it out with the toe of his boot. "Always the funny man. Just wanted to see if it was as good as I remembered. It wasn't. Feels like I licked an ashtray."

Mikhail tried to keep from grinning without success. "Why are you here? Have you been pestering Petra?"

"We haven't spoken since she returned from the Rock Hewn Churches. I'm here to make sure she and Chadwick don't have any trouble returning tomorrow. I'm surprised you aren't going."

"I wasn't invited. Besides, I have work to do here. The senior pastor is not well." He tilted his head toward Zane. "You didn't have anything to do with that, did you?"

"I can neither confirm nor deny that," he admitted.

"Now, who is funny? Don't see many of your kind in the CIA."

"Wanna bet?" Zane smirked. "I guess you've seen in the news how UNESCO and other scientific communities are mystified how the appearance of the Rock Hewn Churches has been restored in such a short period of time. Even those hideous metal roofs have been removed. At least they don't look like a glorified gas station."

Darkness blanketed the street as the sun disappeared on the horizon. Mikhail glanced up at the window that was part of the top floor of Petra's apartment. He lifted a hand to acknowledge her when he saw her smile down at him. "I gotta go. She's cooking dinner."

"Have you seen much of her since Chadwick got out of the hospital?"

"She's been busy taking care of him and work. Maybe a couple of meetups at the coffee shop. It's hard for me to get away too." Mikhail felt he was being interrogated.

"He's good as new. I saw him today working at the museum. He's pretty excited about the trip back to Ethiopia." Zane pushed away from the wall and looked up at Petra's window then back at him.

"Did Petra see you today?" Anytime his friend showed up, something went wrong.

"No. I watched from afar. You know who else I saw at the museum?" Zane lowered his chin in the way he always did when he wanted to drive a point home.

Mikhail shifted his weight to one leg and exhaled his impatience.

"Okay. I'll tell you. That Hawi police guy." Zane's eyebrow arched, and a snide expression took over his mouth.

"She's not interested in him."

"Hmm," Zane said as he tapped his cheek sarcastically. "Wonder why she was giggling so much when he pulled her into the hall to talk. Or was he whispering? Not sure. He was standing pretty close."

Mikhail's face heated, and his heart beat a little faster. "She deserves to have a life outside that musty museum."

Zane laughed so hard he bent over and slapped his

knees. "You're jealous."

"What I am, is late. Anything else you want to taunt me with?"

"I'll think of something. Maybe later tonight we can catch up." Zane gave him a soft fist bump on the shoulder.

"That reminds me." Mikhail reached into the inside pocket of his leather jacket and withdrew a long black feather. "I think this belongs to you." Watching Zane grab it out of his hand gave him great satisfaction. "I spotted this on Petra's desk a few days after we got back. Said she found it stuck to some of Chadwick's things."

"She can't remember seeing me, Mikhail."

"Are you sure about that? For some reason, she can see you when others cannot. Maybe she did discover your angelic form."

"Then, that would be a problem," Zane confessed in a threatening tone. "We'll finish this discussion later tonight."

Mikhail glanced back up at Petra's window then to Zane. Giving his friend a playful shove, he narrowed his eyes. He opened the door to her building. "Don't wait up."

MEET THE AUTHOR

Tierney James decided to become a full-time writer after working in education for over thirty years. Besides serving as a Solar System Ambassador for NASA's Jet Propulsion Lab, and attending Space Camp for Educators, Tierney served as a Geo-teacher for National Geographic. Her love of travel and cultures took her on adventures throughout Africa, Asia and Europe. From the Great Wall of China to floating the Okavango Delta of Botswana, Tierney weaves her unique experiences into the adventures she loves to write. Living on a Native American reservation and in a mining town, fuels the characters in the Enigma, Dark Side, and now the Strong Women series. She has now introduced another set of heroes in the Whispers of Angels series.

After moving to Oklahoma, the love of teaching continued in her marketing and writing workshops along with the creation of educational materials and children's books. Try some of her other books to bring a little adventure to your life.

http://www.tierneyjames.com   Speaking at book clubs, school functions, church and community groups are a few of the things Tierney enjoys doing when not writing her next adventure. She also helps beginning writers in their quest to becoming a published author through her workshops and classes. Family, travel and gardening fill her life with plenty of laughter to share with others.

Tierney has been an Amazon #1 Best Selling author and won awards at the Annual Ozark Creative Writer's Conference as well as the Sleuths' Ink Mystery Writers, and Between the Pages Writer Con.

Other Publications by Tierney

Enigma Series
1. An Unlikely Hero
2. Winds of Deception
3. Rooftop Angels
4. Kifaru
5. Black Mamba
6. The Knight Before Chaos
7. Invisible Goodbye
8. Martyrs Never Die
9. The Hemlock Switch
10. Knight of the Sugar Plum Fairy
11. China Dolls

Dark Side Series
1. Dark Side of Morning
2. Dark side of Noon

Whispers of Angels Books
1. Dance of the Devil's Trill
2. The Unleashed Angel

Strong Independent Women Series
1. The Rescued Heart
2. House of Miracles
3. Whiskey and Sweet Tea (Summer 2025)

Stand Along Books
1. Recipes to Die For – Enigma Cookbook
2. Turnback Creek
3. Lipstick & Danger – A collection of short stories

Children's Books
1. There's a Superhero in the Library
2. Zombie Meatloaf
3. Mission K9 Rescue

Marketing Books for Authors
1. How to Market a Book Someone Besides Your Mother Will Read

Social Media

Personal Facebook Page:
https://www.facebook.com/tierney.james.7/

Author Facebook:
https://www.facebook.com/AuthorTierneyJames/

Facebook Reader Group:
https://www.facebook.com/groups/2430789897157949

The Write Place to Create:
https://www.facebook.com/groups/JustTheWritePlaceToCreate

Twitter: https://twitter.com/TierneyJames1

Website: http://www.tierneyjames.com

Pinterest: https://www.pinterest.com/ptierneyjames/

Instagram: www.tierneyjames7